VANISHED IN THE MIND

DOCTOR WISE BOOK 13

ARJAY LEWIS

MIND
BENDER
PRESS

II

Cover Design: Marianne Nowicki, PremadeEbookCoverShop.com
Editing: Libby Broadbent,

ISBN-13: 979-8989828135

Published by:
Mindbender Press
474 South Main Street
Phillipsburg NJ 08865
www.mindbenderpress.com

IV

DEDICATION

To the cast and crew of
FIDDLER ON THE ROOF
Kelsey Theatre, 2025
From your Tevye,
It was a joy to work with you all

"When the student is ready the teacher will appear. When the student is truly ready… the teacher will disappear."

—*Lao Tzu*

"Patience and perseverance have a magical effect before which difficulties disappear and obstacles vanish."

—*John Quincy Adams*

PROLOGUE

Isabella Fontaine stabbed at her phone, her perfectly manicured nails clicking furiously as her voice rose in frustration.

"How could you leave me in this place? There is absolutely nothing to do!"

Her father's voice remained infuriatingly calm. "Isabella, my darling." His composed tone only stoked her anger. "You've created quite the stir in Hollywood with your... shall we say... headline-grabbing relationship with that actor—"

"Georgio is going to be famous one day," she snapped.

"Fame or not," he continued smoothly, unfazed, "the fact remains that gossip sites splashed images of the two of you — drunken and disheveled — all over the internet. And let's not forget the unfortunate incident with your dress—"

"That was an accident... a wardrobe malfunction!" she huffed, but couldn't help a small smirk. The memory of that night — blazing camera flashes, the roar of paparazzi, the rush of knowing all eyes were on her — felt like a dream compared to her current predicament.

She faced the full-length mirror. She knew she was striking — her tall, statuesque frame exuding effortless grace. Silky waves of chestnut brown hair tumbled over her shoulders, framing her piercing green eyes and high cheekbones. It wasn't vanity. It was simply a fact — she belonged in the spotlight, not hidden away in some remote location.

Her father sighed, the weary, long-suffering sigh that only a diplomat and father of Isabella Fontaine could muster. "Seeing my daughter sprawled across a sidewalk in a less-than-dignified state has caused me no end of distress."

"I don't understand why I have to be a prisoner here!" she protested, her voice edging toward a full-blown tantrum.

"Listen, Isabella," he said, his patience thinning. "My reputation depends not just on my actions, but my family's as well. If I embarrass our country, they will recall me, and then you will have to either return home or fend for yourself."

She scoffed, still admiring her reflection. "I could manage. I could start a brand — become an influencer, start a blog or a podcast… or something."

Her father chuckled indulgently. "My dear, you wouldn't be able to run a lemonade stand even if someone else squeezed the lemons and handed you the money."

She scowled.

"All I need from you is to stay at the Edgewater Resort for a few weeks. Lie low. Let the media frenzy settle—"

"There's nothing to do here!" She flung herself onto the plush sofa, tossing a throw pillow for good measure.

"There are plenty of activities," her father countered, clearly unimpressed. "Perhaps fewer than the ones available at your usual Hollywood soirées, where you… shall we say, 'bared it all'."

Isabella let out an exaggerated sigh, willing herself not to scream.

Her father pressed on. "And if this Georgio fellow truly cares for you, he can visit. Lake Tahoe isn't the end of the world — you're only a few hours from L.A."

"We broke up!" she shot back, bristling. "And how do you expect me to meet anyone new? I'm stuck on a goddamn mountain in the middle of nowhere!"

"The Edgewater is a five-star resort with exquisite amenities, and you have your own private chateau," he reminded her.

"Oh yes, and my only company is Victor, the world's least talkative bodyguard," she grumbled.

"Victor is there to ensure you don't find yourself in another compromising situation. First, the dress incident, then the beach —"

"The beach wasn't my fault!" she protested. "I thought it was a nude beach! In Europe, no one cares!"

Her father groaned. "Just stay put until I say otherwise. Can you do that for me, my little one?"

Isabella clenched her teeth, gripping the pillow tightly. "Fine," she bit out. "But I'm not happy about it."

"Neither am I. But I have crucial meetings this week, so please try not to flood my inbox with complaints. I promise I'll visit soon and take you shopping."

She exhaled sharply. "Yes, Poppa."

"That's my good girl." His tone softened. "I'll call when I'm on my way."

Isabella tossed her phone onto the sofa, where it fell in between the cushions. She let out a long, exaggerated groan.

A knock at the door brought her to her feet, irritation bubbling back to the surface.

"Now what?" she muttered, stalking to the door. If Victor was bothering her with something pointless again, she was going to scream.

She yanked the door open—

And froze.

A tall man in a server's uniform stood in the doorway, a black skull mask covering his face.

Before she could react, he shoved his way inside.

She stumbled backward. "What the hell are you—"

The click of a pistol's safety disengaging cut her off. It had been hidden under the tray the man had carried.

Her heart slammed against her ribs as the man aimed the gun — sleek, black, with an intimidatingly long silencer attached to the barrel.

Three more masked men burst through the door, their heavy footsteps shattering the fragile stillness. Between them, they dragged a figure — Victor. Isabella's heart clenched, a cold pit forming in her stomach as they brutally hurled him to the floor. Victor — the man who had been her shield, her silent guardian through countless dangers, the one who had stood by her side long enough to become more than just a protector. He was her friend. And seeing him like this, vulnerable and broken, sent a wave of fear and helplessness crashing over her.

He groaned weakly, blood soaking into the plush carpet.

"Victor!" she gasped, but the moment she tried to move, a hand clamped over her mouth.

"*Silencio*," one of the masked intruders ordered, his breath hot against her ear.

She thrashed against him, but a quick jab of the gun's muzzle against her temple stopped her cold. The gun felt warm — too warm — as if someone had recently fired it.

"You're coming with us," another voice said, low and devoid of emotion. "Make a sound, and I'll make sure you never make another."

Tears burned at the edges of her vision. She nodded, her body rigid.

The hand over her mouth finally lifted, and she sucked in a shaky breath.

"Come," the man commanded.

Rough hands seized her arms, dragging her toward the door. The cool mountain air hit her like a slap as they shoved her into a white, windowless van idling at the curb.

"What do you want with me?" she croaked.

One man turned his masked face toward her, his eyes gleaming with something dark—something cruel.

"*El Conjurador Oscuro* wishes to speak with you," he said, his voice like gravel.

Her blood turned to ice.

1. LOST TO SIGHT

I *heard the thunderous crack of machine-gun fire shatter the elegant stillness of the ballroom. Chandeliers trembled as bullets ripped through the ornate ceiling, sending a cascade of plaster and dust raining down on shrieking guests.*

Cries of terror burst forth as people dove for cover. I jumped up and used my body to cover Jyanette, my hands over my head.

As I watched, a group of armed men stormed into the room, specters of violence in their black tactical gear and featureless masks. Automatic weapons gripped tightly in their gloved hands; movements precise, practiced — predatory. They spread out, corralling the well-dressed captives like sheep, cutting off avenues of escape with ruthless efficiency.

My breath came fast and shallow, but I forced myself to steady it. My fingers instinctively sought my wife's hand, finding it trembling but warm. My wife. Jyanette and I had only just begun our life together, and now we stood in the midst of a waking nightmare.

One of the terrorists stepped forward, taller than the others, his stance exuding command. When he spoke, his voice was cold, clipped, carrying the faint trace of an accent.

"Some of you will come with us."

The words hung in the air, leaden with finality.

Panic rippled outward like a stone dropped into still water. Guests clung to one another, their faces pale, eyes darting toward exits that no longer existed.

"We are in control of this hotel," the man continued, his calm tone more chilling than if he had shouted, "You will do as we say, or you will die."

I faced my wife and whispered, "I love you."

A voice, soft yet insistent, pierced through the lingering echoes of gunfire in my mind.

"Len, are you awake?"

I jolted upright, my eyes snapping open to find myself not in a ballroom under siege, but in the stillness of a parked car. The dream unraveled, slipping from me like mist.

Jyanette was in the driver's seat, watching me with a mixture of amusement and concern. Her ebony hand — a dark contrast against my own pale flesh — rested lightly on mine, grounding me in reality.

"You were really asleep, weren't you?" she asked, tilting her head. "I thought you were just going to meditate."

I exhaled slowly, rubbing my temples before allowing a sheepish grin to cross my face. "I guess I nodded off."

Outside the windshield, the world remained blissfully untouched by violence. The hotel before us stood tall and stately, its three stories bathed in the golden glow of the setting sun. Multiple chimneys jutted into the sky like silent sentinels, the stonework reflecting an era of old-world grandeur. Beyond the main structure, the lake stretched out like a field of diamonds, its surface catching the last rays of sunlight in a mesmerizing dance of light.

Shaking off the remnants of the dream, I reached for my cane — a sturdy wooden one with an elegant hooked top. It was a recent acquisition, replacing the collapsible cane I had used throughout our week in Las Vegas. That one had proven too flimsy for my needs, prompting a stop at the Las Vegas Mobility Shoppe for something more substantial.

It still wasn't as good as my cobra-topped cane from home, but I couldn't exactly bring a cane that contained a twenty-four-inch sword hidden within it onto an airplane.

Jyanette grinned, her earlier concern melting into something far more mischievous. "Am I wearing you out on our honeymoon?"

I chuckled, playing along despite my lingering unease. "We have been catching up, haven't we, my darling?"

Our playful banter was a comforting thread of normalcy, yet something about the dream still clung to me — something deeper than just the images.

I swung open the trunk, retrieving our luggage while Jyanette leaned against the car with a knowing smile. "Be warned," she teased, "I intend to keep up this pace. We still have another week before we go back to New Jersey."

I grinned, but my fingers curled a little tighter around the cane's handle. Balancing our bags, I also gripped the cane for support. Although I had my knee replaced a few months earlier and could bend it after a decade of it being fused straight, the muscle mass I lost in a car accident years earlier made the leg prone to weakness.

Her eyes drifted toward the hotel, where the setting sun cast a golden glow over the manicured gardens. The air carried the rich scent of pine needles and blooming wildflowers, mingling with the soft, rhythmic rustle of a gentle evening breeze. Birds trilled their twilight songs from the towering evergreens, their melodies adding to the ambiance.

"This is such a refreshing change after that whirlwind week in Vegas," Jyanette murmured.

"Definitely a different energy here," I agreed, my gaze drifting to the vast crystalline waters of Lake Tahoe. The lake shimmered like liquid sapphire under the waning sunlight, a stark contrast to the neon vibrance of Las Vegas.

Together, we made our way toward the grand hotel entrance. "All that running around and excitement feels like something from another lifetime."

"And you chasing after a killer," Jyanette added, her voice laced with admiration. "After all the craziness, I'm really looking forward to just relaxing and enjoying our honeymoon."

I paused mid-stride, setting the luggage down on the stone pathway and pulling her into a warm embrace. She melted into me as our lips met, a gentle hum of contentment escaping her throat.

When we broke apart, her smile was radiant in the soft twilight. "Glad I didn't completely wear you out. But let's get to our room before the romance takes over," she said, a playful gleam in her eyes.

"I can't help it." My heart thrummed at the sight of her. "You're just so beautiful."

"Keep this up, Doctor Wise, and you might get lucky."

I gaped in mock horror. "Are you suggesting I fool around with a married woman, Mrs. Wise?"

"I think it's entirely acceptable at this point," she laughed.

With our bags in tow, we stepped into the vast hotel lobby. The polished marble floors gleamed beneath several chandeliers fashioned from interwoven antlers, casting a soft golden light. Rich wooden beams framed the high ceilings, and oversized windows revealed a breathtaking view of the lake, its surface touched by the last streaks of sunset. Plush sofas and elegant armchairs were strategically placed around a stone fireplace, a small fire crackling invitingly.

"Now that's something we didn't have in Vegas — a private beach," Jyanette noted, peering out the window. "I plan on soaking up the sun for hours every day."

"I'll try to join you," I chuckled, already anticipating my inevitable sunburn. "But I burn easy."

"So do I," she admitted. "My skin just hides it better than yours."

Jyanette's complexion was a deep, rich ebony, an inheritance from her mother, who had emigrated from Africa. In contrast, I was as pale as they came, a quintessential academic whose indoor lifestyle left me deprived of a tan and possibly vitamin D.

We approached the sleek reception desk, where a young brunette greeted us with a bright smile.

"Doctor and Mrs. Wise, checking in," I said.

She nodded, tapping on the keyboard. "May I see your ID and a credit card for incidentals, please?"

I handed over my New Jersey driver's license and my overtaxed Visa card. She swiped it, frowned, and tried again.

"I'm sorry," she said, her smile faltering. "It's declined. Do you have another card?"

I glanced at Jyanette, the flicker of unease in her eyes mirrored my own.

"Did we overspend in Vegas?" she whispered as I rifled through my wallet.

Sighing, I ran a hand through my hair. "It's possible. I didn't factor in the wedding expenses when I set up the automatic withdrawals for our bills. I thought we'd just be attending — not getting married ourselves."

The woman frowned at the computer screen again, then glanced back at me. "Excuse me, can you wait here for a moment?"

"Sure," I replied, beads of sweat forming on my forehead.

Even though both Jyanette and I had decent incomes — and I had received several large financial rewards for my investigative work — we were still burdened by student loan debts, including her law school tuition. We had designed our finances to pay down that debt head-on, but it left little wiggle room for spontaneous expenses. Our trip to Vegas for my brother's wedding had maxed out my credit card, despite my brother generously covering our hotel and flight.

I carefully slid the cards and identification back into my wallet while we waited

Jyanette watched me silently, her gaze fixed on the contents of my wallet as I closed it. "What's that tan piece of paper?"

I glanced down and recognized the fragile sheet nestled behind my driver's license — a small square that had traveled with me for quite some time.

"That?" I replied, pulling the paper free. I unfolded it gingerly, revealing an intricate design etched in a special deep red ink: a circle encased within another circle, adorned with peculiar lettering that danced between the two rings, as well as a series of lines that converged into an odd, almost hypnotic shape.

"I guess I consider it a lucky charm," I explained, my voice dropping slightly. "It's one of the seals of Solomon. Drawn on parchment with Dragon's Blood ink, it possesses the power to frighten demons and imprison them."

Jyanette's expression shifted into a more serious demeanor. "You used something like that... when we faced that... man..." Her words hung in the air, a reminder of the haunting memories we shared.

I carefully folded the parchment and returned it to my wallet, sensing the weight of our shared past. "Yes. It was because we got through that night, I carry this on me now."

I looked into her eyes and saw the shadow there, fully aware that this had stirred a painful recollection. A year and a half ago we shared a terrifying night. We confronted a man possessed by a demon in a desolate insane asylum, a night that had nearly claimed both our lives.

"I'm sorry," I said, squeezing her hand gently as I watched an array of emotions flicker across her face. "I didn't mean to remind you—"

She took a deep breath, her grip tightening around mine. "No, it's all right," she replied, her voice steadier now. "You should carry something like that, just in case. We survived that nightmare, so it's a reminder that we can face anything that comes our way." Still, a pensive look washed over her features. "I'm just wondering why you brought it here?"

"I just keep it in my wallet," I shrugged, trying to lighten the mood. "It might come in handy, if we run into a demon again,"

"Well, there is that," Jyanette chuckled softly, a hint of her humor breaking through the seriousness of the moment. "I suppose it's better to be prepared than to let our guard down, especially with the situations you attract."

That was true. As a parapsychologist, psychic, and investigator who worked with the Mountainview Police Department, I was often pulled into situations that were strange and often supernatural, or just unusual to say the least.

Just then, the receptionist returned with a middle-aged man in a quality suit, his graying hair neatly combed. He exuded quiet authority, his smile cool and professional.

"Doctor Wise," he greeted smoothly. "I'm Mr. Jenkins, the hotel manager. I apologize for the confusion. There is a credit applied to your account."

"A credit?" I echoed, perplexed.

"Yes, sir, and a credit card is connected for your stay from a Doctor Samuel Wise. It fully covers your expenses for the duration of your visit."

Jyanette, her eyebrows arched in surprise, said, "Your father paid for everything?"

I blinked. "He did?"

"And," Jenkins added, "you also have a full spa treatment courtesy of Mr. George Emery."

Jyanette's eyes widened in delighted surprise. "My dad got us spa treatments?"

I exhaled a breath of relief, gratitude swelling. Both sets of parents had gone above and beyond to ensure our honeymoon was perfect.

"Let me get you your key cards," Jenkins said. "Will you need a guest service attendant for your luggage?"

"No, we're fine," I said.

He produced a glossy brochure for the spa. "You will both be receiving the full spa treatment, with gratuities included. Just contact the spa manager to arrange your appointment."

Jyanette's eyes sparkled with anticipation. "This sounds absolutely wonderful!"

As we stepped into the elevator, Jyanette flipped through the spa brochure, grinning. "We're getting a couple's massage, facials, manicures, and pedicures!"

"That will be a first for me," I admitted.

She grinned. "Maybe they can finally tame those toenails of yours."

"I never thought of my toenails as being a problem," I said, laughing.

"You could use them as weapons," she said with a wink.

We reached our suite on the third floor, and the room seemed to stretch on forever. Floor-to-ceiling windows framing an unobstructed view of the moonlit lake with a cozy gas fireplace and a small balcony with deck chairs. Leather sofas and a plush easy chair added to the room's elegance, crowned by a shimmering chandelier that cast a warm glow.

"Wow," Jyanette gasped. "This is fancier than the hotel in Vegas." She wandered over to the corner, where a sleek coffee maker and refrigerator were neatly arranged on a counter. "I guess I get to be Cinderella for a week."

I wrapped my arms around her waist, pressing a kiss to her neck. "I promise I won't make you clean any fireplaces when we get home."

Moving into the adjoining bedroom, I found it equally well-decorated. The king-size bed rested on a pedestal, while the bathroom featured a large round tub and twin sinks adorned with polished marble.

"This is so nice," Jyanette said, her voice a mix of awe and pleasure. "After the flight and our drive from the airport, I could really use a bath."

"I have a few other ideas in mind that would be equally wonderful," I countered, pulling her into my arms.

We fell into a kiss that ignited all the fire we felt for each other. The simple contact stirred desires, fueling my every nerve.

She drew back with a mischievous grin. "I'm glad to see you're still interested."

With a pat on her flawless backside, I murmured, "Not even the slightest bit bored."

Before she could reply, a firm knock echoed through the suite.

Jyanette gave me a curious look before heading to the door. A moment later, she returned, her expression serious.

"Len, there's a man in uniform who wants to talk to you."

Frowning, I stepped forward to find a tall, imposing figure waiting. He was broad-shouldered, clad in a dark green sheriff's uniform with a neatly pressed tan shirt and tie. His salt-and-pepper hair was cropped short, his sharp eyes scrutinizing me.

"Doctor Wise?" he asked, extending a hand. "I'm Captain Lauwers with the Douglas County Sheriff's Office."

I shook his hand firmly. "How can I help you, Captain?" I asked, immediately sensing the weight of the situation.

"I read about your involvement in a recent case in Las Vegas," he admitted. "It's been all over the news. I also had a conversation with Detective Washington from the LVPD—"

"I worked with him, yes." I said, still unsure where this was leading.

"He mentioned you have a unique ability to read a scene," Lauwers continued, a hint of admiration in his tone. "I learned you'd be staying at the Edgewater. We have a situation and your expertise could be invaluable."

"I have some techniques I use," I said.

I felt Jyanette tense beside me. "We're on our honeymoon," she interjected, crossing her arms.

"I understand, Mrs. Wise," Lauwers said with professional calm. "But if you would spare just a few moments, maybe your husband can help."

"What happened?" I pressed.

"A woman is missing," he stated, his brows furrowed with concern. "We've found signs that indicate foul play, but so far, we don't have any leads."

Jyanette looked toward me, her expression firm. "May I speak with you privately?"

I followed her into the bedroom, already anticipating an argument.

"I can say no," I offered.

To my surprise, she wasn't angry. "I'm going with you."

"What?"

"The man needs your help. That's fine. But it's our honeymoon, so, wherever you go, I go," she said, her eyes seared with determination.

"I'm sure this will be—"

She raised her hand, in a familiar gesture which silenced my protests, "This is not a negotiation."

"But—"

She folded her arms defiantly. "We help him now and then get back to what we were about to do. No arguments."

I sighed, knowing I was defeated. "Fine, let's go help him," I agreed, resigned but also intrigued by the unfolding situation. Together, we stepped back into the sitting room.

"We can go with you," I said to Captain Lauwers, casting a glance toward Jyanette, who nodded. "Is it far from here?"

"No, it's quite close. In fact, the scene is within the resort — a private guest chateau."

"Crime scene?" Jyanette echoed, her curiosity piqued.

"Yes," he confirmed, his demeanor somber. "We found a bloodstain and at this point, we don't know whose it is."

A chill passed between Jyanette and me.

Our honeymoon would have to wait.

2. DISSIPATED DREAMS

We followed Captain Lauwers down the main staircase, each step echoing softly in the heavy quiet of the lodge. At the landing, he paused just for a heartbeat, glancing over his shoulder to ensure we kept up, before leading us out through the main doors and into the gathering twilight.

Outside, the sun had already slipped beneath the horizon, leaving the sky a bruised purple and streaked with dwindling ribbons of burnt orange.

It felt unnaturally still, the air tense and laden, as if the fading daylight itself were holding its breath.

The hotel's exterior lamps cast pools of misty golden illumination along the manicured pathway. As shadows deepened, the tall pines loomed closer, silhouetted blackly against the dimming sky, their branches shifting quietly under a breeze too gentle to dispel my own growing sense of unease.

Walking behind the Captain, I studied the angular profiles of the smaller buildings clustered nearby.

They stood like half-seen sentinels in the dusk, strange hybrids of sleek elegance and dignity, each one identical, and each clad in that same uniform slate-gray siding. Their sharply pitched rooftops angled deliberately toward the lake, as if the architect had wanted to frame and force attention to the dark, reflective waters — a view that, tonight, felt startlingly ominous.

Why was I so concerned? I was only being asked to examine a scene, something I had done with my police contact and friend, Lt. Bill McGee, numerous times. Why did this fill me with sudden apprehension?

The memory of my strange dream flickered through my mind, complete with the sound of echoing gunfire.

Ahead, the largest of these residences loomed in prominence. Its facade, starkly illuminated by harsh portable floodlights, stood out unnaturally bright, casting distorted shapes onto the gravel driveway and the neatly trimmed hedges lining the building's approach.

Two uniformed officers guarded the entrance, their postures stiff and silent, expressions impossible to decipher from the shadowed rims of their standard-issue hats. But one look at their rigid stances and the intense vigilance with which they surveyed everyone who drew near was intimidating.

Nearby, the dull drone of a generator thrummed like a distant heartbeat, constant and heavy. It seemed to speak more clearly than the officers' measured silence.

Captain Lauwers exchanged a brief nod with the officers. A moment later, the entryway door creaked open in front of us, revealing an interior that spread out far larger and more elaborate than the exterior would suggest.

Crossing that threshold, I felt a chill pass through me — and knew with cold certainty that we had just walked into a place where something bad had occurred.

"This place is almost as big as Mrs. Higgins' house," Jyanette murmured, speaking of our landlady's residence back home. I think she was trying to lighten the mood, noticing that I was on edge.

She felt it too.

She also was correct in her assessment. The open-concept design allowed the living room to flow seamlessly into a kitchen dominated by a sleek, polished island. Beyond that, an inviting dining area gleamed under the soft glow of recessed lighting. An exposed wooden staircase led to the second floor, its railings crafted with elegant precision.

It was luxurious, yes, and large. But it felt cold, impersonal... distant.

All of my impressions faded into insignificance as my eyes locked onto the large, dark stain marring the center of the carpet. A deep, reddish-brown blotch, unmistakable in its grim nature.

Blood. Dried, but undeniably human.

Captain Lauwers spoke, his tone brisk. "A maid came in this morning, found the stain, and reported it. The hotel staff contacted the police right away."

His voice was steady, but I detected an underlying tension.

"It's a rather delicate situation. The woman guest is missing. Her limousine disappeared as well. Some locals claim to have seen a white van outside early this morning, but as of now, we have no confirmation of its involvement. It could've been nothing more than a delivery."

I frowned, my curiosity piqued. "Then why the heavy police presence?"

Lauwers exhaled through his nose. "Because the woman in question is the daughter of a diplomat. Forensics came in earlier to analyze the scene, and they confirmed that the stain is human blood."

Jyanette and I exchanged a glance. This had just escalated from an odd disappearance to something far more sinister.

"How large is this place?" I asked, scanning the room, trying to gauge the layout.

"Four bedrooms — one on this floor, three upstairs. There's also a den past the staircase."

"How many people were staying here?"

"Only the woman and her bodyguard."

Jyanette, ever one to catch details, asked a question that, under other circumstances, might have seemed out of place. "How much does a suite like this cost?"

"This one runs about six thousand dollars a night," Lauwers replied, as though discussing the weather.

Jyanette and I exchanged another look. "Six thousand? A night?"

"That's what the manager told me."

I wondered just how much my father was spending on our own accommodations, then decided it was best not to dwell on it.

Instead, I went to Lauwers. "Would you like me to do a reading?"

His expression barely shifted, but I caught the slight narrowing of his eyes, the small twitch of his fingers. "Fine with me. What does that entail?"

Jyanette stepped in before I could reply. "Len puts himself into an altered state of consciousness. During this state, he perceives past events as though they're playing out, like a movie."

Lauwers's skepticism was evident in the deepening of the lines on his forehead. "Is that so?"

"Essentially," I confirmed. "If we want to be scientific about it, I tap into the residual energy left behind by emotionally charged events. My mind then interprets those energies as a vision."

Lauwers hesitated. "Do you think this will work?"

"I can't say for sure. Sometimes, I see past events with absolute clarity. Other times, nothing comes through at all."

Lauwers folded his arms. "Right now, we have a bloodstain and a missing heiress. Any insight you can provide would be helpful."

"Then I need you to take notes on what I say. And clear the room — only you, me, and Jyanette should be here."

Lauwers nodded and said to the officers, "Clear out."

As the men filed out, I sat at the small dining table, choosing one of the straight-backed chairs. Jyanette perched herself on the overstuffed chair, watching me with quiet attention.

"Do you need candles or anything?" Lauwers asked, his tone half-joking.

"No, nothing like that," I said, shaking my head. "I just need as few interruptions as possible. Jyanette, if I fall silent, please encourage me to keep describing what I'm seeing, in case Captain Lauwers doesn't jump in."

"I know the drill, Len," she replied, her tone reassuring.

I closed my eyes, inhaling deeply and exhaling slowly, focusing on my breath.

In… out, in… out.

Gradually, I allowed myself to relax deeply, releasing the tension from my body and quieting my thoughts until my mind drifted into a peaceful, meditative state — a state referred to as the alpha state, where the mind is calm and receptive, somewhere between normal alertness and sleep.

In this tranquil state, my surroundings felt distant and muted.

When I opened my eyes again, my point of view had shifted dramatically. Everything about me looked completely different. The previously colorful room now appeared as if viewed through an old-fashioned sepia-toned photograph. The colors had reduced themselves to soft black and white shades, tinted with a brown hue giving the entire scene a dreamlike quality.

Everything around me appeared softer, warmer, as if I had stepped back in time or slipped into another reality entirely.

And in a sense, I did.

I was seeing what had occurred in this room hours earlier that left a strong mental impression.

A woman emerged from the shadows — a translucent figure, pacing anxiously, her phone pressed to her ear. Her mouth moved rapidly, yet I heard nothing.

This was a vision that was merely visual, so I did not hear anything she said.

"I see a woman," I murmured. "Long, dark hair. Striking features — high cheekbones, graceful but athletic build. She's about five-foot-seven. She's walking as she speaks on the phone."

"Do you see the bodyguard?" Lauwers asked.

I scanned the scene. "No. He's not in the room."

The woman admired herself in the mirror as she spoke and eventually sat on the sofa. After a moment, she ended her call abruptly, tossing her phone onto the sofa where it fell between the cushions. She stood, and bent as if to retrieve it, but then hesitated, and walked toward the door.

"What do you see, Len?" Jyanette reminded me.

"She's going to the door," I said, my eyes fixated on the event. "She's opening it."

On the other side of the door stood a menacing figure, though all I could discern was an inky-black silhouette — void of any recognizable features or clothing. My pulse quickened.

"I see someone there, but I can't make them out," I murmured, a sense of unease creeping in.

Three more shadowy figures entered the room, dragging a man between them. He was clear to me — a large, fit man with a shaved head.

They laid him onto the carpet right where the blood stain was located, and I could see the deep brown mark through his almost transparent body.

The bodyguard.

I described what I saw.

The four figures loomed in the dim haze, indistinct shadows that moved with silent precision. Though their features remained shrouded in darkness, their presence alone carried a heavy weight — an air of dominance, of menace. Their outlines suggested strength and experience.

"These men that entered the room," Lauwers asked, his voice edged with urgency. "Can you see their faces? Describe them?"

I exhaled sharply, frustration curling in my gut like a tightening coil. "No. I can't make out any of their features." The words tasted bitter, my own limitations gnawing at me.

One of the shadows stepped closer to the woman, his hand clamping over her mouth, muffling any chance of a scream. Another figure raised his arm, and in the eerie half-light, I caught a glimpse of what looked like a silencer affixed to the end of a gun.

The woman's eyes widened, terror crystallizing in their depths as the men took hold of her, dragging her across the room. The image flickered, then blurred at the edges, as if the vision itself was being swallowed by the darkness from which it came. Just as they reached the threshold, it collapsed entirely, the scene dissolving away.

I gasped as reality rushed back, my body taut with residual tension.

Rubbing my face, I forced myself to breathe, grounding myself in the present. "That's it," I muttered, shaking my head. "That's all I could see."

Lauwers studied me, his expression unreadable, though the disappointment in his voice was evident. "Not much to go on."

"No," I admitted. "But it felt… off. Like I wasn't just seeing a moment in time, but something deliberately obscured."

Lauwers exhaled and ran a hand through his short-cropped hair. "At least the forensic team got photos of footprints on the floor and carpet. Maybe that'll help confirm how many people were in here."

A thought struck me. "She threw her phone," I said, recalling the quick, desperate motion. "Do you have gloves? An evidence bag?"

Lauwers narrowed his eyes. "Why?"

"I want to check if it's where I saw it land."

He didn't question me further. "Hang tight," he said, striding toward the door. He disappeared into the hall and exchanged a few words with an officer outside.

A gentle touch on my arm made me turn. Jyanette's anxiety was palpable in the soft furrow of her brow. "You really couldn't see anything?" she asked, her voice low, careful.

I shook my head, the frustration still simmering. "They weren't just masked or hooded… they were shadows. Like living silhouettes."

Jyanette studied me, searching my face. "Any theories on why?"

"Nothing good," I admitted.

Lauwers returned, snapping on a pair of nitrile gloves. He handed me a set as well as an evidence bag, his gaze already sweeping the room. "Forensics checked under the furniture but didn't find anything out of place."

"Let's see if they missed something," I whispered.

My gloved hands moved to the sofa. Slowly, I let my fingers brush across the worn cushions, feeling every crease and fold as if they might speak to me. Then, suddenly, my fingertips brushed against something unexpected — smooth, cold, unmistakably solid beneath the fabric.

Time seemed to stretch; the room grew quiet. And there it was — a smartphone nestled like a secret treasure. I pulled it out. The pink case shimmered in the pale light, dotted with what I first thought were rhinestones, but when I squinted closer, they glinted with an unmistakable fire. Real diamonds — delicate, dazzling, and hauntingly out of place.

Lauwers' eyes sharpened with interest. He took the phone, pressing the power button. "It's locked," he noted. "I'll have tech take a look."

"Do you have a photo of the victim?" I asked, already knowing the answer in my gut.

Lauwers scrolled through his own phone before turning the screen toward me. The moment my eyes landed on the image, my stomach dropped. Long, dark hair. Striking features. A woman whose eyes now haunted my mind. "That's her. That's the woman I saw."

Lauwers nodded. "Finding the phone is a good lead," he admitted, handing me a business card. "Call me if you get anything else. The Sheriff's department is under a lot of pressure on this case."

Jyanette crossed her arms. "Who is she?"

"Isabella Fontaine," Lauwers replied grimly. "As I told you, she's the daughter of a South American diplomat. Powerful. Wealthy."

Just then, an officer stepped in. "Captain, there are men here to see you. From Washington."

Lauwers stiffened. "Feds."

Before he could say more, a figure pushed past the officer with the force of someone who had long since stopped caring about protocol. He stood tall at around six feet, his athletic build accentuated by a tailored suit that had clearly suffered from a long day spent crammed in the confines of an airplane. His thinning brown hair suggested late thirties, but his presence was ageless in its authority.

"Captain Lauwers?" he demanded, his voice a blade's edge.

"Yes," Lauwers answered, calm but firm.

"I'm Special Agent Roberts with the Diplomatic Security Service," he said, glaring at me and Jyanette. "Who are you two, and what are you doing in my crime scene?"

Feeling the weight of his stare, I stepped forward. "I'm Doctor Leonard Wise. I'm a consultant."

Roberts' expression hardened into a thin line. "I don't allow civilians in restricted areas."

Lauwers held up the bagged phone. "I requested Doctor Wise's assistance. He was instrumental in locating the victim's cell phone when forensics overlooked it."

Roberts seemed unimpressed, his demeanor suggesting he viewed our contributions as negligible. "We'll have my team conduct another sweep of the scene. I'll take that," he said, extending his hand for the evidence bag.

Lauwers handed it over but didn't back down. "When can we expect your team?"

"They're on the way, but it's an eight-hour drive from the Los Angeles Field Office, and a bunch of that FBI team are on maneuvers somewhere. If you'd contacted us earlier today, they'd already be here."

"Agent Roberts, we didn't even know the victim was under Diplomatic Security's auspices until this afternoon," Lauwers shot back, annoyed.

As the two of them continued their crossfire of heated words, I caught sight of an African-American man stepping into the room, dressed sharply in a suit and tie emblazoned with that unmistakable FBI flair. He stood tall and robust, and his shaved head made him instantly recognizable to me.

His eyes landed on Jyanette, and a broad smile spread across his face as he approached confidently.

"Marcus?" Jyanette exclaimed seeing him draw near, her eyes lighting up.

Agent Marcus Calvin, an FBI agent with whom both Jyanette and I had collaborated in the past — and who, coincidentally, had also been her boyfriend during the time when she and I had separated — was now standing right before us.

With his arms wide open, he enveloped Jyanette in a warm hug. A knot twisted in my gut. It had been a while, but the past still had teeth. I mean, who wants to see the man your wife used to sleep with, especially on your honeymoon?

Marcus extended a hand to me. "Len. Good to see you."

I shook it, masking my discomfort.

"Agent Calvin, you know these people?" Roberts asked, impatient.

"Yes, sir. Ms. Emery here used to be a DOJ field agent, and Dr. Wise has assisted the FBI on high-profile cases."

Roberts waved a dismissive hand. "Escort them out."

"Thank you for your time, Doctor," Lauwers called out as we passed, and I offered a nod in acknowledgment.

Once outside, Marcus escorted us to the curb, turning to Jyanette with a warm smile. "I thought you were back at the DA's office in New Jersey. What are you doing here?"

Jyanette intertwined her fingers with mine, and broke into a wide and happy smile. "We got married," she announced, raising her left hand to reveal the rings adorning her finger.

For a fleeting moment, surprise flickered across Marcus' face, quickly shifting into a grin. "Congratulations! That's fantastic!"

Despite our competitive history over Jyanette's affections, I felt a small measure of relief seeing that Marcus was happy for her. Still, it was hard to shake off the memories of the past — the times we had clashed, how close we had come to blows.

"We just got married last week," I quickly added.

Jyanette glanced at me. "Len's parents and my parents pitched in to give us a honeymoon here."

"Wait, you guys are on your honeymoon?" Marcus' brows shot up in surprise. "How did you end up at a crime scene?"

"I solved a case in Vegas that got national attention," I said. "Captain Lauwers asked me to do a reading at the scene."

"Are you two staying here, at this hotel?" Marcus asked.

"Yes," Jyanette replied with an optimism that made me a little uneasy. "Maybe we can have dinner together."

I shot her a glance, trying to maintain a neutral expression. The last thing I wanted was to spend quality time with Marcus. It also annoyed me that I was being so petty. After all, I got the girl.

"Good to know," Marcus said, his enthusiasm seemingly undeterred. "But I can't promise my schedule will allow for it; I'm providing support to Agent Roberts."

"He seems like a real treat," I quipped.

Calvin sighed, clearly exasperated. "Let's avoid that discussion. If I need your help, can I reach out to you, Len?"

"If you want him, I come along," Jyanette stated firmly. "We come as a package."

Marcus nodded in understanding. "Absolutely. I'll keep you posted."

With that, he headed back inside.

Jyanette and I started back along the pathway to the main lodge.

"Time to get back to our honeymoon," she said, breezily.

"Yeah," I grumbled.

Suddenly, Jyanette stopped, facing me with a piercing glare. "Are you upset that Marcus is here?"

Taken aback, I paused, trying to process the emotions swirling within. "I just wasn't expecting to run into your old boyfriend on my honeymoon."

Her eyes widened in surprise. "Oh my God, you're jealous."

I scoffed. "How would you feel if Kate Yearling showed up here?"

Kate was an FBI profiler I'd worked with. When Jyanette and I broke up, she and I became intimate for a few months, both of us emotional and needy.

"That's hardly the same thing," Jyanette countered, placing her hands on her hips. "You still work with Kate all the time."

Fuming, I resumed walking, and Jyanette hurried to catch up.

"Christ, Len, I didn't know you were so insecure."

I stopped and faced her. "Are we having a fight?"

"I wasn't planning on one," she replied softly. "In fact, I was hoping to take you back to our room to—" She wiggled her eyebrows invitingly.

"Renew our vows?" I interrupted, grinning.

She pulled me close. "I think we can figure it out. Now, do you want to be jealous, or do you want to do some renewing?"

As if on cue, my intuition flickered, and I glanced into the surrounding tree-line. A movement caught my eye — a dark silhouette flitted between the branches. Without thinking, I pulled myself free to lift my cane like a weapon. The wood felt solid and real in my grip, as memories of those ominous shapes I'd seen flashed through my mind.

It turned out to be just a man in a bathing suit with a towel slung over his shoulder, casually strolling toward the lodge. I released a breath I didn't realize I was holding, tension seeping from my body as Jyanette placed a hand on my shoulder.

"You're pretty jumpy," she said, concern written on her face.

"Yeah, I guess I am." The images from my earlier visions lingered — the uncertainty worrying me. "Sorry I overreacted. I know Marcus is a part of your past."

"And an old friend." She leaned in, lips brushing my ear. "But I married you. Now, let's go up to our room and let me renew you."

I couldn't help but smile. "Well, since you put it like that…"

3. RECEDING VIEW

*T*he deafening roar of machine-gun fire shattered the ballroom's illusion of safety, a thunderous rat-tat-tat that sent shockwaves through the crowd. Guests screamed, instinctively diving beneath tables or flattening themselves against the polished marble floor. Chandeliers trembled from the vibrations, their crystals jingling like a dying wind chime, while plaster rained from the ornate ceiling in thick, choking clouds. The air reeked of gunpowder and fear.

My pulse pounded against my ribs as I crouched low, scanning the chaos. I knew this wasn't random. This was a message, a calculated display of dominance.

A group of armed men stormed through the large double doors, their heavy boots pounding against the floor with brutal finality. These figures looked sinister as they wore grotesque black skull masks covered in white symbols. The hollow, empty sockets let them stare down at us with eerie detachment.

Death itself had entered the room, and it had a voice.

One of them, taller than the rest, stepped forward and raised his weapon above his head. The room fell into a terrified silence. His voice, thick with an accent boomed over the stunned crowd.

"Move to the center of the room!"

The command was absolute, slicing through the tension like a guillotine's blade. For a moment, no one moved — then the fear took hold. The guests hesitated only long enough for realization to sink in before scrambling to obey, their shoes skidding against the slick marble as they stumbled toward the center.

Husbands shielded their wives, whispers of prayers and choked sobs filling the space between hurried footsteps.

I squeezed Jyanette's hand, feeling the tremble in her grip. She was terrified — but steady.

The leader took another step forward, sweeping his rifle in a slow arc as if daring someone to defy him. "We control this hotel," he declared, his voice carrying an unnerving calm. "You will obey our commands without question, or you will die where you stand."

I could see the hostages around me — eyes wide, mouths slightly open, as if still trying to process the impossible.

My mouth barely opened as I whispered to Jyanette, "I love you."

I shot up in bed, gasping as if I had just surfaced from the depths of a dark abyss, my chest tight with the weight of unseen forces pressing down. The remnants of my dream clung to me like a cold sweat, my pulse pounding in my ears. Shadows stretched long and distorted across the hotel room, shifting as my vision adjusted.

I blinked away the haze of sleep and glanced at the bedside table. The soft glow of the digital clock caught my eye: 6:00 AM. The numbers gleamed in the darkness, as though marking something inevitable.

Sinking back against the mattress, I exhaled. The room was silent save for the rhythmic hum of the air conditioner, a gentle contrast to the racing thoughts going through my head.

Beside me, Jyanette lay in peaceful slumber, her dark curls spilling over the pillow. The sheet had slipped down, revealing the soft curve of her shoulder and the gentle rise and fall of her chest. One perfect breast lay exposed, moving in sync with her slow, steady breaths.

I couldn't help a small smile. Moments like this — simple, unguarded — were what I should focus on. Instead, my mind had fixated on ghosts of the past and shadows with no substance.

I let out a quiet chuckle, remembering how frustrated I'd been just hours earlier when Marcus had shown up. The annoyance had gnawed at me, jealousy creeping into my thoughts.

But now, in the stillness of morning, it felt so trivial. I had married the woman I loved, a woman who had transformed my world with her warmth and light. And yet, like an idiot, I'd wasted energy on fleeting insecurities rather than embracing this new chapter with open arms.

Shaking off the thought, I carefully slipped out of bed, moving slowly so as not to wake her. I found the pajamas I had set aside the night before — the ones I never got around to wearing — and slipped them on.

I eased the bedroom door shut behind me. The room was still, the only sound the faint murmur of water in the lake beyond the window. I flicked on the coffeemaker, but my mind was elsewhere.

The nightmare still clung to me, lingering like the last vestiges of a storm that refused to fully pass. It wasn't just a nightmare — it was familiar, too familiar. It was the same dream that plagued me during the drive to the hotel, only now the details were sharper.

More pronounced. More deliberate.

The figures in my dream hadn't worn simple cloth masks over the lower half of their faces. No. This time, they had worn black skull masks, their hollow eye sockets like specters of death itself. The imagery haunted me, gnawing at the edges of my waking thoughts.

What did it mean?

I wasn't superstitious — not exactly. But I'd spent too many years dealing with the supernatural, and seen things that could make any man question his sanity. I relied on my instincts, and my unusual abilities, and knew better than to ignore a feeling like this. My gut churned with something I couldn't quite name, a deep-rooted unease that I couldn't shake.

The rich aroma of fresh coffee filled the air, bringing me back to the present. With a sigh, I booted up my laptop.

It had been days since I last checked my email — between the wedding, the celebrations, and the travel, everything else had taken a backseat.

My inbox was flooded with notifications. Hundreds of emails, most of them useless — except for a series of messages from Teddy Santos.

Teddy, my Teaching Assistant back at Garden State University in New Jersey, had used the summer preparing Anna Sokolov — a bright, promising student, with astounding psychic ability — to take over his TA position for the upcoming fall semester, as he was leaving to start his career in computers. There was nothing unusual about that. But as I read through his latest email, typed all in lower case as was his habit, a twinge of unease crept in.

doc;

don't know if Anna is going to work out. her grasp of the basic computer stuff is fine, but she can't really handle the uploads. I keep trying to get her to understand how all the programs work, but I'm not getting through to her.

you might need to rethink this.

teddy.

I quickly crafted a response, reminding Teddy that he was a computer science major with years of experience, while Anna was just beginning her journey. She wouldn't grasp every concept instantly.

Patience is essential, I typed, urging him to give her the time and space to learn. I knew Teddy well enough to understand his frustrations. He held himself to high standards and often expected the same from others. But Anna was young, still finding her footing, and I needed him to recognize that.

Before I sent the email, I added a brief update, letting him know that Jyanette and I were married. I kept it casual, letting him know I'd be unavailable for the next week, but would check in when I could.

Teddy's frustration didn't surprise me. Anna was an incoming freshman, after all. She lacked the experience Teddy had when he started to work with me, and yet, I had placed her in the position of teaching assistant.

Was he right? Had I made a mistake?

The idea gnawed at me. Anna's inexperience in computer science was undeniable, but I hadn't selected her for the role based on her technical skills. Something else motivated my decision — her extraordinary psychic abilities.

Anna was one of the strongest psychics I had ever encountered, her raw talent even outstripping my own. Over the past year, I had taken her under my wing, mentoring her in private sessions to refine her abilities. She had the potential to become something truly remarkable, but she still had so much to learn.

Maybe the TA position was too much, too soon. Or maybe it was exactly what she needed to push her to the next level.

Either way, she needed encouragement, and I could at least provide that much.

Glancing at my phone, I checked the time. It was three hours later on the East Coast — she was likely already up.

The phone rang twice before she answered.

"H-Hello? Len?" Anna's voice was hesitant, as though she hadn't expected to hear from me.

"Hey, Anna," I said, keeping my tone light. "Hope I'm not calling at a bad time."

"No, not at all! I just got off the bus," she replied, the faint sounds of the traffic bustling around her. "I'm walking to GSU to meet with Mr. Santos."

"How's everything going?" I asked, genuinely interested.

"I'm doing my best," she admitted, frustration creeping into her voice. "But I don't know if I can handle this job. I mean, I really appreciate you giving me the opportunity — it means a lot — but so far, I feel like I'm drowning in all the computer stuff."

"Just keep at it," I reassured her. "You're smart, Anna. You'll figure it out. It just takes time, that's all."

A silence stretched between us before she spoke again, her tone shifting slightly.

"I'm really glad you called, Len," she said.

There was something in her voice — an unease I hadn't noticed before.

She went on. "I've been worried about you."

That got my attention. My grip on the phone tightened slightly. "Why?"

"I had a dream about you last night," she admitted. "It involved you and Ms. Emery."

A chill ran down my spine.

Did she see the same thing I did?

I hesitated for a beat, considering how to respond. My instinct was to press her for details, but I also didn't want to alarm her, not yet. Instead, I tried to keep things casual.

"I didn't share this with you," I said. "Jyanette and I got married last week."

There was a brief pause on the line. "Wow, really?" she said, sounding both surprised and… something else. Resigned, maybe.

I wasn't sure what to make of it.

"I kind of sensed that," she added.

Of course she had. With her psychic abilities, keeping her in the dark about any major event in my life was next to impossible, but something about the way she said it unsettled me.

"But that's not the important part," Anna continued, her voice suddenly taut with urgency. "In my dream, I saw you in a hotel — a ballroom, big and extravagant. Then a group of men burst in, all armed with guns."

"Really?" I asked, my voice steady despite the unease creeping into my gut. "Were they wearing black masks?"

"No," she said, a tremor in her voice. "It was stranger than that. They weren't human at all. They looked like... shadows. Three-dimensional, but completely blank, no faces — just moving darkness."

A chill prickled at the base of my neck.

Shadows. Faceless figures.

"Are you serious?" I pressed.

"Yes," she said, her tone grave. "Len, I think you're in danger."

I exhaled, my pulse thrumming against my ribs. "I believe you might be right," I admitted. "A similar dream visited me last night."

Silence stretched between us, thick with unspoken concerns. Then, barely above a whisper, she said, "Please, be careful. I don't know what I'd do if something happened to you."

"We'll be fine," I said, though I wasn't sure if I believed it. "Just promise me — if you get any more insights, day or night, call or text me."

"I promise," she said, her voice firm but still shaky.

A beat passed, and I hesitated before adding, "And Anna... if anything does happen to me—"

"Len, don't talk like that," she protested.

"I need you to contact Doctor Kohl, my mentor at the University of Southern California. He can help you learn to harness your abilities."

"Nothing is going to happen to you," she said, her voice thick.

I let out a slow breath. "Anna, I'm counting on you."

A pause. Then, softer: "O-Okay."

Seeking to lighten the mood, I forced a smile into my voice. "Now go out there and master that computer. You've got this."

She let out a small, reluctant laugh. "I'll do my best."

I ended the call.

She had a dream about me. And about Jyanette.

I knew Anna was in love with me. When I first met her, her mind had been completely open to me, leaking thoughts with no control. She all but told me how she felt, even if she never meant to.

I understood it. When she was sixteen, she had been abducted by a gang of sex traffickers. Her psychic abilities allowed me to communicate with her and find her location. This enabled me to rescue her before they could hurt her. So, there was some hero worship mixed in with a teenage crush.

I had always hoped she'd meet a young man her own age, and that with time, her obsession would fade, but that hadn't happened yet.

Before I could dwell on it further, the bedroom door creaked open.

Jyanette's silhouette was bathed in the soft morning light. Her dark skin glowed warmly, and her tousled hair cascaded to her shoulders, wild and beautiful. She tilted her head, a slow, inquisitive smile playing on her features.

"Why is my bed empty?" she asked, her voice still husky from sleep, laced with playful curiosity.

I pushed the thoughts of Anna from my mind. "Sorry, I had a nightmare," I admitted.

Her expression softened instantly, and she wrapped her arms around me, pulling me close. The familiar scent of her shampoo filled my senses — something floral, rich, grounding. As I held her, the tension from the call, from the dream, from everything melted away.

Then her mouth found mine.

Soft. Warm. Inviting.

Her hands slid down, exploring me with slow, deliberate intent, igniting passion deep in my core. The heat of her touch chased away every lingering shadow, leaving only us.

"Honeymoon, remember?" she teased, her voice lilting with amusement.

She tugged at my hand, guiding me back toward the bed, and I followed without hesitation, letting the morning steal me away from the night's lingering unease.

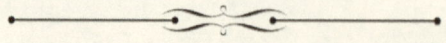

After making love, Jyanette was buzzing with energy, sprawled across the bed with the hotel spa brochure in hand, her fingers idly flipping through the glossy pages. Her brown eyes gleamed with excitement as she took in the offerings — massages, facials, seaweed wraps, even a couples' mud bath.

"When do you want to do this, Len?" she asked, rolling onto her side. "Today? Maybe tomorrow?"

I stretched out beside her, still feeling the warmth of our moment together. "Whatever you want," I murmured, running a lazy hand down her back.

She grinned. "I definitely want to hit the beach today. And I gotta say — I'm really looking forward to that hot tub."

"Does the resort have one?" I asked.

"Are you kidding?" She shot me an incredulous look, flipping a page. "It has three. One of them even has a waterfall."

I chuckled, shaking my head. "Alright, you've convinced me."

Just as she leaned in to kiss me again, a sudden knock at the door shattered the moment.

I exhaled, reluctant to leave the warmth of the sheets. "Who the hell...?"

Jyanette groaned, flopping back onto the bed. "You've gotta be kidding me. Can't we have one morning to ourselves?"

I forced myself upright, slipping on my pajama pants and grabbing the plush hotel robe. The air outside the covers felt cool against my skin, and I sighed as I padded toward the door.

When I opened it, I found Marcus Calvin standing in the hallway, his expression sheepish but expectant.

"I hope I'm not intruding," he said.

No point in telling him he was.

I stepped aside, motioning him in. "Come in, Agent Calvin. Can I get you coffee?"

"That would be nice." He ran a hand over his bald head. "It was a long night."

I led him toward the small kitchenette, grabbing the hotel-provided coffee pods and starting a fresh mug. Just as the rich aroma filled the air, Jyanette appeared from the bedroom, dressed casually in jeans and a simple blouse.

Even with her effortless look, she was stunning.

"Marcus?" she said, eyebrows furrowing in concern. "What's going on?"

Marcus hesitated before nodding toward the sofa. "I wanted to speak with both of you. Mind if I sit?"

Jyanette and I exchanged a glance before settling onto the couch, while Marcus took the single chair facing us.

"You'll have to excuse me," he began, his gaze flickering between us. "I was… surprised to see the two of you last night. But that's not why I'm here. Len, I could use your help."

"That's not exactly the reaction Agent Roberts had last night," Jyanette interjected, a skeptical edge had crept into her tone.

Marcus let out an annoyed exhale. "Roberts is a supervisor in the Diplomatic Security Service. He doesn't work in the field anymore, and frankly, it shows."

"What do you mean?" I asked.

Marcus leaned forward, his expression turning serious. "Len, I don't know how you do what you do, and I won't pretend to understand it. But right now? We have little to go on. And we could really use your insights."

A sudden, vivid flash of my dream surged into my mind.

Black skull masks. Oversized eye sockets. Strange symbols painted in white.

I swallowed hard. "Okay... I don't know if this means anything, but something came to me since last night. It might sound crazy."

Marcus didn't flinch. "Let's hear it."

I sat back and gazed up at the ceiling gathering my thoughts. "I dreamt about men wearing black masks, shaped like skulls. They had these wide, hollow eye sockets and intricate white symbols all over them."

"That sounds familiar," Marcus said, his jaw tightened as he pulled out his phone. "But I don't see how there could possibly be a connection."

"Why? What does it mean?" I asked.

Without a word, he scrolled rapidly through images. After a moment, he offered the screen to us.

A black skull mask stared back at me.

It wasn't just similar; it was identical to what I had seen in my dream. The deep-set eye sockets, the vertical lines cut into the mouth where the teeth should be, and most disturbingly, the cryptic symbols crawling across its surface.

My blood ran cold.

"That's it," I said, my voice sharper than I intended. "That's exactly what I saw."

Marcus's expression darkened. "If so, it doesn't make any sense."

Jyanette shifted beside me, alarm creeping into her features. "Why? What does it mean?"

Marcus leaned back, rubbing a hand over his jaw. "There are rival factions of drug cartels waging war across South America," he said, his tone grim. "One of them is led by a man who calls himself *El Conjurador Oscuro*."

Jyanette frowned. "What does that mean?"

I glanced at her, my unease growing. "It translates to The Dark Wizard."

"Exactly," Marcus confirmed. "His real name is Diego Vargas, but his men call him Don Diego. He's one of the most ruthless traffickers in the region — bloodthirsty, calculating, and utterly devoid of compassion."

"What's his connection?" I asked.

Marcus nodded. "According to FBI reports, his followers wear masks like those whenever they carry out operations in his name."

"Why the masks?" Jyanette asked, brows knitting together.

Marcus sighed. "Vargas claims to possess 'powers' that make him untouchable. Those masks are supposedly part of the mystique — meant to protect his men, and frighten their adversaries."

"Seems like you're very up to date with this guy," I said.

"We had a briefing a couple of weeks ago, that's how I got the photo," Marcus said. "The bureau got an alert that he might be in America."

"Really?" Jyanette asked.

"No. A team was sent to track him, and they found he was still in South America. The whole thing was a false alarm."

"Can you send me that image?" I asked.

"Why?" Marcus said.

"Those symbols are unusual, and I don't recognize them. I want to send the photo to my mentor, Doctor Kohl. He might be able to tell me their origin or what they mean."

"It's a cold lead, but take a look," Marcus nodded, already forwarding it. "Most of the drawings just look like squiggles to me."

I received the image and quickly sent it to Dr. Kohl, typing in the message that I wanted to know where the symbols were from. Then I studied them again, something nagging at the back of my mind.

Marcus spoke up. "Len, I have no problem with you finding out about those symbols, but I have to tell you, there is no way this Diego guy is anywhere near Lake Tahoe."

"Why not?" I said.

"I told you, the FBI are tracking him because they thought he'd slipped into the country, and he didn't. And let's face it, why would he have anything to do with Ms. Fontaine's disappearance?"

I hesitated. He was right. I had not seen anything in my vision, or even my strange dream that would explain a criminal cartel coming up to a resort in Lake Tahoe.

"I don't know," I said slowly. "But when I conducted my reading at the scene, I couldn't make out faces. I couldn't see bodies — just silhouettes. No human features. If those men were wearing these masks… that could explain why."

Marcus narrowed his eyes. "How do you mean?"

I hesitated, attempting to piece it together as I went. "These masks might affect what I do. Maybe they're not just symbolic — perhaps they are designed to block perception, especially psychics."

Marcus rubbed his temples. "You're telling me that you think a bunch of guys from South America invaded Lake Tahoe to kidnap an heiress, because you saw some masks in a dream? I think you were right in the beginning when you said it didn't make any sense."

I glanced between Marcus and Jyanette, reading their expressions: concern. Uncertainty. A hint of unease.

Just then, my phone chimed.

It was Doctor Kohl.

The message was brief. Precise.

Leonard;

The symbols on the mask are from a Latin American occult practice known as Brujería.

Be very cautious when dealing with anyone associated with these designs. They represent the worst kind of dark magic.

Fritz

I read it aloud to my companions.

Marcus listened intently, his brow furrowing. When I finished, he leaned back. "Yeah, that's what I read in this Don Diego's file. He practices Brujeria, genuinely believes he's some kind of wizard." Skepticism laced his tone, yet disgust showed on his face. "The bureau thinks all that supernatural crap is just bluster. A way to scare his enemies."

"Okay, but in my vision, I couldn't see the men who abducted her, but I saw those same masks in my dream."

"So, it's what? Black magic?" Marcus scoffed and folded his arms across his chest, his expression carefully neutral. "I don't really buy into black magic."

I shook my head. "Think of it more like a cult." I locked eyes with him, wanting him to understand the gravity of what we were dealing with. "If this Don Diego is a practitioner of some kind of ritual magic, he isn't just a cartel boss — he'll demand unwavering loyalty. Whether he actually possesses supernatural abilities is irrelevant. What will matter is that his men believe he does. A leader like that? One shrouded in mysticism, promising protection through dark ceremonies? His followers will die for him without hesitation."

I stood and paced the floor in front of Marcus. "But let's step away from the supernatural label for a second. Let's approach it scientifically. Everything has energy, right?"

Marcus hesitated, glanced at Jyanette, then nodded slowly. "I can't argue with that."

"Good." I leaned forward slightly. "What I do at a crime scene isn't magic. It's an ability to read the energetic residue left behind when someone experiences intense emotion. But here's where it gets interesting — people can manipulate energy. Some train their minds to control it, some corrupt it, and others use objects — talismans, artifacts — that carry that energy. It's possible that those energies can obscure my readings, distort my perception. That's why I couldn't see the men who took Ms. Fontaine yesterday."

Jyanette wrapped her arms around herself as she processed my words. Marcus, however, remained stiff, his jaw working as he considered my explanation.

"So why did you see these masks in your dream?" he asked, one eyebrow arching in challenge.

"Because I was asleep," I admitted. "My conscious mind wasn't filtering the information. It didn't get in the way. That allowed me to perceive those men as they really were."

What I didn't say — what I wasn't ready to say — was that I might have experienced a precognitive dream. A vision of something that hadn't occurred yet.

Marcus shook his head. "I'll relay this to Agent Roberts, but I have to tell you I doubt he will follow up on it."

"Sorry I don't have anything more to give you."

He reached into his pocket and pulled out a business card, extending it to me. "If you do dig up anything else — especially if you can pinpoint a location where the girl might be — call me."

I took the card, slipping it into my pocket. "Understood."

Marcus nodded, rose, and without another word, he headed for the door. Jyanette followed, unlocking it for him, and after he left, she fastened the deadbolt before stepping back into the room.

She watched me closely, her expression shifting from the no-nonsense composure she often wore to something gentler, more intuitive.

"You're genuinely worried about this, aren't you?" she asked.

I sighed, running a hand through my hair. "I am."

A pause. She waited for me to continue.

"There's something I didn't mention to Agent Calvin," I admitted, my voice quieter now. "I've been having a recurring dream... or maybe it's something worse."

Jyanette's brow creased. "What do you mean?"

I pictured the shadowy figures in my mind, the ones wearing those eerie masks. "I see men — a lot of them — storming a hotel. They corral the guests into a grand ballroom, weapons drawn. It's chaos. Fear. I can't shake the feeling that it's not just a dream."

She sat down beside me, her knee brushing against mine. "Do you think it's a vision?"

"I don't know. I don't want to jump to conclusions, but if there's even a chance that this is some kind of warning..." I let my voice trail off, the unspoken words lingering between us.

Jyanette shook her head. "What should we do?"

I appreciated she didn't dismiss my concerns, even if she didn't fully understand them.

"You wanted to go to the beach," I said, glancing at the brochure she'd left on the coffee table. "You should go, enjoy it. In the meantime, I'll do some research, see if I can reach out to Doctor Kohl. He might have insights — maybe even a way to shield ourselves from the occult side of all this."

Jyanette's dark eyes held something between amusement and stubbornness. "Let's compromise."

I raised an eyebrow. "Compromise?"

She grinned. "We'll go to the hotel pool. You can work on your laptop while I swim and soak up the sun."

I hesitated. "I'd probably be more productive here."

"And it's our honeymoon," she countered. "So my husband should definitely accompany me. For goodness' sake, Len, you're acting like it's a chore."

I smiled despite myself. "You're right. I apologize."

"That's better."

"Besides," I added, slipping into a playful tone, "if you're planning to wear that bikini you bought in Vegas, I might have to fend off other men."

She laughed. "Not a bad comeback." She glanced down at my legs and quirked an eyebrow. "You should probably bring a towel."

I frowned. "To cover up the scars on my leg?"

"No," she said, eyes twinkling with mischief. "I'm just worried your legs are so pale they might blind everyone at the pool."

I chuckled, shaking my head. "Touché."

We changed into beach clothes, I grabbed my laptop bag and with towels in hand, we headed out — but in the back of my mind, that lingering unease remained.

If my dream was a vision, then somewhere, sometime soon… the nightmare was about to become real.

4. INTO THIN AIR

T he sun hung high overhead, bathing everything in golden light. The scent of chlorine mingled with the breeze off the lake. Laughter and splashes filled the air as revelers indulged in midday drinks, their joy a stark contrast to the dark world I was plunging into as I navigated the murky depths of Brujería.

I was unfamiliar with the full history, though in my studies with Doctor Kohl we had touched on it. As I did a search online, it unraveled before me like an intricate tapestry. Like Voodoo and Santeria, Brujería had its origins in the forced migration of enslaved Africans, their beliefs adapting, merging, and surviving under the guise of Catholic saints, as well as remnants of Aztec mysticism.

Over generations, the practice evolved, splitting into distinct paths: the curanderos — healers revered for their wisdom — and the brujos or brujas — a South American version of a witch — feared and often shunned, unless desperation led people to seek their aid.

But Diego Vargas — *El Conjurador Oscuro* — was something else entirely.

The moment I put his name into my search engine and I saw the results, an involuntary chill skated down my spine. His legacy included more than just crime; it was drenched in blood.

Reports of human sacrifices, killed in dark rituals.

According to one report, a girl, just fifteen years old, was found dead on a stone altar in the desert, her body marked with a black mask tattooed onto her flesh. The report concluded that it was Diego's work.

Another site claimed that investigators discovered that Diego seized another cartel's compound, and sacrificed the men who worked there, leaving fifteen bodies murdered and mutilated.

The number twisted in my mind, nagging at something just beyond my grasp. Fifteen sacrifices. A fifteen-year-old victim. What did it mean?

Vargas's atrocities didn't stop at ritual killings. He also left a trail of murdered police officers across five countries. Over one hundred fifty men and women in uniform had died because of him.

He ruled his empire through terror, and met betrayal with punishments so brutal, so agonizing, that whispers of his name alone were enough to make even hardened criminals shudder.

And then there were the rumors.

There were articles suggesting that he wasn't even real, nothing more than a phantom that the police could never catch. Someone who knew things before they happened, as there was no other explanation how he could do the things he did.

Another story painted him as a true brujo, a conjurer of dark forces, who could outmaneuver his enemies before they even knew he was near.

This troubled me. I knew that no man was invincible, and that no form of magic was that strong.

And yet Vargas had evaded every raid. Every trap.

I snapped my laptop shut. The air felt heavier around me, as if the research itself had tainted my surroundings.

I looked up just as Jyanette emerged from the pool, water cascading down her dark skin, glistening in the sunlight like liquid diamonds. She ran her fingers through her wet hair, then met my gaze with a warm, knowing smile.

"You look like you just read something terrible," she said as she reached for her towel.

She wasn't wrong.

I forced a smile, trying to ground myself back into reality. "Just the usual afternoon deep dive into the occult horrors of drug cartels."

She rolled her eyes playfully and plopped down onto the lounge chair beside me.

"What did you uncover?"

"A bit of the legends of Don Diego. None of it good."

"You don't agree with Marcus that Diego is out of the country and it can't be him."

"Since I saw the photo of that mask, I am convinced it has something to do with this case."

"Okay, let's say he's involved. If he isn't a dark wizard, what is he?"

"A monster," I said simply.

She hesitated before asking, "Do you really think he's a conjurer? I mean, I thought your entire stance on the supernatural was that it's more about mental energy and perception."

"That's still true," I admitted. "But let's break this down logically. Let's say Diego Vargas is a psychic, like me."

"Okay."

"Now imagine that instead of rigorous mental training, he went a different route — ritualistic training, following the traditions of Brujería. He could hone whatever natural ability he had, but not for self-discipline or insight, like I did. He uses it to run an empire. If he has even a fraction of real precognition, it could explain why he always seems a step ahead — why law enforcement can never catch him."

"So, if he gets those little psychic buzzes you do, he'd used them to sidestep traps, avoid arrests. And the more he escapes, the more his followers believe he's untouchable."

I nodded. "Exactly. And belief is powerful. I would imagine his people revere him, as well as fear him. That collective energy feeds into his mystique, making him even more dangerous."

She narrowed her eyes. "Is belief really that important to psychic ability?"

"My belief in myself is." I gave her a dry look. "But I have no intention of starting a cult, if that's what you're asking."

She grinned. "Pity. I was looking forward to being a cult leader's wife."

I laughed. "I don't think I have the patience for flowing robes and cryptic prophecies."

"You never know unless you try."

I shook my head, sobering. "What I know is that Diego Vargas takes this seriously. And I can't shake the feeling that Ms. Fontaine's abduction was for some larger purpose, other than holding her for ransom."

"How so?"

"With most kidnappings for profit, a monetary demand is usually made within twenty-four hours. Yet, neither the local law enforcement nor the Feds have received any demand."

"You don't know that. Law enforcement doesn't have to share their information with you."

I nodded. "True, but if a demand had been made, they would have moved on, set up a field office off-site. Leaving people here means they are still trying to dig up any clues."

"You're really good at this, Mr. Wise."

"Nice of you to notice, Mrs. Wise," I said with a grin. Then I became serious. "I have a strange feeling that Ms. Fontaine's abduction is only part of a much bigger plan, though I don't know exactly how or what that plan could entail."

Jyanette studied me. "Any new insights from that dream of yours? The one where the masked men storm a hotel?"

"Nothing," I admitted.

"Any idea which hotel?"

"No, I haven't found a room that looks like the one in the dream."

She stretched, then stood, offering me her hand. "Let's head back to the room, change, and grab some lunch. Afterward… who knows? Maybe we'll do what honeymooners do."

"Ah yes, board games," I deadpanned.

She smirked. "I have a few games in mind that you might enjoy."

I packed up my laptop, and we gathered our things, setting off along the winding stone path toward the lodge. The sun glowed high above, casting our shadows over the pavement. Just as we rounded a corner, a uniformed waiter emerged from the outdoor bar, balancing a tray of bright, colorful drinks with practiced ease. He headed toward the poolside guests.

I glanced up at him—

And froze.

My breath hitched, my heart hammering against my ribs.

Where his face should have been, there was nothing. Not a shadow, not a blur, but an empty void. A black hole that drank in the sunlight, swallowing every detail of his features into an abyss of absolute darkness.

Jyanette stepped closer. "Len?" she asked softly. "What's wrong?"

I forced my gaze away from the faceless figure, my eyes darting toward the sunlit pool, the lake stretching beyond, waves lapping gently at the shore.

Normal. This is normal.

I looked back—

The waiter was still walking, his back now to us, his posture casual as he weaved through the crowd.

Jyanette followed my gaze, then leaned toward me, concern etched on her features. "Len, talk to me. What is it?"

My voice was barely above a whisper. "That man. I think he's one of them."

She frowned. "One of who?"

"The men who took Fontaine." I hesitated. "I-I couldn't see his face. It was like when I did the reading at the chateau. Just... a blank space. A void."

Her shoulders tensed. "You think the people who took Fontaine are here? At this hotel?"

"I don't know," I admitted. "But if he's one of them, we need to find out who he is."

Before I could stop her, Jyanette turned on her heel and strode toward the bar.

I blinked. "Wait — what are you—"

"Excuse me?" she called to the bartender, flashing a friendly smile. "The waiter who's taking drinks to the pool — I think he served us earlier. What's his name?"

The bartender glanced up from slicing limes. "That's Miguel. Why? Was something wrong?"

"Oh, no! He was great," Jyanette said smoothly. "Just wanted to remember his name. Has he worked here long?"

The bartender shrugged. "Not really. Maybe a month?"

"Thanks so much," Jyanette said, walking back to me with an air of casual confidence.

I couldn't help but grin. "Impressive."

She arched a brow. "Len, I was an Assistant District Attorney. Did you really think I wouldn't know how to get information?"

"Fair point." I exhaled. "We should text Agent Calvin, see if he can run a background check."

Once we reached our room, Jyanette grabbed her phone.

"What are you doing?"

"Texting Marcus," she replied, her gaze never leaving the screen.

I hesitated. "You still have his number?"

She finished typing and looked up, her expression unreadable. "Yes, I do. And I still have a lot of contacts from my DOJ days. Do you have a problem with that?"

"No," I muttered. But to my surprise, I realized I did. That she had slept with Marcus and still had his number bothered me. More than I wanted to admit.

Jyanette studied me. "This jealousy streak is new."

"I didn't realize you kept in touch with old boyfriends," I shot back.

She gave me a look. "Really? Says the man who had a private hypnosis session with his ex-girlfriend during his last New Jersey case."

It was a fair point.

And I hated she had it.

Jyanette's eyes locked onto mine, steady and unwavering. "Len, either you trust me, or you don't."

"I trust you," I said, though my voice wavered slightly. "But Marcus is still in love with you — and he's here."

She blinked, genuine shock crossing her face. "You read his mind?"

"I didn't need to," I muttered. "I saw it all over his face when he saw you."

A small, knowing smile appeared on her face. She shook her head. "You're mistaken. Marcus has never been in love with me. Don't you remember why we broke up? He couldn't stay faithful. He was always involved with other women."

"Maybe losing you changed him."

"I hope so." Her voice softened. "I want him to treat the next woman in his life seriously — the way I thought you would treat me."

Her words landed like a punch to the gut. "What does that mean?"

She held my gaze. "It means I trust you alone with Kate Yearling — darting around crime scenes, disappearing for hours, sometimes days. But the moment Marcus shows up, suddenly you feel the need to compete with him. And on our honeymoon?"

I rubbed the back of my neck, shame prickling under my skin. "I'm sorry," I said.

Jyanette's expression softened. "Len, we're married now. If we're going to make this work, you have to trust me. Jealousy will only undermine us."

"You're right." The weight of her words settled deep. Then, trying to lighten the mood, I added, "But it's hard to ignore that you seem to have a thing for guys with shaved heads."

"I do. But I've grown very fond of your unruly hair," she said with a wink.

I grinned. "Good to know."

She stretched, then tugged at my shirt playfully. "Now, how about you take me downstairs, feed me, and then bring me back up to ravish me?"

I leaned in, my lips brushing against her ear. "How about I ravish you first?"

She tilted her head, considering. "Well… okay. But, feed me soon. I bite, you know."

"Oh, I know…"

Marcus didn't get back to us until we were well-ravished, dressed, and eating a hearty meal at The Bistro. The restaurant exuded a laid-back charm with its rustic wooden tables, warm lighting, and an eclectic mix of art adorning the walls.

Jyanette and I were sharing a vibrant beet salad, drizzled with tangy feta dressing, when her phone buzzed on the table, pulling her attention away from our lighthearted banter.

"Is that from Marcus?" I asked quietly, leaning in to glimpse her screen.

"Yes," she replied, her brow furrowing as she read the message. "He's asking where we are."

"Let him know," I suggested.

Moments later, Marcus and Agent Roberts strode in, their authoritative presence cutting through the cozy atmosphere like a knife.

"We can't stay for long," Roberts expression steely as he pulled over a chair. Marcus followed suit.

"Have you questioned the waiter?" I asked.

Roberts shot me an annoyed glance, his jaw tightening. "Where did you get information about this Miguel character?"

His abruptness caught me off guard.

"Why does it matter?" I replied, trying to maintain my composure despite the growing tension.

"You don't ask the questions," Roberts grunted, his tone leaving no room for interpretation.

"Actually, I think I might have spotted someone resembling him when I examined the crime scene," I said, and it wasn't completely false. In my vision, the men had been faceless, and when I encountered Miguel, he had no features either.

Marcus sighed, his voice laced with frustration. "We've had no luck tracking this guy down."

"What do you mean?" I asked, sensing trouble on the horizon.

Jyanette, her voice steady, said, "He was delivering drinks to the pool less than an hour ago."

"Yes," Roberts continued, his demeanor unyielding, "The main office summoned him five minutes later. No one has seen him since."

"Who made the request?" I pressed.

"According to the bartender, who relayed the message to Miguel, there was a call from Mr. Jenkins—"

"He's the manager; we spoke to him when we arrived," Jyanette interjected, her brow furrowing in concern.

Marcus sighed again, frustration clear on his face. "We spoke to Jenkins, and he claims he made no such phone call."

"That's strange," I muttered.

"I have team members investigating the man's employment records, checking his address, and exploring any connections to the case," Roberts said, still bristling with tension. "So, once again, why the sudden interest in this individual?"

"I told you—"

"Don't bullshit me, Wise," Roberts spat, his irritation boiling over. "Captain Lauwers informed us you didn't see any faces and claimed the men looked like silhouettes."

I set my jaw. "When I saw Miguel, he didn't have a face. There was a black void where his face should have been."

"What the hell does that mean?" Roberts demanded, pinning me with a glare.

"When I first got a look at him, he didn't have a face, just a black hole where his features should have been," I explained, trying to remain calm.

Roberts spun sharply to Jyanette. "Can you back that up?"

"Len's abilities allow him to perceive things in ways we can't."

"This waiter might've worn something that shields him from recognition by psychics," I said, my voice dropping to a hushed tone.

"Where would he get something like that?" Roberts demanded.

"I think this case has a connection to a cult involving Brujeria," I said. "And a man named Don Diego."

"Yes, Agent Calvin mentioned you thought some South American gangster was involved," Roberts said. "That has to be the most ridiculous theory I've heard today."

"Don Diego is more than just a gangster," I said.

"Right," Roberts scoffed. "He's a freakin' wizard!"

"Agent Roberts," Marcus interjected, attempting to redirect the conflict. "This waiter is in the wind. I have to say that suggests that Len was onto something by reporting him to us."

"I want to know how this Miguel could have received a warning to evade us before we even started searching," Roberts said, his frustration palpable.

"Someone must have tipped him off," I replied, my voice steady.

"Brilliant observation, Wise," Roberts shot back sarcastically. "I'm sure that never crossed our minds."

"Agent Roberts," Jyanette said, her tone rising. "My husband attempted to assist you. We don't work for you, the Department of Justice, or the FBI."

Roberts gritted his teeth. He exchanged a glance with Marcus, a silent understanding passing between them, before he muttered, "Sure. If you find out anything useful, that doesn't involve a criminal who is not even in the country or witchcraft, keep us informed."

After a curt nod to Marcus, the two of them left us behind. The tension in the atmosphere gradually ebbed away, replaced by a sense of disquiet. I faced Jyanette, the aftertaste of the confrontation still sour on my tongue.

"Well, that escalated quickly," I said, trying to inject some levity into the situation.

"The nerve of that man!" Jyanette fumed, her cheeks flushed with indignation. She glared across the restaurant, as if she could will Agent Roberts to crumble under her fierce gaze. "He talks down to you as if you haven't conducted more investigations than he has in his entire career! It's infuriating!"

"Easy, tiger," I chuckled, unable to suppress a smile at her unyielding defense. "Thanks for growling at Agent Roberts. But don't you find it peculiar? I spot a suspicious character, report it, and the guy vanishes before they even have the chance to question him?"

Jyanette leaned back in her chair "How do you think that could have happened?"

"I'm not entirely sure. Maybe it was Don Diego himself. There are legends that say a Brujo can shape-shift."

"Is that something you can do?" she asked, with a grin. "That could prove interesting if so."

"It's not something anyone can just do. However, on a more plausible note, anyone could easily impersonate Mr. Jenkins over the phone to push Miguel out of here — just by practicing his voice."

"But that's the thing. How would they know to get him out? Only you, me, and Marcus were privy to that information."

I hesitated, considering another angle. "Let's go with the theory that Don Diego is involved."

"Okay. After all, it's just a theory."

"Right. Now let's say Don Diego really is a psychic. He could have a precognitive flash like I do. Then he took steps to orchestrate the call to get Miguel to leave."

Jyanette's eyes flitted around the bustling restaurant, scanning the room. "Do you think they have operatives hidden in this resort? You saw the attack in your dream, and I take your visions seriously."

"As do I," I admitted, allowing my gaze to sweep over the guests and servers. They all appeared perfectly ordinary, sharing laughter and stories over their meals. "Everyone here looks like the quintessential vacationer, but it's telling that Miguel was the only one whose face eluded recognition."

"And you think that was because he carried something?" Jyanette leaned in closer, intrigued.

"Yes, energy embedded in an item such as a medallion or jewelry — even a ring. If Miguel was wearing something inscribed with those mystical symbols and genuinely believed in their power, it could distort my vision, much like those masks."

"Blurring your ability to see their faces?"

"It's one way to maintain anonymity," I explained. "But it might be more than that. Other people might not even register his features. It's as if a fog surrounds him, obscuring him from my sight."

"What do you mean? I saw him."

"Okay, describe him to me."

Jyanette frowned, her confidence fading as confusion washed over her. "He was average height — definitely not taller than you..."

"Be more specific — his face."

Her frown deepened into a look of concentration. "He had..." She faltered, closing her eyes slightly, as if to summon the memory from the depths of her mind.

"Eye color? Facial hair?" I prompted, hoping to jog her memory.

"I can't picture him," she finally admitted, disbelief mingling with awe across her features. "This is insane, Len. I'm good at remembering faces."

"I know," I replied, concern threading through my voice. "You wouldn't notice it unless someone probed you deeply about it. This does not sit right with me."

"What can we do?"

"I need to call Doctor Kohl and seek his advice."

After settling the bill, we stepped out of the restaurant, the faint murmur of conversation trailing behind us as we made our way down the corridor, heading back toward the lobby and the elevators.

As we walked, something caught my eye — a pair of imposing double doors that seemed to beckon me, an inexplicable compulsion urging me forward.

"What is it?" Jyanette asked.

I opened the doors, stepping into a grand ballroom. The space was vast and empty, with tables set up throughout the room, all void of their customary linens. As I ventured deeper into the center, I spun about to face the entrance.

It was the precise location of my dream.

5. INVISIBLE INVADER

O nce ensconced in our hotel room with a sense of safety, I dialed Doctor Kohl. With Jyanette by my side, I put him on speakerphone so we could both hear his advice.

"Leonard! So good to hear from you," he began, his thick German accent warping his words. "Congratulations on your vedding!"

"Thank you, Doctor Kohl," Jyanette interjected,

"Ah, Jyanette! I vish I could be there to kiss the bride," he added, a jovial twinkle in his voice even through the phone.

"Len's got the kissing under control," she teased back, prompting a hearty chuckle from Kohl.

"Fritz, I sent you the photos of the mask. Have you found anyone who can decipher the symbols?" I transitioned, eager to steer the conversation towards the mysteries that plagued us.

"Yah, I've been consulting mitt a colleague, Doctor Navarro," he replied. "He specializes in South American religions and cult practices. Now, tell me, vhat has happened since you sent me the photo?"

I recounted my recent experiences, detailing my eerie encounter and the elusive man I'd seen without a face.

"Very odd, Leonard. You say you saw a man with no face, yet Jyanette did not see a mask, is that correct?"

"That's right, Doctor," Jyanette said. "I saw nothing covering his face, yet I can't remember what he looked like at all."

"Ah!" Fritz exclaimed. "Doctor Navarro has been examining the symbols on the mask, and they could be used on more than one item. It is possible the man you saw vas carrying vhat is known as an amuleto. In Brujeria, that is an object imbued with symbols and blessings to grant the bearer specific protections. In that case, the ability to hide his true appearance."

I could hear a note of concern creeping into his voice as he went on. "I am particularly vorried about this man you mentioned, Don Diego. He grandiosely dubs himself El Conjurador Oscuro. Such a moniker hints at an inflated ego."

"Not if he can back up his claims," I pointed out.

"Indeed. Doctor Navarro raised a fascinating point: the symbols on the mask you sent could have been created by a Nahualli. This term describes someone who can change form — into another being or even an animal."

"Do you think that is genuinely possible?" I asked, my skepticism warring with curiosity.

"Vhat is possible, Leonard? In my discussions with Dr. Navarro, he suggested that if a Brujo is powerful and has psychic abilities, he could project any mental image, and others would see this projection."

"A mental image?" I repeated, intrigued.

"Yah. He vouldn't physically transform into an animal, say a coyote. But vhen you gaze upon him, you do not see the man before you; rather, your mind perceives him as a coyote or whatever form he desires."

"So you're suggesting that the ability to erase someone's face from memory might be a variation on that power," Jyanette said, piecing together the puzzle in her own analytical fashion.

"A variation, indeed, but much less complex," Fritz said. "I believe his followers, adorned with an amuleto empowered by a powerful brujo, like this Diego, can invoke this effect, even if the individual vearing the talisman lacks any psychic capacity themselves."

"If Doctor Navarro or you can recommend any way of dealing with this man or any information — no matter how minor — please keep me informed," I urged.

"I vill consult mitt Doctor Navarro again, now that I understand better what you seek. I vill forward you some articles he sent me, detailing Brujería and its vorkings," Kohl promised.

"Thank you, Doctor Kohl," Jyanette chimed in warmly.

"Please call me Fritz, my dear," he said. "Once again, my congratulations on your marriage."

With that, he ended the call.

"One day, I hope I get to meet that man," Jyanette mused, admiration in her voice.

"It would be a challenge, considering we live on opposite coasts — us in New Jersey and him in California," I reminded her, though I wished the distance was shorter.

"I should have invited him to the wedding," she said "Everything came together so quickly."

"And I didn't even know it was going to happen," I added, recalling how spontaneous our decision had been.

She stepped closer, her eyes searching mine. "But you're happy we did it, right?"

"Ecstatic. I was planning on marrying you. We just did it sooner rather than later," I replied, the memory flooding back.

"What do you think we should do now?" she asked, her voice laced with uncertainty, as she walked into the bedroom. "Should we just wander around and see if there's anyone else in this hotel missing their face?"

"I doubt they would have left any of their crew behind after what happened with Miguel. If it is Don Diego, or anyone with psychic ability, they would have evacuated everyone. But that gives us another clue. It suggests that they have a base of operations nearby,"

A sly smile crept across Jyanette's face as she strode back into the room, her bikini in her hand. "I think I know what comes next," she declared.

"And that would be?" I asked.

She let out an exaggerated sigh, rolling her eyes as if my question were the most predictable thing in the world. "You're planning to meditate, slip into an altered state, and try to locate where they might hide," she said, her tone teasing yet affectionate.

"Wow, it's almost as if you can read my mind!" I chuckled.

Jyanette, unfazed, smoothly pulled off her top and bra, tossing them onto a nearby chair. I stared in awe, overwhelmed once again by the realization that this stunning woman was now my wife.

"That's usually what you do when you're stuck with no leads. It's that or you go for a drive and see where the road takes you," she explained, slipping off her slacks and panties, a delightful teasing glint in her eyes, fully aware of the appreciative gaze I had fixed on her.

"And what's your plan, then?" I asked, my voice a mix of curiosity and admiration as I watched her don the bikini top, her curves barely hidden beneath the fabric.

"I'm heading to the hot tub to have a glass of champagne," she declared, a sparkle of adventure flickered in her eyes.

"You don't mind if I stay up here?" I wanted to be considerate, especially since she made it clear that she expected togetherness during our stay.

"Len, this one I'll give to you. I married you just as you are. I've grown accustomed to your habits. On the other hand, there's no way I'm letting you ruin my honeymoon because you're busy chasing after a case."

"So our honeymoon became your honeymoon?" I said.

"Of course! That's our life. Sometimes we do things on our own. And hey, if you can piece together some intel before anyone makes a move against this resort, then I'm all for it. Besides, who knows? I might just get some insight while soaking in the hot tub."

She fastened her robe snug around her waist, the soft fabric grazing her skin as she slipped on her sandals, each movement imbued with a fluid grace that captured my attention.

"I love you," I managed to say.

"Me, too," she replied. Her smile ignited my heart as she headed for the door, the quiet click of the latch echoing in her absence.

Once solitude wrapped around me, I shifted my focus inward, attempting to corral the swirling disorder of my thoughts and zero in on the task ahead.

In psychic readings I have done focusing on a specific person typically required an item that belonged to them. This helps me connect with them. However, in this instance, Ms. Fontaine's possessions lay under police watch, a frustrating barrier.

The only item I had recently handled was her phone. I called to mind the image of that phone, closing my eyes and concentrating on my breath, allowing myself to drift away from the physical world.

In…out. In…out.

Gradually, I slipped into an alpha state, the world outside fading into obscurity. I envisioned the phone: its soft pink rubber cover, glimmering with delicate rhinestones that caught the faintest light in the dim chamber of the chateau.

I urged myself to focus on its owner — Isabella Fontaine.

As I slipped deeper into meditation, I felt the world around me vibrate with energy, the hum of voices threading through the veil of my consciousness. Men spoke, their words spilling forth in rapid Spanish, layered with urgency, yet the context eluded me.

I felt I was with her, experiencing what she was going through. It was Isabella's perspective, but not entirely.

My awareness was clouded, shrouded in darkness — perhaps a blindfold pressing down over her eyes, restricting her vision.

Desperate to immerse myself further in her experience, I tried to discern my surroundings. Was she seated? It was hard to tell. Were her hands bound? A fleeting intuition suggested they were.

I pushed against her limitations, straining to sense the environment rather than remain confined to her restricted awareness. The background noise crescendoed — an unsettling cacophony of mechanical noises and hushed conversations composing a discordant symphony that churned restlessly in my mind.

And then it hit me. The whirring I heard was pneumatic wrenches. Isabella was possibly trapped in a garage or auto repair shop.

Suddenly, an unexpected voice thundered in my mind, rending the fabric of my concentration.

WHO ARE YOU…?

I recoiled slightly, the force of the thought crashing into my consciousness, like a jagged bolt of lightning.

What…?

I could only manage a whisper, my brain struggling to adapt.

I SENSE YOU, FEEL YOUR THOUGHTS, POKING IN WHERE YOU DON'T BELONG…

The words crashed through me, each syllable creating a resonating pain behind my right eye — a tremendous headache blossomed as I fought to retain control.

Who are you…?

YOU KNOW WHO I AM, LITTLE MAN. I HAVE SENSED YOU TRYING TO REACH OUT, TRYING TO FIND ME...

I attempted to erect mental barriers, fabricating a fortress of concentration around my thoughts. But I floated in a delicate alpha state too permeable to defend against this overwhelming assault.

Don Diego...?

I AM EL CONJURADOR OSCURO...

His proclamation rolled over me like a torrential wave. I felt a strange mix of dread and defiance.

I'm not impressed ...

YOU SHOULD BE...

In an instant, reality twisted, shifting around me. I was suddenly in a car; the vehicle navigating over rain-slick asphalt. My knuckles gripped the steering wheel, a numb weight settling on me as I sped up.

"Still want to get married so soon? Right before we start our residency?" I looked over to see Cathy Garber, my fiancée from a time long past — a bright, effervescent blonde whose presence seemed ethereal against the encroaching shadows of memory.

Dread hit me. I recoiled, lifting my foot off the accelerator, unwilling to witness the impending tragedy about to unfold.

I knew that a figure loomed in the road ahead.

"No, no, no!" I shouted, terror clawing at my throat.

There in the center of the road was a grotesque demon, skin molten and fiery red, its massive form topped with horns twisted like a bull's. Its yellow eyes fixed on me, burning through my very essence as it stood resolutely in our path.

As in my memory from a decade past, the steering wheel slipped from my grip, the car veered into a skid, the world a rush of color and noise, each agonizing second stretching painfully as I lost control of the vehicle.

With a deafening screech, we crashed through the guardrail. Time twisted around us as the car soared through the air, our descent a twisted nightmare. The ground rushed up to meet us, each heartbeat syncing with the speeding pulse of terror in my chest.

Then came the bone-jarring impact — our car collided with a tree, the world exploding into fragments around us. The airbag deployed, slamming me backward against the seat, disoriented.

Dazed, I blinked through the wreckage of the car and memory, grappling with the reality of hanging upside down, my seatbelt a vice around me. Pain flared in my right leg. My gaze flicked to Cathy, hanging from her restraints, her face pale and slick with blood.

She was going to die.

No, this isn't real. This happened ten years ago...

I squeezed my eyes tightly, willing myself to sever the ties binding me to that fateful night. It was a trick; somehow, through some kind of mental manipulation I couldn't comprehend, the man whose mind I had touched unearthed a memory and resurrected it around me.

In a disorienting haze, desperation surged as coarse fabric suddenly held my limbs. I struggled against the restraints as pain tore through my body. I was injured, possibly beaten. I opened my eyes and found I was… somehow… lying on a hard floor imprisoned in a straitjacket.

My breath scorched my lungs as I fought for clarity. I rolled against a cold stone wall, trembling with panic. A dull pain throbbed around my right eye, and there was swelling that nearly closed it.

Slowly, reality sharpened around me. A small, circular room that felt constricting, its wooden beams jutting toward a peak. Dust hung in the dense air, giving everything an oppressive weight. An open trap door with a ladder was the only way in or out of the prison.

The sole illumination emerged from the flickering candles perched on ornate gothic metal stands, casting restless shadows that danced across the stone walls.

This was the tower room of the asylum where Jyanette and I had battled for our lives. Memory clawed at my mind, mingled with fresh waves of fear that constricted my chest. How had I found myself here again?

Overwhelmed, I shoved myself up the wall to stick my head out the open tower window, the relentless rain outside transforming everything into an unsettling blur.

There, on the rain-slicked pavement, lay the lifeless body of Jim Stevens — a man ensnared by the suffocating grasp of demonic possession that led to his destruction. Nearby, the figure of Sergeant Stant, the courageous officer who had once stood beside me, lay motionless, a silent witness to the darkness that had enveloped us.

"This is impossible," I muttered, disbelief clawing at the back of my mind.

"Get me out of this!" Jyanette screamed from behind me.

I spun, dread surging through my veins. There she was — my beloved Jyanette, tightly bound to a massive wooden chair, leather straps biting into her skin. Bruises marked her face, each one a testament to struggle, yet within the agony, a spark of defiance gleamed in her eyes.

"This can't be happening," I stammered, terror winding itself around my heart. The palpable reality of the situation pulled at me.

"Come on!" she snapped, irritation mingled with pain in her voice. "My arms are killing me!"

I instinctively shifted back, terror filling my heart and plunging deep into my core. "No, no, this isn't what happened. I can't be here."

A harrowing presence sneered, a rough voice emanated from Jyanette's lips — an insidious incarnation from within her.

"Untie me," it rasped, her eyes igniting with a blood-red glow.

I closed my eyes, steeling myself against this haunting vision. It wasn't reality; merely a twisted fragment of memory pulled forth.

I will not fall for your tricks...

YOU HAVE LITTLE CHOICE...

The scene warped again, and suddenly I stood in a stark hospital corridor, the sterile air thick with antiseptic. Medical equipment hummed nearby, a monotonous backdrop to the heavy atmosphere.

Fluorescent lights cast shadows, and beside me stood Bill McGee, my steadfast friend and Mountainview Police Lieutenant. He was my height, but built like a linebacker, his brow creased in profound worry.

Mrs. Higgins, my Irish landlady, little more than five feet tall, stood nearby as well with arms crossed, her vibrant spirit dimmed by the grim reality we confronted.

A doctor approached, his purposeful stride echoing with gravity. He was of Indian descent, dark intelligent eyes assessing the situation. The tension surged, each of us awaiting the inevitable exchange.

"You're here for Ms. Emery?" he asked, a slight accent softening his words.

"No, not this," I choked, grief clawing at my throat as tears brimmed in my eyes. "Anything but this."

He didn't hear me, but he inclined his head. "Are you the father of the child?"

"Please, no," I sobbed, the heaviness in my chest was so strong I felt as if my heart were fracturing.

His expression became grave. "I'm afraid she lost the baby."

As Mrs. Higgins stepped closer, the infinite hallway stretched interminably, its harsh fluorescent lights cast shadows along the sterile walls. Medical staff rushed past, oblivious to the tragedy unfurling in my heart — the acrid scent of antiseptic mingled with the bitter taste of grief surrounding me.

Amidst the flurry of emotion, the sinister voice rumbled through my mind, thick with a chilling resonance.

STAY OUT OF MY WAY...

I jolted awake, eyes snapping open to the safety of my hotel room, light pouring through vast windows that overlooked the tranquil lake. I wiped away tears from my cheeks, relief flooding my chest as I took in my familiar surroundings.

"What the hell?" I murmured, overwhelmed by a wave of gratitude for my reality.

I pushed myself upright, but my rubbery legs buckled as I reeled back into the chair, nearly toppling over. Drenched in sweat, I gasped each breath as fatigue heavily settled in my bones.

What had I just endured? I had faced psychics before, but nothing could compare to this staggering invasion of my mind.

He had claimed he was El Conjurador Oscuro — which was the name Don Diego used.

Whoever he was, he delved into my innermost shadows, dragging forth reminders of agony, resurrecting the vivid memories of the car accident that almost claimed my life, the merciless night in the tower of the old asylum where I almost died, and the heart-wrenching death of the child Jyanette and I lost.

I tried to understand the things I had experienced. The pain I suffered in the vision must be psychosomatic; my mind's cruel way of manifesting emotional turmoil as physical suffering. Yet, my body ached, even after I returned to reality.

Through the torment emerged a vital fact: I needed to relay what little I had discovered to Marcus Calvin. Shakily, I staggered toward the table, snatched the card he had given me, and grabbed my phone. With trembling fingers, I hastily typed out a message:

Isabella Fontaine might be held in an auto repair shop.

Something in the area, not too far.
Please check.

Upon sending the message, I felt like the weight of the world pressed down on my weary spirit. With heavy limbs, I collapsed onto the bed, fury and dread swirling within me as I faced the brutal truth about Don Diego, if he was indeed the man I had faced.

How could I combat a man capable of delving into the darkest corners of my soul, taunting me with the most harrowing memories? Faced with such a formidable opponent, my resolve wavered.

Did I truly stand a chance against *El Conjurador Oscuro*?

6. DIMINISHING TIME

I was lost in the depths of sleep, until my bride gently shook me awake. The moment consciousness returned, I shot upright in bed, my heart racing and a wave of panic washing over me as I scanned the dimly lit room.

"Calm down, it's just me," she said, her voice a mixture of concern and surprise at my sudden alarm.

"Sorry," I mumbled, struggling to steady my breath. "I just had a really... unpleasant experience trying to find the missing woman."

"What do you mean? What happened?"

"I believe I encountered the Dark Conjuror."

She shook her head. "I don't understand."

"He sensed me reaching out to Ms. Fontaine — he interrupted my attempt, and somehow, he forced me to relive some of the darkest moments of my life," I explained, my throat tight. "Each recollection had an intensity that felt as if it were the first time happening all over again."

"Which memories?" she asked, her eyes narrowing and staring deeply into my eyes.

I hung my head. "Cathy's death in the car — and that night in the asylum, the confrontation we had with that possessed man —"

At the mention of the asylum, Jyanette flinched as if struck. She took a step back, her expression a mix of fear and sorrow.

"That night still haunts my dreams," she confessed, her voice barely above a whisper.

I continued, pushing past the knot in my throat. "And then there was the night we lost... the baby." The memory lodged in my chest like a splinter, an ache that never truly faded.

I could still remember how the hospital hallway had overwhelmed me, filled with sterile smells and the muffled sound of distant footsteps, the harsh reality crashing down with an unforgiving finality.

It was because Jyanette lost the baby that she had broken up with me, relocated to Virginia, and left me desolate. It was only her and I working on a case with the FBI that brought us back together.

She blinked rapidly, tears threatening, but her resolve hardened.

"So, you think he's here. That he does have something to do with Ms. Fontaine's disappearance?"

I set my jaw. "I'm sure of it, now."

"Then, you need to stop this guy," she said, the steel in her voice cutting through the heavy cold of our shared shadows. Her eyes met mine, fierce with determination.

"I have a problem. I've never encountered someone with power like this," I said, a sense of defeat creeping into my tone.

"He must be a psychic, but his abilities exceed my own, and I don't know how."

"What can you do?"

"I'm sure my mental barriers can keep him out when I'm conscious. He only breached my defenses because I was in an alpha state, reaching out for Ms. Fontaine. I think they've got her in an auto shop or some place like that. I could hear pneumatic wrenches in the background; she's blindfolded."

"Did you tell Marcus?" she pressed, her voice urgent.

"Yes, right after it happened."

"Then you've done all you can," she said, though I sensed a lingering worry in her voice.

"I need to do one more thing," I asserted, moving toward my laptop, seeking the articles sent by Dr. Kohl. "I need to figure out how he could invade my mind."

"Let me throw on some clothes," she said, darting into the bedroom as I opened the link to articles Dr. Kohl forwarded, detailed and illuminating information for me.

I read that practitioners of Brujería operated in the realm of dreams, one of the fifteen layers of reality. My heart skipped a beat when I noticed that number again: fifteen. Could it be a crucial part of his plan? Was it tied to the sacrifices he'd been making, all linked to the number fifteen?

I pushed forward, delving deeper. It detailed how a sorcerer could manipulate reality through dreams, causing ripples in the fabric of existence — like tossing a stone into still water.

The articles further explained that some of the Brujo harnessed the power of spirits to aid in their craft. Those spirits did not take a single form; they included the ethereal essences of plants, elemental forces like fire and water, and even the lingering souls of the deceased. People believed these practitioners possessed a unique ability to communicate with these spirits and forge bonds enhancing their magical work.

But far worse, there were accounts of certain Brujos summoning and binding formidable demons. The Brujo's compelled these beings, often thought to be agents of disorder, to serve their will, performing tasks that ranged from delivering messages to enforcing spells. Through these profound connections, they wielded both the wisdom of nature and the shadows of the beyond, making them powerful figures in their communities.

The entire situation unraveled in my mind as Don Diego's audacious invasion of my meditative state began to make sense. He had accessed the dream world. The human mind has several states: alpha, beta, gamma, theta, and delta. Beta and gamma are our normal waking minds, though one is more focused than the other. Delta is the sleep state, but both alpha and theta are meditative conditions, where the mind is relaxed, and it is what I used to reach out mentally to people and events.

It was in that state of mind that he seized control, dragging forth my most private memories, manipulating them like puppets in a grotesque display of his power. I had felt utterly helpless, ensnared in a web of his making. The thought of encountering him again sent icy tendrils of fear slinking down my spine.

Just as the weight of my thoughts bore down heavily, Jyanette emerged — dressed in an elegant yet comfortable pantsuit, her phone clutched in her hand.

"I got a text from Marcus. He wants me to call him."

I sat up. "Maybe my tip paid off."

She held the phone to her ear. "Hey, Marcus, we were just—" Her tone faltered as she listened, a deepening frown etching lines across her forehead. "If that's what you have to do…" Another pause stretched across the conversation, and when she spoke again, her voice was subdued. "Alright. Nice seeing you. Thank you."

"What's going on?" I asked.

"He wanted to let us know he's leaving town, and to congratulate us again on our wedding," she replied.

"Leaving?" I echoed, a sense of unease filling me.

"It seems the woman and her bodyguard surfaced… in San Francisco. She lost her phone and could only get in touch now."

"That's not possible. In my vision I saw the bodyguard on the floor of the chateau. He was dead."

In response, Jyanette shrugged. "Marcus says the entire team is leaving to drive to California to meet Ms. Fontaine."

Frustration boiled inside me. "None of this is right. She's not in San Francisco; she's nearby."

"You mentioned how this conjuror got into your head. Maybe he misled you about her location?" she suggested.

"Or maybe he's directing Agent Roberts to the wrong place." The eerie thought blossomed in my mind, a dark seed of doubt that thrived in the grim reality we were facing.

"Do you think he could?"

"Jyanette, I distinctly saw the woman throw the phone on the sofa, where I found it. But I also witnessed her abduction. I also can't shake the image of her bodyguard lying in a pool of blood."

"I'll call Marcus back," she said, glancing at her phone.

"It won't help. Marcus isn't calling the shots. Agent Roberts is running this operation."

"Should we go to the chateau before they leave?" she suggested. "Talk to them directly?"

"It's worth a shot."

We stepped out into the warm afternoon air, our footsteps purposeful as we navigated the winding path that led us toward the chateaus. We tempered our pace, mindful that any sign of haste might attract unwanted scrutiny.

The resort was buzzing with life, guests milling about in casual conversation, laughter spilling from the courtyards, and the scent of gourmet meals roasted on outdoor grills wafting through the air.

However, as we approached the chateau, the atmosphere shifted dramatically.

The scene before us was a whirlwind of activity. Apparently after we'd been involved, Agent Roberts had called for backup. Men in suits rushed about, their expressions focused and intense. Large black step vans loomed nearby, their doors wide open, filled with a myriad of equipment. Apparently they had set up a base of operations on the site, which they were now packing up. Cables were being coiled, crates were being loaded, and the air crackled with an undeniable tension as preparations for departure reached a fevered pitch.

A federal agent stood sentinel at the entrance, tall and imposing in a sharply tailored black suit. A curled wire connected him to an earpiece, and behind his dark sunglasses, his eyes scanned the premises for any signs of danger.

As we approached he lifted an arm to stop us. "I'm sorry, this area is closed off," he stated, his tone dismissive.

"We need to speak with Agent Roberts," Jyanette told him.

The agent's posture stiffened even more, and with a swift motion, he pressed a button on the wire leading to his ear. "Agent Roberts. Can you come out front?"

Moments later, Roberts emerged from the chateau's depths, irritation evident on his face. "You two?" he shot back, glancing at the federal agent as he snapped, "Finish packing up. Wheels up in five."

The agent nodded and vanished back inside, leaving Roberts to face us alone.

"Agent Roberts, I have to tell you, I think you're being led in the wrong direction," I blurted out, desperation lacing my words.

"Oh, really?" he scoffed, "And how do you know that? Did the spirits whisper to you, and tell you where she is?"

"I don't know her exact location," I replied, urgency clawing at my throat. "But I'm certain she's close, not in San Francisco."

"For the rest of us who rely on facts rather than imagination, I can assure you she is at a reputable hotel in San Francisco. I spoke directly with her; she provided me with the correct code words to confirm her identity. She simply misplaced her phone, as you well know, seeing as you found it," he said, annoyance in his voice.

"I think someone is manipulating you, using this to pull you out of the area," I insisted. "If they captured and tortured her, she would easily give up codes or anything else they demanded."

Roberts let out an exaggerated breath, frustration radiating from him. "Agent Calvin mentioned you suspected some South American drug lord was behind all this. Look, I can't draw conclusions without evidence. I've seen the file on this Don Diego character. He's a lunatic, but I can assure you he has cast no spells on me. Ms. Fontaine made contact as protocol dictates, and our job now is to retrieve her and secure her safety until her father arrives."

He strolled away, but then hesitated, glancing back at us with a tone that dripped with condescension. "Why don't you two go enjoy your honeymoon and leave this to the professionals?"

I instinctively tightened my grip around Jyanette's hand, sensing that the fire brewing within her would push her to chase after the insufferable man and unleash her fury.

"Let me go, I'm going to tell that idiot off," she growled, her eyes blazing with indignation.

I held on with a gentle yet firm resolve. "My darling, it's our honeymoon, and I'd rather not spend it in federal lockup."

She huffed, clearly torn between her instincts and the absurdity of the situation. "I'd prefer to slap him upside his head. He doesn't get to treat us like that."

"Which is exactly why I'm holding your hand," I replied, with a grin. "The only thing that would come from you confronting him would be a swift ride to the local jail."

With a resigned sigh, we headed toward the lodge, the weight of his dismissive words hanging in the air.

"I can't believe he treated you like that," she said, her frustration simmering just beneath the surface. "It's as if neither of us has ever dealt with high-stakes cases before. We've both faced down danger."

"He's just a bureaucrat who needs to feel like he's in charge," I replied, trying to soothe her frustration. But deep down, I was more troubled by the implications of his departure. "But all of them leaving worries me."

"Your dream about an attack?"

"Yes," I admitted. "If I were planning something like that, the first thing I would do is ensure all the federal agents were out of the picture and that only the local police remained to face whatever threat was coming."

"Captain Lauwers seems to know what he's doing."

"I sincerely hope you're right," I said. "But with the stakes so high, we can't afford to underestimate the danger. We need to stay vigilant."

Together, we walked towards the lodge, my mind a storm of worry, fueled by the uncertainty that was overshadowing our supposed paradise.

Dressed in a sleek suit without a tie, attempting a look of casual elegance, I walked alongside Jyanette, her hand in mine, my heavy wooden cane in the other. In her stylish pantsuit and high heels, she commanded attention with every step.

I was grateful that my leg had not given me much trouble, but then again, I'd been mostly sitting and lying in bed, so the strain on it was minimal.

The air in the Alpine Reflections, the resort's premier dining establishment, carried the subtle scent of rosemary and seared butter, mingling with the quiet hum of polite conversation. Candlelight flickered across polished glassware, casting soft shadows over the elegantly set tables.

I savored a spectacular eggplant dish bursting with vibrant flavors, while Jyanette chose seared scallops nestled in a creamy saffron sauce — an artistic creation that matched her own style.

Despite the idyllic setting, my mind drifted back to my recent encounter with Don Diego, a shadow lingering over my thoughts, coupled with a knot of anxiety concerning the absence of the law enforcement agents stationed on the property.

As Jyanette enjoyed a chilled glass of champagne, I opted for plain water, swirling the ice in my glass, my mind elsewhere.

Dinner had calmed her nerves, and the atmosphere invited us to relax, but I still felt something was wrong. It wasn't just paranoia; it was the distinct pull of unease, a silent alarm just beneath my consciousness.

"So, are we off the case?" Jyanette queried, her gaze searching mine.

"As far as I know," I replied, retrieving my smartphone from my pocket, placing it conspicuously on the table between us. "Unless Marcus or Captain Lauwers calls us."

"You should be nicer to Marcus," she chided gently, shaking her head with a playful smile.

"I feel no need to extend kindness to men who've pursued my wife," I retorted, unable to mask the hint of possessiveness in my voice.

The phone…

I was getting a buzz — which is what I call a glimpse of precognition. Those brief messages have sometimes saved my life. My eyes flicked to my phone, expecting an urgent message, but the screen was blank.

"Maybe it's good for you to know that other men find me attractive," Jyanette mused, tilting her head as she met my gaze with a teasing grin.

"Any straight man with a pulse would find you attractive. You're stunning," I remarked, picking up my phone again to check the screen.

"That was the right thing to say."

My brow furrowed as I glanced at my phone, noticing that it had no signal. "My phone isn't getting any bars. I'm connected to the hotel Wi-Fi, but nothing is coming through."

"We're near the lake. Maybe there's no nearby tower?"

"I had four bars earlier today."

She frowned and retrieved her own phone. "You're right. I'm not getting anything either." With a sigh, she slipped it back into her purse. "Look at it this way — one less distraction."

"Sorry, I'm still unsettled by my encounter with Don Diego," I admitted, my voice lowered, more serious than before.

Jyanette raised an eyebrow. "If it was him," she pointed out.

"That's true; I have no definitive proof," I conceded. "But given his reputation, he appears to be the most logical suspect."

With a slight shift in tone, she redirected the conversation. "Shall we look at the dessert menu?"

"Definitely," I replied, eager to indulge in something sweet to lighten the mood.

Len...

The voice echoed in my mind, startling me. It was Anna Sokolov. I blinked, my heart racing as the reality of my surroundings settled back in.

Jyanette, sitting beside me, sensed my abrupt shift in demeanor and leaned in closer. "What is it?"

"I'm not sure," I said. I reached out with my mind.

Anna...?

Her presence washed over me, and I felt the urgency in her voice.

Len... you're in danger... They are coming for you...soon...

What? Who...?

You have to run... you have to hide...

Meeting Jyanette's inquisitive gaze, I felt a sense of dread bloom in my chest. "I'm getting a message from Anna."

"Really? What is it about?"

That's when my own buzz burst through my brain. A violent warning that sent my pulse spiking.

Danger...

I scanned the restaurant, eyes darting over unsuspecting guests sipping wine and laughing at inside jokes. Yet beneath the normalcy, something was wrong. The air felt charged, like the seconds before a storm.

I motioned for the server, signing the bill quickly. "We need to leave. Now."

"What? Why?" Jyanette asked, her eyes darting around, seeking some threat.

"Anna warned me, and I just got a strong buzz." I stood, my movements controlled but urgent.

Jyanette hesitated for a moment before nodding, standing beside me. We moved with deliberate calm yet purposeful haste toward the exit. As we stepped into the hallway, my mind echoed with warnings.

DANGER…

I impulsively took Jyanette's arm, steering her past the elevators and into a nearby set of double doors leading to stairs.

"You've got to be kidding!" she exclaimed, her shoes clicking against the floor. "I'm in heels!"

"Trust me! We need to get out of sight — right now!" My voice carried an edge of desperation, and she must have sensed it. We ducked into the stairway, which was stark and bare, concrete underfoot instead of the plush carpeting of the lobby.

The stairs created an unlit space under them. The space was half full of chairs piled one on top of another in columns.

"Quick, go in there," I whispered.

She squeezed past the chairs and into the shadows. In the darkness, I couldn't see her.

"That's good," I said, following her and sliding a stack of chairs over to hide us better.

I pressed against her in the confined space, heart pounding against my ribs.

"This is cozy," she muttered. "You want to tell me what this is all about?"

"That's just it, I don't know."

She sighed. "You really need to find out what these buzzes of yours are about before we—"

Without a sound, the lights in the stairway suddenly flickered and then extinguished. An impenetrable darkness enveloped the entire room, leaving both of us momentarily speechless.

Each second stretched into what felt like an eternity, a quiet suspense wrapping itself around us. Then, the emergency lights flickered on, casting a muted glow that barely illuminated the doorway and little else.

Though the light was dim and eerie, it pierced through the darkness enough to reveal the outlines of our surroundings.

"Did the hotel just lose power?" she asked.

"I think so. Maybe the entire resort."

"I don't see why we had to hide because of—"

But before she could finish, a violent eruption of gunfire shattered the air. Jyanette stiffened beside me.

"Was that—?" she gasped.

"Shh!"

The double doors slammed open, and two men rushed in. Over the chairs, I caught a glimpse of them.

They wore black masks, styled to resemble skulls, covered with symbols painted in white. One man gripped his black submachine gun by the handle, while the other held his, ready to fire; both guns had long, menacingly gleaming barrels.

They shouted to one another in rapid-fire Spanish, bounding up the stairwell over our heads, urgency and menace radiating from them.

"Did you see them?" I whispered, my voice barely above a breath.

"Yes," Jyanette replied, her voice tremulous. "They're carrying Barrett M-81s."

My jaw dropped. "You recognize the guns?"

"I prosecuted a case involving one," she said, her breath hitching. "They're horrible — capable of penetrating bulletproof vests."

We fell silent, hearts pounding in unison, as an additional pair of masked men smashed through the doorway, their movements precise and methodical. They swept the area before bounding up the stairs.

"I'm going to reach out mentally, see if I can find out what's going on." I whispered.

"Be careful," she murmured.

I shut my eyes, lowering my mental defenses just enough to tap into the frenzy swirling around us.

Being psychic is a double-edged sword; If I am not careful, I can be perpetually bombarded by the thoughts of those nearby. In earlier days, I sought solace in alcohol to drown out the constant noise, which nearly led to my downfall until Doctor Kohl taught me how to construct mental barriers. Now, however, I needed to cast them aside to receive the thoughts and fears surrounding us.

The fear rushed over me as I sensed the emotions rippling through the resort. Panic thrummed through nearly everyone's minds.

Oh, my God, it's men with guns…

What will we do…?

Where are the police…?

The panicked thoughts were all around. I also detected the terrorists, but I couldn't read their thoughts, which was probably a result of the masks. Agent Calvin did not accept the idea of black magic, but I was rapidly becoming a believer.

I focused harder, striving to gain insight into what was happening. Men were going through the restaurants, the rooms, forcing guests to head to one central location — likely the large ballroom I recalled from my dreams.

That's when I sensed… him.

Desperate, I sought someone in his vicinity whose mind I could infiltrate. I hesitated, as invading a person's mind felt like a violation. But, with these stakes, I had to risk it.

The masked men were impervious to my mental abilities, but I felt one person near the front lobby, trembling with fear — a woman. With a push of determination, I slipped into her mind. Through her eyes, I beheld the lobby from behind the main desk. It took me a moment, but I realized my mental host was the woman who greeted Jyanette and me upon our arrival.

Six men in black uniforms filled the lobby, but since I wasn't seeing them with my actual eyes, they appeared to me as the dark silhouettes like in my vision.

There, amidst them, was their leader — a tall figure clad in fatigues with a long black cloak. His face, unlike those of his compatriots, was visible. Dark hair framed his jawline, adding an air of sinister authority fitting his reputation.

With a swift motion, he shoved a woman forward. I immediately recognized her — Isabella Fontaine, her hair wild and mascara streaked with tears, looking battered and terrified. She hunched protectively, flinching away from the man who menaced her.

I glanced to my right and saw a black silhouette standing next to me... my host body was being watched.

Don Diego smiled and looked around the room. He gestured to Isabella, who was cowering down on one knee. A few words in hasty Spanish, one man grabbed her and took her around the front desk and into the offices hidden away behind.

Diego paused and focused his attention to the woman with whom I was linked.

She wanted to avert her eyes, but I forced her to maintain contact. Diego walked over, his steps deliberate and calm, while I struggled to maintain control.

His hand gripped my host's chin, yanking her gaze toward him. "I see you hiding in there," he declared sweetly in accented English. "Come out and play."

I recoiled, breaking the connection and re-establishing my mental barriers with a surge of effort. I gasped, shock coursing through me like an electric current. Nobody had ever challenged me in such a way before.

"What just happened?" Jyanette whispered, her breath warm against my ear.

"I saw him — Don Diego — he's here at the hotel with Isabella Fontaine, and she's in rough shape."

Her eyes widened in horror. "You gasped when you came out of it."

"I know," I replied, panting. "He knows I'm here. He felt me."

An icy dread settled in my gut as the reality of our situation loomed over us like a shadow.

The resort was being taken over, and we were trapped.

7. DUTIFUL DISAPPEARANCE

"What can we do?" Jyanette whispered urgently, her eyes wide with fear.

"We have to separate," I replied softly, my voice barely above a murmur. "If he knows I'm here, he'll tear through this hotel until he finds me. If you stay quiet and hidden, they might overlook you."

"I'm not abandoning you," she hissed, her tone a mix of defiance and concern.

The sentiment cut through me like a knife, but also filled me with fear. I could feel her concern, a mirror to my own, but reason had to prevail.

"If anything happened to you, I'd be lost," I murmured, desperation creeping into my voice. "Please, don't fight me on this."

"What if something happens to you?"

"I can keep going as long as I know you're safe," I said. "I love you."

"I love you too. Just… don't make me a widow," she replied, fear threading through her words.

"I'll do my best," I promised.

I slid out from our hiding place, moving quietly in the stillness of the dimly lit space. With as little noise as possible, I slid the stack of chairs and maneuvered one chair off the top, handing it to Jyanette. She sank down onto it, and I quickly rearranged the stack, ensuring her concealment.

"That's good. No one can see you," I hissed.

I stepped away, opening my mind slightly to sense the surrounding danger.

Up...

I felt the buzz, and ascended the staircase slowly, my wooden cane clutched tightly in my grip, moving as quietly as I could manage. Reaching the landing of the second floor, I placed my hand gently on the doorknob, extending my senses outward, trying to decipher the hazards that lay just beyond.

Step back...

Instinctively, I pressed myself flat against the wall just in time as the door swung wide, a gust of air brushing against me. I was fortunate enough to catch the doorknob, using the door as a makeshift shield to stay hidden from view.

Through the narrow gap, I caught fragments of a heated conversation — a woman's frustrated voice clashed against the harsh accents of two men barking orders.

"Move, move," one urged brusquely, his tone commanding.

"I'll have you know, I'm an influencer and I'm going to give this resort a terrible rating!" the woman shouted defiantly.

"Shut up and move," growled the second man.

Their footsteps echoed down the stairs, accompanied by the woman's continuous protestations, fading out as they exited through the double doors into the lobby.

My heart raced as adrenaline surged through me. I was grateful they hadn't looked back to see that the door I was behind remained open.

Taking a moment to calm myself, I reached out with my mind once more, sensing that it was safe to proceed. Stepping through the doorway, I noted that all the room doors stood open, a sign that the terrorists had systematically cleared each occupant from their quarters.

There was a method behind their madness; these individuals weren't just armed, but highly trained.

I entered the first room I encountered, consisting only of a small front room with a sofa, a bedroom, and a bathroom. I pulled out my phone, but it became quickly apparent that there were no bars on the cellular network, and there was no longer access to the hotel Wi-Fi.

Of course not. With the power down, modems and routers couldn't operate.

My heart sank further as I picked up the house phone to find it completely dead.

This was no random act of terror but a meticulously orchestrated operation designed to sever all lines of communication. They had either disabled the nearby cellular towers or found some way to jam the signals. The power was down, and it was clear they were methodically herding the guests down to the first floor, treating them like cattle on their way to the slaughter.

But why?

What profit could they possibly gain from holding an entire hotel of guests hostage? The diplomat's daughter was the high-value target, and they already had her in their grasp.

I needed to find their true motives.

More importantly, I had to determine how to intervene. Armed and prepared for battle, they possessed the advantage, as I had nothing more than a cane. I'd trained in Aikido, familiar with self-defense moves, but that was little use against high-powered automatic weapons.

I had observed they travelled in pairs, which also complicated any plans I might come up with. Isolating one of them without the other interceding would require a level of cunning I doubted I possessed.

Voices echoed to me from further down the hall. Another shrewd tactic; they were double-checking the rooms to ensure they didn't overlook anyone. They were bound to discover my presence in mere moments, and I stood no chance against two heavily armed men.

Closet...

I got the buzz and shook my head in disbelief. That was such an obvious place. But not having any other plan, I slipped into the closet and quietly shut the door, leaving just a crack so that I could monitor the room.

The air in the closet felt stifling as I stood in silence.

The sound of heavy boots thudding against the floor sent adrenaline coursing through my veins. Two men entered, their faces obscured by those ominous skull masks that rendered them both menacing and bizarre. The long-barreled rifles strapped across their shoulders added an element of cold efficiency.

As they scanned the room, I silently prayed they'd overlook me for just a moment longer.

They walked past my closed door. As they spoke in quiet voices, the taller of the two took the weapon off his shoulder and handed it to his companion, who took it with an air of casual authority.

"Tengo que orinar," the man announced.

My rudimentary grasp of Spanish was enough to let me know the taller man needed the facilities.

The other man remained in the room, and my mind raced with opportunity. I knew two things: the mask the man wore gave him limited peripheral vision so he could only focus straight ahead. With his hands occupied, he couldn't raise the weapon to shoot me easily.

The man in the room with me shouted at the door to his companion, carrying on a conversation through the door.

This was my chance.

Offering a silent prayer of gratitude and with hesitant but deliberate movements, I pressed through the closet door and crept into the room, heart pounding.

My pulse quickened as I approached, staying low and silent. Just as I drew within striking distance, the remaining man rotated, chuckling at his companion's comment.

Our eyes locked, and his amusement morphed into shocked disbelief as he fumbled with his rifle. I seized the moment, swinging my heavy wooden cane with all the strength I could muster. The hook of the cane connected with his temple, knocking him down to one knee. I could sense my chance slipping away — one rifle dropped from his grasp as he struggled to lift the other weapon.

I pivoted on my heel and swung the cane again, this time delivering a crushing blow that knocked him face-first into the carpet. Without hesitation, I knelt beside him, yanking off the mask to ensure he was unconscious. The sound of the toilet flushing reminded me of the looming threat inside the bathroom, igniting a flare of urgency within me.

The voice of the remaining man rang out, asking what the noise was.

Unbuckling the fallen man's strap, I called out, lowering my voice to a gruff growl. I quickly told him in Spanish that I had dropped his gun. I hoped this ruse would stall the second man long enough for me to act.

This elicited several curses from the unseen man.

I hurriedly stashed both rifles in the closet, adrenaline sharpening my focus, and rose, readying myself as the bathroom door swung open.

The second man emerged, mask in one hand while the other adjusted his tactical vest.

"*¿Cómo puedes ser tan torpe?*" he chastised, complaining how clumsy I was, frustration clear in his tone. Our eyes met, and without a second to spare, I raised the cane to defend myself.

He lunged, grabbing hold of the cane with both hands, but I was ready. Channeling the techniques taught by my Aikido instructor, Ashwan, I propelled myself forward, leveraging his pull on my cane to twist it into a vertical position. In that position, I brought the end of the cane up with a stunning strike aimed between his legs, eliciting a sound that was part gasp, part moan as he crumpled to the floor on his knees.

Even in pain, his hand went to his tactical vest, and he pulled free a nasty-looking knife.

With newfound determination, I wrestled the cane from the weakening grip of his other hand and swung, striking him squarely on the head, sending him sprawling to the ground.

I paused, fighting to catch my breath as uncertainty flooded my mind. I had incapacitated two armed men and seized their weapons, but how could I ensure they remained subdued?

I opened the closet, scanning for any items that might help restrain them. There, among the hangers, were some hotel robes, but little else that could help me secure the threats now lying at my feet. Time was of the essence — I needed to act swiftly and decisively.

As I eyed the two men, I realized their attire might afford me an opportunity. The shorter one was well under my height, while the one who had been in the bathroom was stockier and nearly the same size as me.

I could walk around freely if dressed like them, and wearing one of their masks. That might give me the opportunity and anonymity that I needed.

I rolled the unconscious man onto his back and swiftly stripped him of his tactical vest, replacing the knife into it, and fatigues, both pants and shirt, revealing only a pair of boxers beneath.

Grabbing a pillow from the bed, I removed the pillowcase and headed back to the closet. I took a bathrobe belt and shoved a washcloth into the man's mouth, securing it with the pillowcase tied around his head.

Struggling as best as I could, I bound his arms behind his back, bending his legs and fastening the cloth belt around his ankles and wrists with a knot designed to tighten under the slightest struggle. I didn't think this was a perfect solution, but it would slow him down.

Next, I repeated the process with the second man, tossing his clothes into the closet and securing him in the same manner. I donned the green uniform and stashed my suit containing my wallet and useless cell phone under the bed. An odd sensation washed over me as I left behind my former identity.

I sat on the bed, catching my breath for a minute, recovering from the exertion of tying up the two men.

Once suited up, I examined the contents of the tactical vest. There were ammunition magazines for the rifles and the knife was held in a specially designed sheath. I also found a small flashlight. It was a hard choice, but I reluctantly put my wooden cane under the bed; right now, I needed to rely on the uniform and the tools it contained.

I hoped my weaker right leg wouldn't give out on me.

I retrieved both rifles from the closet. Their cold metal felt uncomfortable and imposing.

I grabbed the mask. It was a full over the head mask, and would not only cover my face, but the back of my head and my hair. I gazed at the elaborate symbols, and they seemed to leer at me, igniting an unsettling sense of dread.

I took a deep breath and placed the mask over my face and head.

A rush of warmth caught me off guard, surging through me and spreading like wildfire through my veins. A deep, commanding voice resonated within my mind, dictating my duties with an authoritative clarity.

Take the guests to the ballroom, all of them...

I let go of the weight of responsibility I had carried, feeling an exhilarating surge of power and belonging - as if I had finally found where I truly belonged.

I pulled the mask off, tearing myself away from that revelatory moment, and sucked in several deep breaths to dispel the remnants of the intoxicating influence.

What had just happened to me?

Somehow, the mask had connected me to Don Diego, allowing me to feel his commands and influence. No wonder his followers revered him — merely wearing this bizarre mask evoked a sense of euphoria, a feeling of being part of something greater.

I had underestimated their unwavering devotion to him.

Quickly checking to make sure my prisoners remained unconscious, I went out into the front room. A hesitant glance at the hallway revealed an open door across the way, which was a utility room. With one rifle slung over my shoulder, I stepped into the utility room and set down an extra rifle for now, my mind racing with thoughts of my next steps.

I considered getting the unused uniform and mask to Jyanette, but I dismissed it. She was almost as tall as I am, so the uniform wouldn't fit. Also, if the mask affected me so deeply, it might overwhelm her entirely. Not to mention, her high heels would be a glaring giveaway to anyone inspecting her.

I took a moment to scrutinize the mask that lay before me, my fingers tracing its intricate details. The craftsmanship was remarkable. Inspecting the inner surface, I realized it was constructed from soft leather, expertly stitched and finished. The design was open at the bottom, allowing for an easy fit over one's head, and I could feel the supple material give slightly under my touch, hinting at its intended comfort.

On the exterior, the artistry became evident. Intricate carving and meticulous etching of the mouth lines allowed the wearer easy breathing through both mouth and nose. The rich, dark hue of the dyed leather added depth; it wasn't just a color, but a deep abyss that seemed to absorb light.

It was more than just an object; it felt like a tether connecting me to Don Diego supernaturally. Any lingering doubts I had about Diego's mastery of Brujería and its dark powers evaporated as I studied the symbols etched on the mask's surface.

This was no ordinary artifact. These markings, rather than enhancing my natural abilities, suppressed minds like mine, thus tightening Don Diego's control over his adherents.

I would have to completely shut down my psychic capabilities to don the mask — an act that would effectively render my precognitive abilities and other mental "buzzes" dormant.

There was only one way I could shut off all my mental abilities, and I knew what it was.

Returning to the room where I had dispatched Diego's men, it pleased me when I looked into the bedroom and saw that the bed concealed the pair from view.

Tiptoeing to a small refrigerator nestled within a desk, I pulled out two slender bottles of vodka from the minibar.

With the bottles in hand, I returned to the utility room, broke the seal that secured the first, and looked at it. I peered at the container, feeling a mix of relief and trepidation. I had learned the hard way that alcohol could mute my psychic senses. At one time, drinking was the only way I could stop the overwhelming input of other people's thoughts after my abilities manifested.

However, it came with a price — I had battled an alcohol addiction that nearly consumed me. I paved my road to recovery with the dedication of Alcoholics Anonymous and the unwavering support of those who cared for me.

I uncapped the bottle, feeling a familiar thrill and surge of dread at what lay ahead. I tilted the bottle back, the harsh liquid burning my throat. The taste, vile and yet glorious, filled my mouth. That was the trick of addiction — it beckoned me with promise even as it threatened to drown me.

That was the cruel reality of being an alcoholic: the urgency of craving something I desperately didn't want.

I paused for a moment, then cracked the seal on the second. Drinking them down one at a time, I tossed the empty bottles in an oversized plastic trash can on wheels. I sat waiting, afraid that I didn't even feel any effect from the alcohol at all. I had an amazingly high tolerance, as many alcoholics do.

Then a warm haze began to settle over me.

With a sigh, I realized my psychic senses had faded away. Now the pressing question remained: Would this newfound detachment shield me from the mask's influence if I dared to wear it?

I slid the mask over my head once more. To my astonishment, nothing happened — no alien voices grating at my thoughts, no sensations of euphoria.

It appeared I could now wear the mask without the shadow of Don Diego encroaching on my mind.

Armed with one gun slung over my shoulder, I picked up the other from the floor, glancing cautiously down the corridor to ensure it was clear. Reluctantly, I left the doors of both rooms ajar, understanding the risk involved but knowing it had to be done; if I closed it, another terrorist might find the bodies, jeopardizing my plan.

I cautiously descended the stairs to the first floor and made my way toward the stack of chairs barring the opening where Jyanette was hiding.

"Jyanette," I whispered. "It's me, Len."

"Len?" she said. "Where did you get that outfit and that mask?"

"I took out a pair of the bad guys," I said and put the extra rifle on top of the stack of chairs. "Take this."

The weapon vanished into the darkness, swallowed by the shadows.

"Len, what do I do with this? I don't know how to handle a weapon like this."

"You use a gun at home," I said.

"A handgun," she clarified, urgency rising in her voice. "One that I trained with at the police shooting range for hours."

"Keep it with you. I need it out of circulation. If you don't want to use it, stash it under a stack of chairs."

"I can do that," she agreed, her voice steadier now. "What are you going to do?"

"I'm going to see what I can find," I responded. "If I can figure out a way to get us out of here, I'll come back for you."

Her voice had a stern tone to it. "If you don't come back soon, I will come looking for you."

"No, you can't," I said, trying to keep my voice down as panic gripped my heart. "You must stay hidden. If Don Diego knows you're my wife, he will use you to get at me."

"How could he know?" she said.

"The same way I know things. Look, I am wearing a disguise, no one will notice me. You must stay here as long as you can."

"I'll do my best," she finally agreed.

I ventured out into the lobby, navigating the dimly lit corridors, where only the flickering of emergency lights pierced the oppressive darkness. The transformation from daylight to night had deepened the atmosphere of dread, making the once benign spaces feel threatening.

The strategy made sense; it would dissuade guests from attempting to escape down shadowy corridors.

My goal was clear: I had to enter the ballroom I'd seen in my dreams, as it was the place where they held the hostages. I had enough Spanish at my disposal to communicate with any of the terrorists should a confrontation arise.

I kept my weapon low as I approached the door, spotting two men guarding the entrance. They held their weapons at the ready, and I sensed they wouldn't hesitate to pull the trigger if provoked. With a nod to the men, I pushed the door open, adopting a facade of confidence and authority as I stepped inside.

The interior was tense — a handful of masked men took a moment to assess me before returning their attention to the huddled cluster of terrified guests. Anxiety hung thick in the air. They all looked terrified, and several of the women were crying quietly.

My gaze swept the room, searching for any sign of Don Diego, but he was nowhere in sight.

I glanced toward the windows where it was clearly night, the outside world mostly in darkness.

Something caught my eye — a flicker of light beyond the window's frame. With an authoritative air, I slowly circled the room, staying near the wall, as if obeying orders.

I reached the wall of windows and pulled the curtain aside to look out.

In the open field, several hundred yards from the hotel, the helipad was lit up.

The lights remained operational. Did it have its own power supply, or had they kept it lit?

What were they planning?

Drawing my attention back to the trembling crowd, I stood rigid, mimicking the intimidation that other armed men exuded. Each second weighed heavily as I tried to formulate a plan to rescue Jyanette, devise an escape, and ensure we contacted Captain Lauwers without further escalating the situation.

But — what could local law enforcement realistically do against a group armed with military-grade weapons and deep-seated connections to Don Diego's dark influence? Involving them could hasten disaster.

What were my options?

I had a firearm but lacked the training to use it effectively. If I were to fire indiscriminately, I'd blow my cover, and I'd endanger the lives of the hostages.

Time was not on my side. The discovery of the two incapacitated men would only expedite the terrorists' action, pushing them to uncover their missing comrades.

What if I was to grab Jyanette, pretend she was my prisoner, and make a break in the cover of darkness to the woods surrounding the hotel?

Not a poor tactic, yet, the idea of abandoning the terrified hostages twisted in my chest. I shivered at the thought of Don Diego mercilessly executing his captives — something I had read about in articles highlighting his brutal rituals of sacrifice, including his execution of a fifteen-year-old girl.

It suddenly clicked.

Fifteen.

In numerology, fifteen resonates with powerful alchemical vibrations; transformations and the manifestation of magic. Would Diego view the massacre of fifteen hostages as necessary to amplify his dark powers?

Probably. He was a purveyor of the sinister side of Brujería, and he would believe that the death of hostages would empower him and his abilities.

I shuddered at the implications of such a scenario, realizing he needed to be stopped — soon — and with as few casualties as possible.

But how?

8. EVAPORATING OPTIONS

I didn't see any advantage in returning to the main area of the hotel, so instead, I switched my attention to the expansive wall of windows behind me.

Just a few panels to my right was a door leading out to the hotel grounds — an invitation I found hard to resist. The darkness of the night outside promised not only concealment but also the chance to embark on a reconnaissance mission; I envisioned myself circling the hotel, stealthily peering into the windows of various rooms.

The shadows offered cover to strategize, to gather information, and to locate Don Diego to dismantle whatever scheme he was brewing within these walls, if I could.

Was I being too bold? Definitely, but I needed to know more than I currently did, and I wouldn't learn it by remaining in the ballroom.

My heart pounded in anticipation as I pushed the curtain aside, the moon's silvery glow spilling into the interior. I hastened toward the door, but just as my fingers brushed the cool metal of the handle, a guard shifted his attention towards me, his brow furrowing in suspicion.

"¿Adónde vas?" he demanded in a curt tone, asking me where I was going.

Thinking quickly, I replied in my best high school Spanish that I had spotted someone lurking outside. I pushed the door open, stepping out into the night. The guard cast a wary glance at me before the door slammed shut with a resounding thud.

I darted around the corner of the building to remain hidden and hastily removed my mask. Although the alcohol had dulled my psychic senses, I focused my normal ones on my surroundings.

A guard with an automatic weapon stood near the helipad.

Reassessing my approach, I slipped the mask back over my face and proceeded toward the front of the hotel. My earlier observations proved accurate: the forward-facing eyeholes of the skull mask severely restricted my peripheral vision, forcing me to turn my head excessively to check for any potential threats. The soft, warm glow from the nearby windows provided just enough light to guide my cautious steps as I navigated the building's perimeter.

As silence enveloped me, I couldn't resist stealing glances into the windows as I passed. My first glimpse revealed the Alpine Reflections restaurant. It was now a dimly lit space filled with shadows. Flickering candles cast a ghostly glow around the tables.

Jyanette and I had left just in time.

Fueled by adrenaline, I pressed on, glancing into more windows overlooking dreary meeting rooms and navigating towards what appeared to be a row of shops. The absence of back windows and metal doors suggested spaces designed for deliveries.

Testing my luck, I approached the first door — locked tight.

But fortune favored the bold, and I found the next door slightly ajar.

After a brief search, I found a small rock and wedged it into the gap, ensuring it would stay accessible. With the door propped, I continued on my way, as I needed to assess the situation at the front of the hotel.

Moving with caution, I advanced to the building's façade, peering around the corner. My breath caught in my throat at the sight before me: two men, also in skull masks, leaned casually against a luxurious stretch limousine. Their weapons hung loosely from shoulder straps, emanating an air of careless confidence that made my skin prickle with awareness.

The vehicle itself was striking. I scrutinized its license plate more closely. A green border framed it, something unfamiliar and unmissable.

Then it hit me like a jolt of ice water: it was a diplomatic plate.

Diplomatic vehicles enjoyed immunity, free from searches and seizures, allowing their occupants a pathway to evade the grasp of law enforcement for acts beyond reproach.

I finally grasped Don Diego's calculation. This operation relied on this immunity.

No one could search the car.

It also clarified Isabella Fontaine's role in this twisted game — and that he needed her alive. She was the key to that vehicle. Now, I understood her abduction; if anyone stopped the vehicle, she would talk to the authorities. She represented both a bargaining chip and an exit strategy for Don Diego.

From my vantage point, I looked the vehicle over a second time. Although it was a diplomat's transportation, it lacked the heavier, bulky frame of an armored vehicle. Such vehicles have tires that cannot go flat, but from where I stood, the tires were standard issue.

This made sense, as it was not the limousine the diplomat himself traveled in. His daughter would hardly be subject to the dangers the diplomat himself might face.

So even though it had diplomatic plates, it was basically an ordinary car — though longer and requiring a professional driver.

With this new information, I retraced my steps back along the building, locating the door I had propped open.

Sliding inside, I ensured the lock clicked securely behind me,

Darkness blanketed me, and I fished out the small flashlight from the tactical vest, illuminating the surrounding space.

The room appeared well-organized, cluttered yet tidy — a stock area overflowing with merchandise. The beam from my flashlight rested on a door leading into the shop's sales floor.

Turning off the flashlight, I slowly opened the door, peering into the dimly lit shop. Security gates barred any unwanted visitors coming into the main entrance.

A pang of longing for Jyanette struck me like a knife; I could envision bringing her here to safety. But the ordeal of just getting myself into this position had been challenging enough.

With determination pulsing in my veins, I scanned the back room for anything useful. My gaze landed on a box filled with letter openers, glimmering like whispers of potential danger. While they could inflict some damage in a pinch, I knew the fighting knife I had tucked away in my vest was the more effective weapon.

I sank into the manager's chair behind the desk; the springs protesting under my weight. There were photos and clutter on the wall. In the corner stood a crutch someone had used at one point.

I considered the situation. The helipad was the only thing lit by floodlights. Nearby was a sleek stretch limousine bearing diplomatic plates.

Pieces of Don Diego's plan aligned in my brain like a sinister puzzle, forming a clear image of what this was about.

A drug delivery.

If Don Diego was orchestrating a massive shipment via helicopter, the critical question loomed: how would he transfer the illicit goods to his buyer? The answer was as simple as it was audacious. He intended to load everything directly into a stretch limousine with no hint of concealment. Just pile the drugs into the back seat and trunk since a diplomatic vehicle was exempt from searches by state or local law enforcement.

As long as no one immobilized or tampered with it, local authorities had no legal grounds to intervene.

This daring plan relied on the fortunate confluence of two rare elements: the existence of a lavish limousine and the availability of a nearby helipad. Yet crafting a successful plan required more than mere logistics; it required control over the environment.

For Don Diego, the resort had to be completely his, a fortress without interruptions. Guests wandering about, snapping photos or stumbling upon an illicit deal — even at three in the morning — were a risk he could not afford. But why not use stealth? Why this all out assault?

But lurking behind the tangible threat of the drug operation was a much darker undercurrent. Don Diego was a man who thrived on power and control, unrestrained by conscience. He had every reason to eliminate any liabilities that could derail his operations. His notorious methods included human sacrifices to the gods of Brujeria.

So far, he hadn't resorted to such extremes. I had seen the guests confined to the ballroom.

Perhaps he was keeping them alive as hostages — bargaining chips against any law enforcement that dared to show up.

Or maybe he was simply waiting for the right moment to offer a sacrifice to the forces he used.

It was only a matter of time before someone concerned themselves with the absence of the two men I had incapacitated.

I had to decide my next move. The weight of urgency pressed down on me, clamoring for immediate action.

What to do?

One potential strategy floated in my mind: disable the car. But I had to act quickly and deliberately. Slashing the tires with the knife would be a logical starting point — if I could get close enough unchallenged. The guards stationed by the vehicle were formidable, alert, and heavily armed. A single misstep against the car would guarantee swift retaliation.

As I contemplated my options, the backroom of the gift shop flickered to mind as a potential trap for the guards. If I could lure them inside and subdue them quietly…

I shook my head, dismissing the idea. The thought of going one-on-one with two highly trained men was ridiculous. My first encounter had been a stroke of luck; I had caught the pair upstairs off-guard and separated. The element of surprise had been my greatest ally then. This time, however, it would be different. Here, in the cramped confines of the backroom, it would be a direct confrontation — one where precision and experience would be on their side.

For now, maintaining my cover was essential. Blending in with this hostile group seemed my only viable option until a better plan crystalized.

While I weighed these strategies, a familiar sound broke through my thoughts, gradually increasing in volume until it was unmistakable: helicopter rotors.

I pulled on the mask as my heart raced. I made my way to the door and stepped outside, placing the rock to make sure I didn't lock myself out.

The helicopter approached, cutting through the darkness with its powerful searchlight.

I darted behind the building to remain concealed. My heart sank when I spotted six more men exiting the hotel to join the two by the vehicle. That made eight armed men in plain view with three or four more lingering among the guests in the ballroom, and the two I had already incapacitated. Was Don Diego's force comprised of thirteen men?

I paused and reconsidered this.

It would be fifteen — Don Diego, after all, had an affinity with that number.

I walked over to join the group of men, positioning my rifle on my back and attempting to mimic their relaxed postures as best as I could.

Fortunately, the commotion caused by the approaching helicopter drew their attention, enabling me to slip in unnoticed. Each one wore a black skull mask, their expressions hidden as they collectively craned their necks skyward. The roar of the helicopter drowned out any need for conversation, providing me with a vital veil of invisibility.

As it neared the helipad, its searchlight illuminated the open field. Leaves and debris danced wildly in the wake of its powerful blades. The group of masked men and I watched as the aircraft finally touched down, its landing gear absorbing the impact with a muted thud.

The engine noise faded, giving way to a quieter hum from the slowing rotor blades.

Out of the corner of my eye, I caught Don Diego watching from an office. The wall appeared to be nothing but glass, so I could see his entire form, his silhouette stark against the brightness within.

As the helicopter's rotors stopped, the first man reached the rear of the craft and swung open a door, revealing a broad loading ramp.

He reached inside and pulled out a sizable blue box adorned with vibrant snack food packaging. The labels promised a 'Variety

Pack,' and the colorful graphics advertised offerings, such as potato chips, cheese puffs, and corn chips.

As each man stepped forward to claim a box, it became clear from their grunts and shifts in posture that these boxes were much heavier than snacks.

I made my way slowly to the front of the line, following the men as they each took a box. I was handed my box, hefted it up, feeling its substantial weight — definitely packed with something more significant than party treats.

The men surged forward, forming a tight row as they made their way toward the limousine. One man stood at the rear of the vehicle, ready to stow the boxes. Another man opened the rear door as the cargo began its transfer. The elevated trunk lid shielded the activity from anyone's gaze inside the hotel, especially from the watchful Don Diego.

If I was going to act, now was the moment.

We walked so close that our shoulders almost brushed against one another. As the man in front of me finished handing off his box, I feigned a stumble, jostling the man behind me. I dropped to one knee, cradling my box against the rear driver's side tire to keep hold of it.

"Lo siento, amigo," I murmured, gesturing for him to pass his box into the vehicle. As his attention shifted away, I seized the opportunity, my box obscuring my hands as I discreetly slid the knife from my vest.

Suddenly, a pair of white vans pulled up close to the helicopter. The men's attention diverted to the new arrival — an opportune moment for my clandestine move.

I took my chance, delivering a swift, calculated cut to the tire, the razor-sharp blade slipping into the rubber and fabric, creating a tiny incision that would slowly leak air.

Quickly re-tucking my blade, I struggled under the weight of my box and handed it to the man at the vehicle's rear entrance.

I slipped back into the crowd as it split in two. Some kept unloading the helicopter; I joined those moving toward the white vans.

The back doors swung open, revealing several massive fifty-five-gallon drums—each heavy enough to need two men.

I paired with a masked man to lift the first barrel. The sour smell of jet fuel thickened as another unscrewed the cap and a second brought over a long metal pipe.

Nervous, I mimicked their precise movements. One man slid the pipe into the drum and attached a pump with a hose running to the helicopter's fuel tank.

They worked with practiced rhythm, emptying the first barrel before rolling it away and loading empties into the second van.

Each drum went through this same choreographed process, the henchmen executing with cold efficiency.

All around, armed men stood alert, eyes slicing through the shadows for any threat.

The urgency I felt skyrocketed — I needed to slip away before they noticed the deflated tire. The longer I stayed, the more I feared leaving would draw suspicion.

When the last barrel drained, the driver of the first van pulled away. The men's attention shifted to loading the final boxes into a waiting limousine.   Once more, I clutched a box, making my way back along the path to the limousine.

Just as my box passed into the vehicle, the thunderous roar of the helicopter engines broke through the din, the rotors swirling with escalating noise, stirring dust and debris into the night.

I stole a quick glance around to ensure no one was watching me.

With the helicopter rising into the blackness above, I seized my opportunity. I quietly slipped back toward the hotel, stepping into the shadows of the building. I pivoted and made a beeline toward my hidden sanctum in the back of the gift shop.

Just as I reached the corner, I nearly collided with the formidable figure of Don Diego, who had just stepped outside.

Towering above me at six foot six, he emanated authority, his curly hair framing a smug smile, the face of a conqueror savoring victory.

My heart thundered.

Don Diego paused, looking around as if something caught his attention. His eyes moved from man to man, then he looked away, stepping past me to watch the sky as the helicopter's blades tilted forward as it transitioned into horizontal flight. He kept his eyes on the machine as it swiftly ascended and disappeared into the night sky over Lake Tahoe.

I discreetly made my way around the corner and slipped into the building, seeking the safety of shadows.

Cries rang out, piercing the charged atmosphere. *"Sabotaje!"* echoed through the night, followed by the chilling proclamation, *"Hay un traidor entre nosotros!"*

The panic swelled in my chest; they had discovered the sabotage, and the ominous words echoed in my mind, and the man who yelled that there was a traitor in the group sounded like Don Diego himself.

The stakes had just escalated.

9. FADING FAITH

Once I slipped safely into the gift shop, I caught my breath; the door creaking lightly behind me as I slid the heavy bolt into place. The solid click of the lock echoed in the small, dimly lit space, providing a brief sense of security that allowed the thrum of adrenaline to ebb away.

I hastily yanked off the mask that felt suffocating against my skin, a thin sheen of sweat clinging to my brow. I stumbled toward the solitary chair tucked in the corner, sinking heavily into its embrace with a deep, shuddering sigh.

My right leg throbbed with a persistent ache, a grim reminder of the knee replacement surgery I had undergone just a few months prior. Even though I had dedicated myself to physical therapy religiously, working tirelessly to regain strength and mobility, the muscle mass I had lost nearly a decade earlier from that fateful car accident still limited how much stress I could put on it.

In moments like this, my cane became indispensable — a useful crutch for when my leg faltered. Hauling heavy boxes a hundred yards and wrestling with fifty-five-gallon drums had been less than smart; still, the adrenaline surging through my veins had kept me going.

Now that I was sitting and relaxing, I was aware of the pain.

I again noticed the crutch in the corner of the room and deeply wished I could use it to take some of the weight off my leg, but quickly dismissed the idea.

During my hasty act of sabotage, I had successfully suppressed my fear, shoving it deep down. Now, fear surged within me, crashing over me like an unforgiving wave, overwhelming my senses and leaving me reeling. The gravity of my situation settled in, and I felt utterly unprepared, dwarfed by the consequences I had unwittingly unleashed.

For years, my work alongside Bill McGee and other law enforcement officers had revolved around piecing together events after they had already unraveled: the aftermath of crime scenes, the meticulous gathering of evidence.

But this time, I was not merely a bystander. Firmly entrenched in the wave of turmoil itself, my decisions bore down on me.

I had lost Jyanette before, after she miscarried the baby. I had been in dark despair in those months, barely able to function. We came back together on a case and both of us realized we were meant to be together. The idea of her getting killed flashed through my mind and it terrified me.

I thought about my sabotage and what it had accomplished. I created a minor setback — a slight delay that would take time to change a tire. Did that disrupt their timetable? They would undoubtedly search the hotel and recover the two men I had dispatched, starting a thorough manhunt for me.

I glanced at my watch; it was about ten at night, though I was so exhausted, it felt like three in the morning had come and gone. Time seemed to stretch and warp, trapping me in a moment that echoed the darkest hours of night.

Midnight...

Surprised, I lifted my head at receiving the buzz. I had underestimated how long the effect of the alcohol could dull my psychic abilities.

The effect was wearing off, and quickly.

Closing my eyes, I took a few deep breaths, centering myself and built my protective mental barriers again.

Glancing around the room, I wondered if the gift shop had any alcohol; I needed to wear the mask to go outside, but I despised the way it affected my mind while wearing it. I needed some way for it to no longer influence me, but what could I do?

My gaze landed on a mug filled with colored markers atop the desk, and a glimmer of hope pierced through my anxiety. I rummaged through the cup and quickly retrieved a metal nail file, a black permanent marker, and a white paint marker — likely used by the manager to correct price tags.

The mask's mystical symbols contained energy, undoubtedly vested by Don Diego himself. This allowed anyone who wore it to be connected to him. His followers accepted it willingly, but I had no desire to let that monster into my head.

Yet, in ritualistic magick, one usually performed their incantations within an enchanted circle, a precautionary measure against darker forces. I understood this technique. In my training, I learned that a magic circle was simply a physical representation, similar to my mental barriers. It is a focal point of the energy of the user's mind. The barrier is all a mental projection, but drawing the circle on the floor gives the mind an image to use.

The symbols on the mask connected directly to Don Diego's mind so his men could receive his orders. Breaking or taking control of that connection was crucial. In ritual magic, the ritual ends by breaking the circle, which requires erasing part of it.

I found the very tools I needed to make the symbols ineffectual.

There was a circle in the center of the forehead, filled with lines and curves to form the cryptic symbol. I carefully examined it, as well as the other intricate shapes and symbols.

Fortunately for me, they had painted the symbols on the mask, and not carved them into the leather. With precision, I took the metal nail file and delicately scratched away at the paint in the circle's perimeter. I needed to be careful to choose locations where the imperfections would be unnoticeable.

The black permanent marker followed suit, effectively concealing the scratches. I worked methodically, but with a sense of urgency driving me. Carefully, I altered the symbols. I used the fine white marker to add subtle lines, effectively transforming the designs into something entirely different.

I set the mask down and scrutinized my handiwork. The changes were subtle enough that someone would have to look closely. I doubted anyone would get near enough to notice. Gritting my teeth, I pulled it over my head.

For a moment, nothing. No overwhelming rush of energy, no haunting whispers or mental communications. It was as if I were wearing an ordinary mask.

Slowly, I relaxed my mental barriers, cautiously testing the waters, and it surprised me to discover that my latest attempt at sabotage had succeeded. Damaging the symbols disrupted the mental connection where Don Diego was pushing orders into my mind.

With my mental barriers lowered, an unsettling tingling crept up the back of my neck, tinged with a strange awareness that I was being sought after. It felt as if an unseen force was prying into the depths of my consciousness, and I recognized it instantly: Don Diego, with his formidable psychic abilities, was hunting for me.

Where are you, little mouse…?

The whisper echoed in my mind, slithering through the fabric of my thoughts.

Wouldn't you like to know…

I responded, then summoned all my energy to reinforce my mental defenses, sealing my mind away from him.

The last thing I wanted was for him to discern my location. Just that moment of connection had been dangerous. I was certain he understood the threat I posed. After all, I had sabotaged the car tire, and his crew would scour the hotel looking for me.

I yanked the mask off my face and inspected it, my thoughts racing.

I'd received a buzz about midnight. Was it a warning? If so, it likely signaled that something bad was going to happen at that hour.

They could easily repair the tire by then and be ready to execute their plans. My act of defiance inflicted nothing more than a minor inconvenience. But it may have only served as an alarm, alerting them to my presence and putting them on guard to prevent any other attempts to stop them.

My thoughts shifted to Jyanette. Sitting alone in the cramped back room, surrounded by shadows and stiff, stale air, few options were available to me; if I aimed to ensure my safety, I could sit here like a trapped animal, enveloped by dust motes dancing in the faint light. But if I hoped to actually thwart their plans, the time to act would soon be at hand.

I longed for a way to reach out to Marcus, Agent Roberts, or even Captain Lauwers. However, my psychic abilities wouldn't allow me to communicate directly with them.

I paused, considering my options. There was someone I could connect with mentally — someone who had already reached out to warn me.

Anna Sokolov.

It would be tricky; if I opened my mind carelessly, Don Diego might sense me. However, the psychic bond I had with Anna was strong, and if I focused on her exclusively, I believed I could keep Don Diego at bay.

I leaned back in my chair, closed my eyes, and slowed my breathing. Concentrating intensely, I envisioned Anna — her long blond hair, impish smile, and all the little nuances that made her real to me.

Anna…

I kept repeating her name in my mind, almost like a mantra, willing her to hear me despite the thousands of miles separating us.

Len…?

Her voice materialized in my consciousness; I could feel her reaching out, though she felt distant, likely roused from a deep sleep because of our link.

Yes Anna, it's Len…

A flood of mental chatter surged from inside her, a scrambled torrent of fear and confusion.

I was so scared; I knew something bad had happened and I've been so worried…

And on and on. Her mind was dashing about in a mental cacophony, all aimed at me, and I found it overwhelming.

Anna, focus your mind the way I taught you…

Her mental chatter stilled, and I could sense her organizing her thoughts.

I'm sorry Len. Are you all right…?

No, I'm in grave danger. Terrorists with guns have taken the hotel, just like you saw…

The weight of my words sent a tremor through her psyche, and I felt her panic flare momentarily before she wrestled it back under control.

It made me smile. She had taken my lessons seriously and was learning to direct and control her mind.

What can I do...?

I need you to phone Bill McGee. I gave you his number. Do you have it on your phone...?

Yes. But it's late... after midnight...

That's fine. Tell him I am at the Edgewater Resort in Lake Tahoe...

I informed her of the situation, ensuring she repeated it back to me for clarity. I relayed further instructions for her to tell Bill to reach out to his contacts in the FBI and to use his powers of persuasion to convince them to send a heavily armed team.

I couldn't help but notice the shadow of self-doubt that lingered in her mind.

But how will I convince him? He thinks I'm just a kid...

Bill is aware of your abilities. I need you to convince him you were in touch with me...

I'll try...

You can do it. Anna. It's a matter of life and death...

I sensed her panic rise, then felt her replace it with a steely determination.

Okay...

I'll be in touch when I can. Thank you...

I exhaled deeply as I withdrew, bringing myself back to full consciousness and severing our brief connection and pushing my mental barriers into place.

I hoped she would accomplish the task. Bill knew I had been working closely with Anna and I had faith that as a former FBI agent, he would know the right channels to contact, and have them on the move to my location.

My one concern was that they wouldn't get here quickly enough.

Going up the chain of command, our situation might land in the hands of someone like Agent Roberts, which could delay any action. If my buzz about midnight was any sign of what was to come, we had very little time left to stop them.

I slipped my mask back on, the leather snug against my skin, as I proceeded cautiously toward the door. I reached out with a gentle extension of my consciousness.

Go…

I opened the door, wedged the rock in place, and stepped out into the darkness. The threat of discovery loomed like a specter. It comforted me that if those men stumbled upon the unlocked door, I wouldn't be there.

I felt adrift, following the outer wall of the hotel like a ship lost at sea. My sole aim blazed in my mind: to rescue my woman and survive the night that lay ahead. The lack of a solid plan only amplified the weight of uncertainty that settled on my shoulders.

It made sense to return to the ballroom — the very heart of this twisted nightmare. I knew that was where they kept the hostages, and if anything vital were to unfold, it would certainly happen there.

I continued along the wall and saw that they had extinguished the helipad's lights, leaving it in darkness. Soon, the faint glow from the ballroom windows came into view, allowing me to find my way.

As I approached the door, the urge to knock surged within me, but a soft buzz of intuition held me back.

Knock twice, pause, then knock once...

I complied with the mental directive; I did so, and the door opened slightly, revealing a guard who quickly questioned me in Spanish if I'd seen anyone outside.

I shook my head and assured him in my broken Spanish that I had seen no one, and received instructions to return to the ballroom.

He nodded, his gaze drifting back to the hostages huddled in the room. I mimicked his defensive stance with my rifle, scanning the faces of the terrified guests.

I was here; I had made it.

My heart sank as I took in the appalling sight: once-proud guests were now trapped like cattle, expressions twisted in fear and confusion. They clustered together at the tables, eyes flickering with desperation, searching for a glimmer of hope amid the desolation. The man who had let me in stood stoically by the door, a grim, silent sentinel.

Two men kept watch halfway down the ballroom, while another pair guarded the ballroom doors with frigid, watchful eyes obscured by their chilling masks.

Nervous whispers filled the air, a collective murmur of confusion and dread — an atmosphere thick with paranoia and fear, as if the very walls were closing in around us.

Just then, the atmosphere shifted as Don Diego strode into the room. Clad in fatigues and now wearing a tactical vest, his presence instantly altered the dynamic. A handgun hung menacingly from his belt, like an old Western gunfighter, ready to be drawn at a moment's notice.

He scanned the room, absorbing the sight of captives and his armed associates. I couldn't shake the feeling he was searching for me. I focused on strengthening my mental defenses, desperate to keep myself hidden from his perceptive gaze. The anonymity of my mask and uniform was my only shield.

To my surprise, a familiar figure stood from one table.

It was Mr. Jenkins, the resort manager I had met upon our arrival. His tie was loose, his hair disheveled, yet he held himself with a semblance of authority. With determination in his stance, he approached Don Diego, each step thickening the already palpable tension in the room.

"Are you in charge here?" Jenkins asked, his voice unsteady as he neared the imposing figure of Don Diego.

At that moment, several of the armed guards shifted protectively closer to their leader, but Don Diego waved them off, allowing Jenkins to approach unimpeded.

"I am," Don Diego replied, his accent heavy as he regarded Jenkins with a predatory smirk. "And who are you, *Gilipollas*?"

He just called Mr. Jenkins a bastard.

"I'm Mr. Jenkins, the manager of this resort," Jenkins declared, now within arm's reach of the cartel leader, straightening his back as much as possible. "I demand to know how you plan to care for the guests. We have not had water or access to restrooms since being forcibly brought here."

Don Diego's sinister grin widened, entertained by the manager's bravado. He gestured dismissively toward the hostages. "And you're concerned for these rich people and their needs?"

"I am responsible for ensuring everyone here receives fair treatment. If you could tell me your demands—"

"My demands?" Don Diego interrupted, drawing his weapon in a fluid motion that sent a chill down my spine. He held the barrel inches from Jenkins' face. I could feel the collective intake of breath from the room, the atmosphere shifting into a tableau of fear.

Jenkins raised his hands, the color draining from his face.

"My demands are that you sit down and be quiet before I blow your damn head off," Don Diego sneered.

Jenkins staggered back, his face ashen, and Don Diego's brutish laughter erupted, echoing against the walls. The guards joined in, their laughter cruel and mocking.

The fearful man returned to his table and sat meekly.

"Anyone else want to know my demands?" Don Diego taunted, raising his weapon again before pulling the trigger. The gunshot ripped through the air, shattering the fragile silence, screams erupting as plaster and dust cascaded from the ceiling above.

I forced myself to stay composed, reminding myself that I had to maintain the facade of the dispassionate observer. I realized that my grip on my gun was so intense it was hurting my hands.

Relax, I have to pretend I see this all the time.

Just then, a man pushed open the door, allowing another figure to be shoved into the room.

Jyanette.

I felt as though someone had wrenched my heart free and cast it aside. I focused intently to keep my breathing steady, and not panic. Yet, I found my finger moved closer to the trigger on my gun. I would rather shoot Don Diego and die in a hail of bullets than allow that monster to hurt my woman.

The two men gripped Jyanette's arms tightly, dragging her unceremoniously forward to Don Diego. It took every ounce of restraint to remain still, my instincts screaming for me to intervene as they approached the tyrant.

I wondered what happened to the gun I had entrusted to her.

Don Diego appraised Jyanette, who kept her eyes on the big man, meeting his gaze with defiance.

I overheard one of the armed men speaking in rapid Spanish, narrating how they had discovered her walking up the stairs to the second floor.

She left the hiding place... that sounded like my lady. She could have stayed safe, but I was in danger, so she came out to find me and help me.

Don Diego focused his stony gaze on her. "Where were you going?"

"I was trying to get back to my room," she replied, her voice strong and challenging, her bravado simmering just beneath the surface.

With a swift and forceful motion, Don Diego grasped her chin, compelling her to meet his penetrating stare. "Do not lie to me, girl."

Her eyes were full of hate.

His satisfaction was palpable. He inhaled deeply and smiled. "You were with the one I seek. You wear his energy all over you. Where is he? Don't make this harder than it needs to be."

"I don't know," she said, her eyes staying on him, despite the struggle against his grip.

One of her captors piped up, suggesting he "give her to us, and we'll make her talk."

Don Diego shot him a furious glare, commanding him in Spanish to stay focused on the mission.

As he studied Jyanette, his expression shifted from fury to contemplation. "I believe you," he eventually said, releasing her chin. "He will come for you. He will not leave while you are here."

"He'll also come for you," she said defiantly.

Don Diego grinned. "I look forward to it."

Gesturing decisively to his men, he ordered them to escort Jyanette to a nearby table. They complied with little care, practically lifting her off her feet and shoving her into a chair, the sound of metal scraping against tile echoing in the large room.

I moved my hand away from the trigger of my rifle.

Don Diego faced a man and spoke in rapid Spanish. "Go, search the hotel for the one who causes me trouble. He is nearby. Search every room again!"

The man nodded sharply and swiftly departed the room; the door creaking shut behind him. An oppressive silence settled over the space, thick with the unspoken fears of the guests.

10. DWINDLING OPPORTUNITY

Don Diego surveyed the room with a practiced eye, his piercing gaze landing on the masked henchmen who filled the corners. My resolve stiffened; I concentrated on fortifying my mental barriers, determined to keep every thought locked away, lest a flicker of fear betray me.

Suddenly, the door swung open once more, and two men stumbled in, wearing only their t-shirts and boxers, led by one of Don Diego's enforcers, still adorned with his menacing skull mask.

I recognized them. The two men I had subdued earlier, with a quick blow and dumb luck on my part. Apparently, Don Diego's men had scoured the hotel and released them from where I'd left them.

The two captives spoke in rapid Spanish, their voices rising in urgency as they attempted to recount their recent misadventures — their capture, the confiscation of their weapons.
Frantic and desperate, they gestured wildly, but their words seemed to flounder in the air, barely impacting the situation at hand.

At last, Don Diego raised a hand, and with a snap of his fingers, he commanded, *"Silencio!"*

Instantly, silence reigned in the room as the men froze, rigid and anxious. The two subordinates stood before him, visibly sweating despite the room's cool temperature.

In a voice laced with cold menace, Don Diego spoke, "You have failed me."

The two men protested, hastily assuring him in a torrent of Spanish that they were loyal, that they would do anything he commanded. One man added fiercely that he would hunt down the one responsible for their capture and kill him like a dog.

Before the man could finish, Don Diego acted with lightning speed and pulled out his handgun, the smooth motion betraying a calculated ruthlessness. "You will not fail me again."

Don Diego's pistol roared twice in rapid succession, each shot echoing like deafening cannon fire, shaking the very walls of the grand chamber.

The first man's head shattered in a grotesque explosion of blood and bone, his body collapsing in a twisted heap. The second man, struck squarely in the chest, stumbled backward before crumpling to the floor, a dark crimson stain blooming across his shirt like a deadly flower.

The room erupted with gasps and terrified screams from the captive guests, their faces frozen in a mixture of horror and disbelief. Yet with a chilling, unyielding glare, Don Diego commanded silence — a cold, ruthless authority that silenced the chaos as surely as his gun silenced his enemies.

"Take them out," he commanded in Spanish, directing the men stationed by the door.

Obediently, the pair slung their weapons over their backs and each seized one of the dead men by their feet, dragging them out of the room. The headless man left a wide trail of blood and brain matter, a thick dark ribbon trailing behind.

Don Diego walked towards the exit. He paused and gazed at everyone menacingly. Then he shouted orders to his men. *"Prepárate para la medianoche. Sabes qué hacer."*

His words struck me like a stone dropped into a pond, sending ripples through my mind. He had given his men orders to prepare for midnight, and it became abundantly clear that they knew exactly what that meant.

Midnight…

What did he have planned? I was desperate to think of anything that could help me stop whatever twisted plan was unfolding. Yet, here I stood, paralyzed by a profound sense of helplessness, unsure of how to proceed.

If I allowed myself to become mentally vulnerable, Don Diego could infiltrate my mind. He was already hunting for me, and if I opened the door even a fraction, he might pinpoint my exact location. I had fortified my mental defenses as much as possible, and thankfully, whenever he cast his gaze in my direction, he somehow overlooked me.

That provided me with a sliver of insight. Don Diego designed mystical symbols for the masks his men wore to invade their minds, control them. Yet, when I tried to see them in an altered state, I couldn't.

Don Diego must have chosen the magickal symbols to keep out psychic intrusion from outside the mask, but a closed loop within the masks where he could send commands, and no psychic could read them.

That meant that the symbols on the masks did not grant him access to their thoughts.

This made sense. If Don Diego could read the thoughts of his men, he would've caught me immediately, as he would have perceived nothing from me. It appeared the mystical designs acted as a barrier, preventing thoughts from being read even though it allowed Don Diego's orders to come through.

While he could send information, he couldn't receive any from those wearing the masks. I had damaged the symbols on my mask, but my own mental barriers kept him out.

I had something that Don Diego lacked: my mask no longer limited my own mental abilities, and I had undergone extensive training in how to use them.

Don Diego had skills to manipulate the dream world and invaded my thoughts, pushing all my emotional buttons when he faced no resistance. At the time, I had been too stunned to fight back, swept away by the mental games he employed against me.

However, if he could enter my mind, then logically, I could breach his defenses as well. I could bar him from my thoughts, but did he have the expertise to keep me out of his mind?

Resolute, I relaxed my mental barriers, extending my consciousness outward. Closing my eyes, I sought to prevent him from discovering my precise location while simultaneously allowing him to engage with me. After all, I would rather have him following a phantom than track me.

You call yourself the dark conjuror. I have to say I expected better…

As my mental presence flickered outwards, I sensed a momentary pause. I could feel his consciousness reaching out, searching for me like a predator stalking its prey.

Little mouse. Have you finally come out of your hole to face me…?

I felt a smile creep across my lips; I had baited him on my first attempt.

Why should I? You're the one who gives himself fancy titles, I'll let you find me. If you can…

I will…

The moment his response echoed in the recesses of my mind, I braced myself for his forthcoming assault. I sensed his intention to invade my consciousness, dredging up memories to distract me. But I was not in a state of deep meditation this time; I was alert and ready. I fortified my mental barriers, closing him out before he could reach out.

With my mental shields restored, I opened my eyes and scanned the dimly lit room, ensuring no one had noticed me. The soft, muffled whispers of hostages reached my ears; one woman's quiet sobbing pierced the anxious atmosphere. Remarkably, the masked terrorists remained stationary, oblivious to anything I had done.

I had successfully thwarted his advance, a minor victory, but one I felt could rattle him. After all, he was rarely so easily spurned.

If I could provoke him enough to redirect his resources towards searching for me, it would create confusion and hopefully disrupt whatever plans he had set in motion until Anna could contact Bill to send agents on a rescue mission. I could only hope that Bill would have a contact who could help.

I needed Don Diego to perceive what I wanted him to see. Casting a glance at the wall of windows, I pretended to spot something unusual beyond the glass, drawing the curtains aside with feigned curiosity.

Moving swiftly, I approached the man near the door that led outside.

"Did you see anything?" I asked in Spanish, feigning urgency in my tone.

He stared out the window. "No, I didn't," he replied dismissively.

Seizing the moment, I lifted my gun and told him I would be right back. With that, I pushed the door open and stepped outside. The darkness enveloping me was almost palpable.

I hesitated at the corner of the building, heart pounding in my chest as I cast my gaze toward the helipad. Two tiki-style torches flickered ominously, their flames dancing and casting long, shifting shadows that clawed at the ground.

Below, illuminated in the eerie glow, were two figures kneeling side by side — masked men, their faces hidden behind those menacing masks. Their hands moved with deliberate urgency, manipulating something just out of sight in the darkened space between them.

What on earth were they doing down there? Whatever it was, it couldn't be good. Not good at all. The silence was punctuated only by the crackling torches and the faint scrape of hard surfaces as they worked.

I pushed back the sense of worry gnawing at me, and with my eyes focused on the dark woods, I opened my mind, deliberately allowing Don Diego's consciousness to sense me as I dashed into the night.

I swiftly stopped and shut him out of my mind. Then I returned to the building and made my way to the glass door of the ballroom. My heart raced in tandem with my footsteps.

I gave the special knock that would allow me re-entry. Once inside, my companion glanced at me with curiosity.

"What did you see?" he asked in Spanish, his voice low.

I kept my responses deliberately terse, offering only the essential fragment of information: "A man running out there without a mask."

I knew that the moment I slipped into longer sentences, my accent would betray my true origins — an outsider among their ranks.

The directness of my answer appeared to do the trick. He waved to the two men stationed at the center of the room. They exchanged urgent glances and rushed over, weapons lifted.

The guard stationed there quickly relayed my claim, and before I knew it, the pair were out the door, ready to confront whatever threat lay outside.

With the two men captivated by their mission, only two remained by the ballroom doors and one oversaw the outside door next to me.

I thought for a moment, closed my eyes and let down my mental barriers. The phrase formed clearly in my mind.

Once I get to the woods, I'll be free...

I quickly fortified my barriers again, my heart pounding as I opened my eyes. Deep down, I was certain that Don Diego had caught my mental transmission. I was hoping he would think it was a loose thought he'd received from me.

I shifted my gaze outside and observed several men moving stealthily into the woods, converging from different angles. No doubt Don Diego had mentally commanded them to search the woods.

That was what I'd wanted.

I pivoted to the man stationed at the door. *"Deberías ayudarlos!"* I urged, the words flowing effortlessly. I was telling him to go help his comrades.

His eyes, the only part of his face visible through his mask, widened slightly in surprise. He hesitated for just a moment, darting a cautious glance at me before he nodded, pushed the door open, and sprinted into the dark.

That left me with only two men: both younger, stronger, and undoubtedly more dangerous than I. An icy wave of apprehension washed over me. Engaging them in a direct confrontation was out of the question, especially with the guests clustered between us. A firefight within such confined quarters would be disastrous.

To my surprise, one of the two men at the door spoke to his companion, then went out the large door into the hall of the hotel. That left me at the outer door and the one man at the large double doors.

No doubt Don Diego was joining his men, searching the woods, trying to capture me.

The people around the room were still frightened and I could see that they were far too scared to attempt anything.

I opened the door as if someone had knocked and pretended to talk to someone. The curtains that hid the outside offered a cover so the man at the other door could not see what I was doing.

The men outside were busy rushing about and combing the grounds.

I nodded several times, then closed the door, glanced over at the man guarding the other door. Raising my arm to him, as if I had an important message, I made my way to him, my rifle hanging loose on its shoulder strap. I scanned the room as I went, as if to make sure no one was moving while I was away from the door.

I walked toward him, and the man, wanting to know what I was going to say, hissed out, "*¿Qué es?*"

I stepped close, gun angled low, and bent to whisper like I had news. His curiosity drew him in. That's when I struck.

In that split second of hesitation, I drove the butt of the gun upward with brutal force, smashing it square into his chin. The unexpected blow snapped his head back sharply, and he stumbled, caught completely off guard. Instinctively, his hand scrambled to raise his weapon.

But I was faster. His flailing arm grazed me just before a savage right hook landed beneath my eye. A brilliant flash of pain exploded across my vision — stars burst in my sight. Gritting my teeth, I clutched the gun's barrel and swung it like a club, the heavy metal connecting solidly with his skull.

He crumpled with a thunderous crash onto the floor; the sound echoing through the room and drawing gasps from the hostages nearby. Silence fell for a heartbeat, tension thick in the air.

I loomed over him, heart pounding, and quickly grabbed the strap of the machine gun slung over his shoulder. I slipped it over his head, wresting the weapon free from the fallen man's grasp.

I pulled the mask off and yelled out, "Someone take this weapon and guard that door!"

I looked over the crowd, but the sudden turn of events froze everyone in place, shocked too much to do anything.

Jyanette was the first to speak. "Len?"

"Come on," I yelled to the crowd. "I can't get this guy's other weapons if I'm holding these guns!"

Mr. Jenkins stood up and hurried over. He accepted the weapon I held out for him. "You know how to use this?"

He nodded. "I served in the army a long time ago, but I'm familiar with it."

"Good," I said. "We need to remove this guy's vest. He has a handgun and a knife and I don't know what else."

A second man with white hair came over. "I'll get it off him. Can we tie him up?"

By this time, Jyanette had run to me, pulling me into a hug.

"How did they catch you?" I asked, holding her.

"I went looking for you," she said, hugging me.

Everyone was standing and chattering, and the noise level in the room was increasing.

"Quiet, quiet," I said, then quickly lowered my voice. "If they hear you talking, they'll come to find out why. Everyone stay quiet." Finally I merely yelled, "Silencio."

The room fell silent.

An older woman raised a hand. "Can we escape?"

"No," I said, keeping my voice low. "There are men in the hotel, and others searching the grounds."

"What are they looking for?" said the man to whom I'd given the machine gun.

"Me," I said, picking up my mask again. "Now, I've got to put on the mask and everyone needs to sit, so if they look into this room, it looks like you're all still prisoners."

"We *are* still prisoners," one man complained.

Mr. Jenkins spoke up. "If you want to get out of here alive, I suggest you listen to this man."

I faced Jyanette. "You need to sit down, too."

She nodded, and I could see her eyes were wet with unshed tears. "I was afraid they caught you or killed you."

"Not yet," I assured her.

She headed back to her seat with a backward glance at me that made my heart ache.

The older man that had been removing the vest and weapons spoke up. "There are restraints in one pocket."

He handed flex cuffs, a pair of sturdy zip ties attached and used like handcuffs. He removed the vest from the man and rolled him over, and got ready to use the restraints to secure his hands.

"Wait," Mr. Jenkins said. "We need to take off his camo jacket and mask." He looked at the older gentleman. "You can wear them and look like a guard as well."

"Great idea," I said. "What's your name? I'm Len."

"Ken, Ken Hastings. My wife and I were celebrating our anniversary."

I forced a quick grin. "It was my honeymoon."

With Mr. Jenkins' help, Ken pulled the camo jacket off the unconscious man and pulled it on.

I removed the mask and gasped as I saw the face of the man wearing it. His youth shocked me. He looked like he was only eighteen or nineteen.

Ken had pulled on the camo and was now slipping on the vest with the gun and knife. He held out his hand and said, "Give me the mask."

"No," I said, and pulled the knife from my own borrowed vest. I took the mask and quickly scratched breaks into the symbols that covered it, scraping the lines and changing the symbols as best I could to break any power they might have. Ken might not be a psychic, but if the mask contained the ability to influence him, I wanted to make sure it wouldn't work.

"Okay, it's safe now," I said, handing it to Ken.

"Was that really necessary?" Mr. Jenkins asked.

"Better to be safe. Let's get this guy under a table so he's hidden by the tablecloth."

Mr. Jenkins and I pulled the unconscious man by the arms and maneuvered him beneath the nearest table. One of the onlookers reached down, and tugged at the tablecloth to drape it over him, hiding him from view.

Danger...

I felt the buzz and pivoted to face the entrance, anxiety creeping into my voice. "We need to secure that door."

"Use the restraints around those large door handles," Mr. Jenkins suggested. "It might not completely stop them, but it will definitely slow them down."

I nodded, knowing he was right. "Good call."

I grabbed my mask, preparing to pull it down over my face.

Just then, a crashing sound echoed through the space. Everyone faced the entrance as the enormous double doors burst open with violent force, the hinges screaming in protest. The atmosphere in the room shifted abruptly, a wave of tension washing over us as the crowd held its breath in stunned silence.

Don Diego stood in the doorway, framed by the dim light and flanked by several heavily armed men.

Don Diego's eyes glinted with a mix of amusement and malice as he surveyed the scene, his smile widening into a grotesque grin.

"So, little mouse," he said, his voice dripping with mockery. "We finally meet at last!"

He snapped out several orders in Spanish, and six armed men marched into the room.

Ken raised his hands, and one man pulled the mask off his face. I watched in alarm as the thug hit Ken in the stomach with the butt of his machine gun, knocking Ken to the floor, where they stripped the vest off him.

"There's no need for that," I snapped.

"He's lucky we didn't shoot him," Don Diego said with a glance at Mr. Jenkins, who slowly raised his hands in the air. "I thought you knew your place."

One of his men struck Mr. Jenkins in the head with his rifle, and the manager fell to the ground.

Two men pulled the machine gun off my shoulder and the handgun from my belt.

Don Diego pulled the mask from my unmoving hands. He turned it over as he examined it. "Clever! You changed the symbols." He smiled again and met my eyes. "You truly are remarkable."

He snapped out words in Spanish so rapidly I couldn't follow them, and two men all but picked me up and pulled me towards the door. I glanced back to see Jyanette, tears in her eyes and her face awash with fear, as the men carried me out of the ballroom.

11. FADED MEMORIES

They hauled me through the lobby, my feet barely grazing the polished floor as they ushered me forward. This was quite a feat, considering I'm over six feet tall. The men had a firm grip on my arms, propelling me around the reception desk and into a room that I could only assume was the manager's office.

They deposited me unceremoniously into one of the two chairs positioned opposite an imposing desk, then stepped back a few paces and raised their rifles. I remained seated, frozen, sensing that any misstep on my part could lead to them shooting me.

Another man entered the room, carrying a length of rope. With deliberate precision, he anchored the rope to the legs of the chair. He then wrapped the rope around my torso, pulling it tight with force and increasing the tension. I grunted from a mix of annoyance and resignation.

After ensuring that he'd secured my chest, he focused his attention on my arms. He fastened them to the chair's sturdy arms, the coarse rope digging into my skin as he tied off the last knot.

I surveyed my surroundings. Most striking was the wall of glass that dominated one side of the room. It showed the facade of the hotel and the circular roadway in front, the outside world right beyond the glass.

I could still see the sleek limousine waiting under the building's canopy through the tinted glass. It was a stark reminder that they would soon leave with their supply of drugs.

Beyond the desk was a bookcase with a clock that read: 11:00. *Midnight...*

I was rapidly running out of time.

The man who tied me finished and left the room, but I heard the sounds of laughter and boisterous voices echoing down the hallway.

It was the unmistakable voice of Don Diego.

As he entered the room, he appeared to be in high spirits, his presence dominating the atmosphere. He barked out a series of commands to the men who followed closely behind him — figures cloaked in those ominous masks.

As the men filed out, they left behind only one who remained at the door.

Don Diego sat behind the desk, obviously in control. Clutching the mask I'd been wearing, he examined it for a moment, as if toying with it like a predator considering its next move.

He slammed the mask down on the desk in front of me. I flinched involuntarily.

Leaning back in his chair, Don Diego observed me with a smirk playing at the corners of his mouth, a glint of amusement dancing in his eyes — reminiscent of a cat that had cornered a hapless mouse, relishing the thrill of the hunt and eagerly expecting the cruel games that would come next.

This was not a moment of simple triumph for him, but a prelude to what this madman might do next.

I had to keep him occupied, no matter the cost. My survival was uncertain, but if I could buy enough time, perhaps Bill could send a rescue team. If that happened, maybe Jyanette and the others would live to see another day. That thought fueled my determination, pushing me to consider any way to stall him.

"You have been quite the troublesome *ratoncito*," he purred, using the Spanish word for "little mouse," a cruel smile on his face. "I had to kill some very useful men because of you."

I clenched my jaw, forcing myself to meet his gaze. "I'm actually sorry about that," I replied, my voice steady despite the dread coiling in my stomach. "But I didn't kill them. You did."

He leaned forward and slapped me across the face. He didn't put much effort into the blow, but it stung.

"Mind your manners, little mouse," he said as he leaned back.

The shocked look on my face only seemed to amuse him further.

I'd forgotten about the man's ego. "I meant no disrespect. I was only stating a fact."

He erupted into laughter, a sound that echoed off the walls and made my skin crawl.

"True," he countered, the mirth in his voice fading almost instantly. His expression shifted to a grim seriousness that sent a chill through me. "You know, it would be only fair for me to bring your woman in here and with you watching, put a bullet in her head."

His words hung in the air. The threat felt all too real as I fought to maintain my composure.

"I'm the one you want," I replied, forcing myself to remain calm and in command of my emotions.

"I want to see the man you are," Don Diego said. "Here, I thought you were a worthy adversary. I am disappointed. I expected a man of action, but you are nothing more than a college professor."

I was sure a look of surprise was on my face, despite my best efforts to mask it. Of course, Don Diego had done his homework after our first encounter. A quick search online and he could have unearthed more information about me. That notion unsettled me further.

Leaning back slightly in my chair, I played the card of nonchalance. "Researching me online? How... unremarkable for someone of your reputed skills. I would've expected a more impressive method from *El Conjurador Oscuro*."

I watched as a flash of anger ignited in Don Diego's eyes, and I winced as he raised his hand to slap me again. Instead, he lowered his hand and spoke, his voice low and laced with menace. "Do not disrespect me. One word from me, and you will find yourself a corpse."

I straightened, dispelling any hint of fear as I leaned forward, closing the distance between us. "True, you can kill my body, but I present a far more intriguing puzzle to your mind. While I do not possess the powers of *Brujeria*, I stand before you, fully present, not lost in a meditation. Can you meet me, mind to mind?"

For a moment, he fell silent, settling back into his chair, contemplation clouding his features. It was as if my challenge had stirred something deep within him, drawing him into a mental duel where the stakes were more profound than mere physicality.

"You're the first person I ever crossed paths with who might pose a challenge," he said, his eyes glimmered. "But just to make things more interesting, I propose a wager."

This took me aback. "What kind of wager?"

He leaned back in his chair, his posture casual, yet there was menace beneath his demeanor. "If you win, I will spare your life," he replied, shrugging as if it were a light matter.

"And if I lose?" I asked, dread settling in the pit of my stomach.

He rose slowly from behind the desk and leaned over it, invading my personal space with a menacing intensity. "If you lose, I'll bring your woman in here and take her in front of you right on this desk, before I put a bullet in her head. I'll make sure you watch the entire time."

He pulled a knife from his tactical vest. It wasn't the standard one the others wore, but a wicked-looking weapon with a black blade. I could sense an energy around it. He placed it on the desk. His voice dropped to a chilling whisper. "Then, I will kill you with a knife, slowly, so that the others know I'm not to be trifled with."

His words hung in the air like a noose tightening around my throat.

"No," I said firmly, the word tasting bitter on my tongue.

"It's not up for negotiation," he answered with a low chuckle.

"Do what you want with me, but let her live," I pleaded, my voice barely disguising the desperation within.

He returned to his chair, that insufferable smirk still etched on his face, as if he relished the torment in my eyes. "Then you'd better win, *ratoncito*," he taunted, his tone serious.

Cold sweat trickled down my neck, pooling at my collarbone. There it was — the excruciating situation laid bare before me. I had to defeat this monster if I wanted to spare Jyanette.

But even if I triumphed, there was no guarantee he wouldn't break his promise. He could just as easily decide that killing me was worth the risk of breaking his word, an ultimate act of defiance against anyone foolish enough to challenge him.

This was not just my life, my pain, but the life of the woman I loved. I had lost so many people in my life. I couldn't bear the idea that after finally marrying Jyanette, I might lose her.
Either I emerged victorious, or I would watch the light fade from Jyanette's eyes, knowing I was powerless to stop it.

I couldn't allow that to happen.

I took a deep breath, forcing myself to calm down. If I was going to even be a challenge to Don Diego, I needed to focus my mind, as Doctor Kohl taught me years earlier.

"Very well," I croaked and looked down at the ropes holding me in place. "It's not like I'm going anywhere."

This made him smile. "That is true."

I glanced back at the guard still at the door. "Tell me, is the guard invited to take part as well?"

"Wait outside," Don Diego barked, and the masked man hurriedly went out the door. Then he faced me. "You do not wish to have him see you reduced to a sobbing child?"

"I just want to make sure I'm not shot while we're in the dream world."

"So, you speak of *Brujeria*. It appears you have done some research as well," he said and leaned his chair back. "It will not help you."

He closed his eyes, and instinctively I followed suit. Focusing on my breathing, I shifted my consciousness into an altered state, lowering the barriers I typically held up against unwelcome intrusions. I could sense Don Diego slipping past those defenses, and I allowed him in.

If I let him in, I could get into his mind as well.

The darkness enveloping me dissolved, and I found myself in a familiar dining room. It was Mrs. Higgins' abode in Mountainview, New Jersey — a place that held precious memories.

In the soft glow of candlelight, Jyanette sat across the table from me, elegant in a black velvet dress that stirred a recollection in my mind. Mrs. Higgins' finest china adorned the table, and a delicate bouquet of roses served as the centerpiece.

Rather than savor the ambiance of the setting, I felt an urge to discern when this scene was unfolding. This was no ordinary dinner; it was a memory that Don Diego had orchestrated, a painful tapestry of my past.

Jyanette's gaze lingered on the roses and flickering candles, and I found I held a small box in my hand.

It was the box that held the diamond engagement ring I purchased for her. The decision was born from desperation — to convince her to marry me after she had unexpectedly become pregnant.

Pregnant. The word echoed in my mind like a haunting refrain.

I locked eyes with her, and I sensed that there was something wrong with her eyes.

A wall was blocking me from touching her mind, just like when I attempted to do a reading on someone in a deep state of hypnosis.

"What's the matter, Len?" she inquired.

I slid my chair back, fully aware of what was about to unfold.

"Why would I do that?" she said, answering a question even though I had said nothing. At the actual event I spoke, but reliving the memory, I was too shocked.

Anger clouded her features. "Oh, you mean that nonsense you fed me so I wouldn't see the truth?"

She stood, the glimmer of a gun in her hand, and her hollow laugh echoed around the room. "You really think I don't know you and that old woman are trying to take my baby?"

In a heartbeat, she leveled the gun at me, and her voice rang out, "You'll never have my baby! Never!"

The deafening crack of the gun erupted, and instinctively, I wrenched myself away from the haunting tableau back into the cocoon of darkness within my mind.

Once again, Don Diego pushed me into a painful memory. The time when Jyanette was under the control of a therapist who was trying to kill me, and programmed her to do the job. The echoes of that fateful moment reverberated when Jyanette, hypnotized by a manipulative therapist, had tried to take my life.

That was the night she lost the baby.

Another person I'd lost — and never even had a chance to meet.

Grief was a luxury I could not afford; reflection would have to remain a haunting refrain for another day. Time to change my strategy, to pivot my energy from mere defense to a calculated offense. I would no longer be a pawn in his twisted game; I would seize the initiative.

If he had the power to excavate the depths of my past, then I would use that same power, turning his tactics against him. I pushed against the walls of my psyche, feeling the world around me shimmer and warp, each thought a ripple in a darkened pool as I moved my consciousness into his mind.

Shapes coalesced, twisting into shadows that whispered forgotten secrets. I felt myself slipping into a new reality. As the darkness faded, I could see a place — a modest one-room adobe home. Its crooked thatched roof sagging under the burden of time. The scent of damp earth and the warmth of a sun long gone enveloped me as I stepped inside.

In the dim light, a small bed sat silently in the corner, its significance heavy with unspoken stories. Beneath fraying covers lay a frail girl, her delicate form an echo of innocence marred by the scars of experience. Her lips parted slightly as she breathed, each inhale a tentative plea for solace in a world that had offered her none. I watched as a young boy leaned over her.

I stared, amazed. This was Don Diego as a child, and I was sharing his memory.

She stirred, murmuring a single word — "brother."

The boy reached out, clasping her tiny hand, and I felt it too, as if I was holding her small hand. I felt the boy and me both whisper assurances to the child in Spanish.

A sudden sound pierced the heavy silence, a faint but unmistakable creak that made the boy and me snap our heads toward the worn wooden door. Slowly, it inched open, as if pushed by some unseen hand.

From the shadows beyond stepped a figure — tall, cloaked, and unnervingly calm — a village shaman whose presence hung thick with whispered legends. Revered and feared in equal measure, he moved like a shadow drawn from ancient rites long buried, his very existence a quiet rebellion against the priest's rigid doctrines that dominated the village. There was something about him — something almost otherworldly — that set the air taut with uneasy anticipation.

I watched, transfixed, as he knelt on the dirt floor, scratching strange symbols into the dirt, then lighting a small candle that pierced the dimness.

The boy clasped his sister's hand, which I felt as well. But even more, I sensed an inexplicable tension mount in the air, an icy chill creeping through the room. It coiled around us, thrumming with an unnatural energy as shadows seemed to move in the corners, like lurking predators waiting for the right moment to pounce.

As the shaman chanted words I couldn't comprehend, his voice rose above the stillness, beads of sweat dripping down his forehead.

Suddenly, chaos ignited without warning. Oppressive energy charged the air as shadowy clouds appeared inside the house! They twisted and thickened, swirling around the boy and his sister like living smoke. A strange, suffocating presence seeped from the darkness itself — there, inside the heart of the house. Something ancient, something unseen, was awakening.

I could sense voices whispering sinister secrets all around the young boy.

Diego's sister's cries pierced the air, fear radiating from her as she gripped the boy's hand tighter. The shadows converged with wicked intent.

An unseen force ripped through the room, hurling objects around us and snuffing out the candle's light.

The girl's screams wailed through the air as understanding went through my mind. This was something that was seeking Don Diego. It had used the Shaman's spell to try and reach him but failed, and instead took the girl's life.

The girl died in that room, and her death irrevocably changed Diego. He learned that the veil between life and death was fragile and that not all spirits were benevolent.

Like me, he had experienced a profound loss.

Get out of my head, little mouse...

I heard his voice echo, commanding me, full of venom. The surrounding scene faded. I had struck at him, and pulled up one of his own memories. He had not expected me to strike back using his very techniques.

Suddenly, the ground beneath my feet shifted, and I felt the frigid grip of metal around my wrist, chaining me to a wooden chair. The darkness around me pulled away and I blinked in confusion before realizing I sat in a chair, trapped in an RV. I could see Jyanette being pushed down the narrow hallway by a hulking man, her wrists bound by the long chains of a pair of handcuffs.

"You can't do this," I cried out in desperation. "I did what you asked—"

"Calm down, Jew boy," the man barked in reply, his voice a growl. "We're just gonna have us a little fun."

I struggled to stand, but someone shoved me swiftly, sending me crashing back into my seat. He slapped my face; the sting searing my skin as I lifted my gaze to Jyanette. Anger and fear burned in her eyes, reflecting my despair.

This memory was hard. It recalled a time when a group of white supremacists captured Jyanette and me. It was a night filled with terror and helplessness. The man had attempted to assault Jyanette in the back of that RV.

I understood why Don Diego pushed this memory into my head, because it was a time when I felt helpless.

Which is what Don Diego wanted me to feel now.

I shoved the memory away, retreating once more to the darkness of our mental void.

I pushed back, rising from the depths, and a new scene unfurled around me.

It was a sultry night in a lush jungle. The scent of damp earth and verdant foliage enveloped me. I heard the sounds of wildlife mingling in the darkness.

I watched the young man, now older as he knelt before a small dirt altar, surrounded by boys no older than eleven or twelve. I knew them. They were boys from the village, sharing this secret place under the moonlight.

His hands were still small, not the big hands of the man he would become. I watched as Don Diego ignited a candle on the altar. Once again, like in the house years earlier, I saw shadows flickering around us, as if alive with a will of their own. The temperature dropped, and I glanced around to see the other boys exhaling visible clouds of mist that mingled with the echoes of their hushed whispers, filled with both excitement and fear.

Then, without a hint of warning, the very ground beneath us convulsed violently, shaking the forest to its ancient roots.

From the swirling shadows, a grotesque figure emerged — a twisted abomination forged from pure, unrelenting malice. Its skin was a sallow, mottled gray, stretched tight over spindly bones, and its hollow, abyssal eyes bored into our souls like twin voids, sucking away every ounce of hope. A malicious grin, dripping with decay and adorned with jagged, yellowed teeth, spread across its face — a smile that promised torment beyond comprehension.

Panic erupted as the other boys screamed, their voices tearing through the still night air as they bolted in every direction, stumbling over tangled roots and underbrush. Their terror was a stampede, chaotic and raw, as the forest swallowed them whole.

But the young Don Diego remained — rigid, paralyzed by a fear so deep it felt like chains wrapped around his very heart.

I sensed the entity's dark, suffocating presence coil around him like a serpent tightening its grip. Its malevolent essence seeped into his mind, poisonous and insistent, drowning out all other thoughts. The creature inched closer, looming over the boy like a shadow brought to life, until its voice — a voice as chilling as the grave — whispered directly into his very soul:

"I am Vexarath," it hissed, each syllable dripping with venomous promise, "and I can grant you anything your heart desires…"

Suddenly, the world around me began to dissolve, colors bleeding into darkness. I fought to anchor myself to the scene, to resist being pulled away, but I felt my mind slipping back into a merciless void.

No, no, you must not, you must not…

Yet as the shadows faded, I understood the depth of Don Diego's fear. He was not merely a brilliant leader with psychic powers. This entity was the root of his power, the very source that had granted him his dark abilities, and it had a name: Vexarath.

This was a chilling revelation: I had uncovered the very source of his extraordinary abilities.

Over a year earlier, I battled a man who had succumbed to the ruthless grip of demonic possession. The malevolent entity that ruled him had utterly devoured his personality, leaving behind a hollow shell, a puppet dancing to the whims of a sinister force. The unfortunate soul I had met was a victim, his mind lost forever.

But Don Diego was different — radically, terrifyingly different. Where I had resisted every dark temptation, he welcomed it with open arms. There was no semblance of struggle or hesitation in him; rather, he thrived on the power and unnerving abilities that the sinister entity had bestowed upon his very soul. This dark being wasn't a parasite to Diego — it was a partner, a symbiotic force that elevated him beyond mortal limits.

I had no psychic gifts of my own until the night I unwittingly unleashed a demon into our world. The creature manifested on a rainy road, its presence chilling the air like a creeping frost. It was the demon that orchestrated the crash that killed Cathy and left me broken, with a bad leg. For years, I chased that malevolent spirit as it roamed from host to host, sowing ruin and terror — until I finally exorcised it, casting it back into the abyss.

Don Diego, however, had taken a path I could never fathom. He had accepted his demon — invited it in, let it fuse with his essence, allowed it to weave its dark influence into every fiber of his being.

In truth, the man I faced was no longer truly Don Diego. The adversary I had to confront was the ancient, insidious creature that had shadowed him throughout his life, binding him in a grotesque partnership. If I could banish that entity, erase it from existence, then perhaps I could weaken my adversary.

And then it struck me like a bolt of lightning — a profound, terrible realization.

Don Diego's powers had blossomed just as mine had, nurtured through struggle and adversity. The difference was stark: where I fought against the darkness clawing at my mind, Diego had embraced it fully. The man before me was a twisted reflection — a shadow version of myself. While I had sought the light through parapsychology and working alongside the police, Diego had descended into the underworld as a master of Brujería and a ruthless drug lord, wielding his sinister gifts to command fear and devotion.

Our destinies were intertwined, mirror images splitting off into diverging paths of light and shadow. And now, those paths collided.

Suddenly, the real world came crashing back in, as I heard the office door slam open, and a man's frantic voice pierced through the disorienting haze, shouting in rapid Spanish.

Although the words tumbled out in a chaotic stream, one phrase cut through the noise like a knife: "FBI."

12. CONTRACTING CHOICES

I opened my heavy eyelids, jolting myself back to reality.

As the blurry surroundings came into focus, Don Diego rose from his desk, his eyes blazing with fury. Yet, flickering behind his anger was a hint of fear that sent a thrill coursing through me. I relished that moment — I had unsettled him.

Without uttering a single word, he bolted from the room, taking the other man with him, leaving me alone, tied helplessly to the chair, and his black knife on the desk in front of me.

I needed to recover, to regain my strength after the intense battle of wills I fought with Don Diego in that dreamlike realm, but I couldn't afford the luxury of rest. There were people depending on me, and if a team of FBI agents was storming the resort, they would likely need every bit of assistance they could get.

Of course, first I would have to get out of this chair.

I thought about my twin brother, Tom. Ever the showman, he had become a celebrated magician in Las Vegas, dazzling crowds with his talents.

Magic had been Tom's passion, and when we were teenagers, I joined his act, going along for the ride. But he taught me a great deal in our collaboration. One of the most vital skills we had mastered was the art of escape.

Tom idolized Harry Houdini, the legendary magician, who made his name by extricating himself from an array of precarious situations. One of Houdini's signature tricks involved allowing audience members to bind him with a long rope. Houdini always escaped, because the secret lay not in the knots but in the technique he used.

I had learned that the trick was to gain slack in the rope while being bound. By expanding muscles and hollowing my chest, I could create a little give. How tightly the person tying the rope, or how many knots they used, was irrelevant. This was what Houdini had done so successfully.

I relaxed my muscles, feeling for the slack that I allowed to build up during my binding. I focused on moving my wrists, each tethered to the armrests of the chair, searching for any opportunity to free myself.

The process was painfully slow as I pushed and pulled against the ropes, using leverage to inch closer to liberation.

Through the smoky glass wall, I could see that turmoil reigned. Figures darted around in the dim light, and the limousine drove out of view. Were they leaving, making their escape while they could?

Midnight...

The buzz sang in my head, and a rush of clarity accompanied it. No, they weren't leaving; they were simply repositioning the vehicle to make it less conspicuous.

Don Diego was resolute in his plans, still intent on carrying out his grotesque ritual at midnight despite the FBI's intrusion.

From a strategic standpoint, this seemed not just foolish but utterly insane. Yet, I now understood what drove him — a warped alliance with a demonic entity that demanded human sacrifice.

This horrific ritual was not merely an afterthought; it was the cornerstone of his entire operation. More important than the drugs or money, the lives he intended to take would feed the malevolent force that lurked behind him, hungry for the death of innocents.

I gazed up at the clock. 11:30.

I intensified my efforts.

With each pull and twist, I felt the grip of the rope relent. Finally, after what felt like an eternity of struggle, I freed my right hand from the initial loop of rope that had confined it.

I freed my arm from the binding.

Though the terrorists had stripped me of the guns and the knife, Don Diego had conveniently left me his own.

My chest still tied to the chair, I reached for the blade, the tips of my fingers just brushing against it. I stretched my arm out a little more and slid the blade closer to where I could finally take it in hand.

I looked at the blade for a moment, and realized it wasn't an ordinary knife, but a ceremonial blade. Made of metal coated in some kind of black matte, giving it a deep, shadowy sheen. Black leather was wrapped around the handle and displayed intricate symbols similar to those on the masks.

It seemed to pulse beneath my touch, a dark heartbeat echoing through time. Suddenly, my vision blurred and shifted — not with light, but with shadowed faces locked in terror and anguish.

I saw a dozen sets of eyes — wide, desperate, resigned — each belonging to a victim. There was the anguished cry of a woman, the silent pleading of a child caught in a nightmare, the grim acceptance of a warrior fallen in ritual sacrifice. The air filled with whispers — anguished murmurs, frantic gasps, curses — that rippled through my mind like a relentless tide.

I dropped the knife to the desk and pulled back, aware that it was a vessel of pain and death. I stared at the weapon, knowing that Don Diego intended to use it on me as well.

Strengthening my mental barriers, I grabbed it, and used it to slice through the ropes binding my other arm and my body, freeing myself. Images of moments of bloodletting, ritual chants murmured by masked figures, the blade slicing through flesh with unstoppable inevitability, flashed through my mind. I shoved the knife into the empty sheath in my tactical vest and released it, the haunting visions fading as I did.

I leapt to my feet, but as I stood, pain shot through my right leg, and the knee buckled unexpectedly beneath me. I stumbled awkwardly, barely catching myself against the edge of the desk, its solid surface providing a momentary anchor.

The throbbing ache in my knee was a painful reminder of the toll this night had taken on my body. My exertions had pushed my leg muscles to their limits. A wave of longing washed over me for my cane — my dependable companion that would have lent me the support I needed.

I pushed myself up again. This time, I steadied myself more successfully, though the throbbing ache felt like fire coursing through my joint.

With utmost caution, I approached the closed office door and eased it open just enough to peek out. The hallway beyond was eerily empty, underscoring my uneasy feeling. I surmised that everyone inside was likely preoccupied — either preparing for an imminent attack or the ritual sacrifice that was about to unfold.

Don Diego had been playing with the mask I had donned earlier in the evening. In his haste to marshal his men, he had forgotten about it. I snatched the mask and pulled it over my head.

I stepped out into the hall, not trying to be discreet, but boldly moving out with confidence as if I belonged there. After all, I was one of Don Diego's men, and no one would notice me.

Going down the dim corridor, I glimpsed into one of the shadowy offices. There, huddled in a chair, was Isabella Fontaine. She had been wearing a jacket when Diego brought her in, which she now grabbed to hold in front of her. Although her face was unmarked, I saw prominent bruises on her arms stark against her skin, glimmering like unsettling shadows in the low light. My heart sank, and I stepped into the room,

"Please, don't hurt me," she whispered, her voice barely audible.

I quickly glanced back into the hallway, checking for anyone approaching, before pulling the mask off my face.

Isabella flinched as if I had struck her, her eyes widening in stark terror.

"Ms. Fontaine," I said, lowering my voice to a hush. "I'm not a cultist. I'm Doctor Leonard Wise, part of the team of investigators looking for you."

Her eyes flickered with uncertainty as she processed my words. Then she jumped to her feet and enveloped me in a tight embrace, weeping uncontrollably. It was clear the captors had not restrained her.

They had merely taken away her will to resist.

I gently disentangled her from my arms and guided her back into the chair

"Listen to me," I urged, taking her trembling hands and looking deep into her eyes. "We are not out of danger. But I think I can buy us some time, and get you to a hiding place, if you're willing to help."

She stopped sobbing and nodded slowly, hope flickering in her weary eyes.

"They need you to ride in the limo in case they run into any obstacles. But I know a place where we can hide you," I explained, trying to rally her strength.

"He hit me." She bit her lip and added. "He — did things to me.

A fierce wave of protectiveness and fury surged through me as I knotted my hands into tight fists. I knelt beside her, my voice steady, whispering promises I hoped I could keep.

"The FBI is on their way," I assured her. "If we can stow you away for just a little longer, it will give them time to mobilize and bring enough firepower to put an end to this madness."

If we can just get past midnight, I thought.

Isabella nodded, unsure. "W-What do you need me to do?"

"I can lead you to a safe hiding place, but I have to wear the mask, and you will have to pretend to be bound — hold your hands behind your back as if you're in restraints. Can you do that?"

"Y-yes," she stammered, her voice steadier now.

I pulled the mask back over my face, transforming myself into an agent of darkness once more. "Alright, stand up and follow my lead. Let's get you out of this room."

She hesitated for a moment, then stood, pulled on the jacket and clasped her hands together behind her back.

"I'm ready," she said, her voice held a whisper of courage.

I led her into the hall, out a door, and past the main desk. The lobby was equally desolate, except for a solitary man with a machine gun stationed at the entrance, his eyes scanning the surroundings. As I nodded to him, I roughly pulled Isabella along in an authentic display of urgency. She let out a faint whimper, lending an air of realism to our ruse.

Continuing down the dimly lit corridor, I caught sight of two guards stationed just outside the ballroom, where they held the hostages. Their gazes sharpened as they noticed our passage. I quickly pivoted, guiding her toward the stairwell door and, with an urgent push, ushered her inside.

Once shrouded in the empty space, I ripped off my mask.

"You did wonderfully," I said. "I apologize if I was rough with you back there."

"I understood what you were doing," she replied, her eyes darting anxiously toward the darkened stairway.

I slid aside a stack of chairs beneath the stairs, revealing the hiding space prepared for Jyanette. The solitary chair remained untouched and on the floor was the rifle I'd taken from the terrorist earlier.

"Please, take a seat in there," I instructed, gesturing toward the claustrophobic nook. "I'll rearrange the chairs to conceal you. Stay silent, and no one will even realize you're there."

Gratitude washed over her features as she nodded. "Thank you."

"Don't thank me yet," I urged, my voice low but firm. "We're still in grave danger, so you must promise me you'll remain absolutely quiet."

With a determined glint in her eyes, Isabella slipped into the makeshift hiding spot. I quickly set about repositioning the chairs, ensuring that they formed a barrier, obscuring her from view.

Once satisfied that she was hidden, I crept to the stairwell door, opened it slightly, and peered into the hallway. The corridor was still devoid of movement, save for the two guards stationed resolutely outside the ballroom.

What was happening outside? I didn't hear any gunfire, which left me puzzled. Had the FBI arrived, like that man had said? Why didn't they storm the resort? Did the terrorists shut off the entrance somehow?

I had the temptation to stretch my mind outwards, to sense the upheaval beyond the walls, but I resisted — now was not the time for distractions. I needed to stay focused on where I was and what was going on around me.

I desperately wanted to head into the ballroom, to confront the reality of my wife and the hostages, but given the two men guarding the entrance, such a move would be foolhardy. I had been lucky to evade detection once, but I dared not test my fortune further.

The guards would scrutinize anyone entering the ballroom, and even masked, I knew I couldn't withstand their examination.

Time was slipping like sand through my fingers. Soon, Don Diego would execute at least fifteen people, their lives snuffed out with brutal efficiency. I felt my stomach twist at the foreboding thought that he might just march into the ballroom and kill the hostages at random.

Don Diego was harnessing power from a demon, inciting him to perform these grotesque sacrifices. What he sought wouldn't be mere bloodshed — it required the energy of a ritual, something far more elaborate than mindless slaughter.

Just then, I heard boots hitting the polished floor just before the men themselves came into view. I counted at least eight of them, marching in formation behind Don Diego, who now brandished an automatic weapon himself.

His face was taut with anger and desperation, undoubtedly aware that he was losing control of the situation and racing against time to complete his gruesome plan.

He stormed toward the ballroom, and the guards pulled the double doors open for him.

I couldn't let this opportunity slip away. As the doorway filled with masked men, I stepped into the group, seamlessly blending in as I followed them through the ballroom doors.

Once inside, the atmosphere crackled with tension. Don Diego raised his rifle, firing a series of deafening shots into the ceiling. The echoes reverberated around the room; the plaster rained down from above as panicked screams filled the air. People instinctively dove for cover, shielding their heads from the imminent threat.

Very much like in my dream.

Don Diego beckoned to his men to grab hostages. I rushed toward Jyanette, desperate to pull her to safety. She hesitated at first, fear holding her back, but soon she complied as I guided her through the disarray, hoping to find a window of opportunity.

Don Diego snatched her other arm and halted our escape.

"No, este es mío," he barked.

This one is mine.

I released Jyanette's arm and stepped back.

In the fracas, I spotted Mr. Jenkins. He slumped over a nearby table, a swollen lump on his head grimly reminding me of the violence he'd suffered. I pulled him to his feet. He moved slowly, pain etched on his face. I wished I could comfort him, but this was not the moment.

Don Diego pulled Jyanette, who lost her balance and stumbled. He grabbed her hair and yanked her to her feet as she screamed.

A surge of rage coursed through my veins. The world around me became a fiery red, consumed by my desire for revenge. My jaw clenched as I watched him drag her along. The group of men and hostages followed him. I looked over at the people and realized that with Mr. Jenkins included; the total was fifteen.

We headed down the hallway, away from the lobby, and passed the gift shop — the very place I had hidden earlier. Security bars rolled down like a fortress.

The tension in the air grew thick as we approached a set of glass doors that led outside.

As we went through the doors and out into the night air, the chilling glow of torches flickered in the distance, their flames casting unsettling shadows that danced like the turmoil raging inside my mind.

The closer we got, the more horrifying the scene became. They had arranged torches around the helipad, transforming it into something far more sinister.

They had created a massive inverted pentagram encased in a rudimentary circle on the worn asphalt using some kind of green powder.

In its upright position, the pentagram is a sign of protection. Inverted, it becomes a sinister emblem of demonic worship. The circle seemed to pulse with a dark, malevolent energy.

Surrounding this main glyph were additional symbols — strange, arcane markings reminiscent of those seen on the masks worn by the terrorists. The symbols were unmistakable: Brujeria invocations, forming a direct connection with Don Diego's demon, Vexarath.

Two men stood with automatic weapons, watching the people moving toward them.

From afar, the eerie sound of squealing tires pierced the air. Moments later, there was a bone-jarring crash, the unmistakable sound of metal colliding with metal. The noise broke the silence like a dark omen.

Don Diego and his men froze in place, as all heads turned toward the noise.

A figure broke away from the shadows — a man without a mask, his face gleaming with sweat and his eyes wide with urgency. He held a walkie-talkie in his hand and ran to Don Diego, speaking rapidly in a torrent of Spanish, but his words were too low for me to catch.

Don Diego, still gripping my wife fiercely by the arm, shot back a vehement reply filled with impatience, "I don't care! Stop them!"

With that, he dragged Jyanette closer to the dreadful circle outlined on the ground. Drawing close, I could see that there were herbs and leaves mixed in the green powder.

It was almost midnight.

In the distance, the crack of gunfire shattered the stillness of the night, giving me hope the FBI was not far away.

Several of the masked men halted momentarily, uncertainty in their movements.

"Pay no attention!" Don Diego's voice boomed out in Spanish, a commanding shout that cut through the murmur of confusion. "We have work to do!"

Like marionettes responding to their puppeteer, the men shook off their hesitation and resumed their approach to that enormous symbol where Don Diego intended to execute the captives.

Panic gripped me like a vice, compelling me to act, to leap into action and do something.

Wait...

The buzz in my mind was intense, a cryptic warning that both beckoned and paralyzed me. What did it signify? My hesitation could allow them to extinguish lives in mere moments.

Wait...

A part of me screamed to charge forward, to fight with every ounce of strength I had for Jyanette, for the vulnerable hostages. But I forced myself to stifle my roaring instincts, pushing me to engage, and instead, I kept walking calmly, silently pulling Mr. Jenkins along with me.

Each step felt like a betrayal, and yet it was my only lifeline. I knew I had to remain unnoticed, to bide my time until the perfect moment presented itself — when striking could turn the tides in our favor.

13. WANING WOES

D on Diego was the first to reach the ominous circle. He paused just outside its boundary, handing Jyanette — terror etched across her face — to another of his clan.

The man grasped Jyanette's arm with a firm grip, another hostage in his other hand, stopping at the very edge of the green outer ring.

The other terrorists fanned out around the circumference of the circle with their captives.

I followed suit, my heart pounding in my chest as if it were attempting to break free, a rush of adrenaline coursing through me.

Wait...

Once the men and their prisoners formed a human chain encircling the pentagram, Don Diego stepped boldly over the boundary, crossing into the realm of the mystic circle.

He strode confidently to the center, dropping his weapon and raising his arms high above his head, as if in acceptance of the sinister bounty delivered from the heavens — or, considering the terrible source of his powers, perhaps from hell itself.

I sensed a palpable energy pulsating all around me, a vibrant green light beginning to rise like spectral walls along the edges of the circle.

I stole a glance at the others, but the hostages seemed unaware of the phenomenon. Only my psychic abilities allowed me to see it.

With my eyes fixed on Don Diego, I saw… *it*.

The entity was a grotesque amalgamation of smoke and shadow, swirling and shifting like a dark mist caught in a tempest. It possessed no tangible body; instead, it shaped itself into an amorphous form that slithered around Don Diego, slipping over him like a shroud, intertwining with his very essence. Within the depths of its inky tendrils, sickly green flashes flickered, radiating a toxic energy that pulsed intermittently. Their dance was a foreboding symbiosis, one that hinted at the monstrous things to come.

That was how Vexarath currently manifested.

Together, they stood — Don Diego, with an unsettling smile plastered on his face, arms still raised skyward. He appeared to be gathering his strength to offer his hostages as sacrificial fuel to the creature that encircled him.

The understanding of what I had to do pierced my mind with a surge of clarity.

I glanced at the dark woods beyond the torchlight and made my decision.

I leaned my masked face close to Jenkins' ear and whispered. "Mr. Jenkins, it's Leonard Wise." He turned his head, and I said, "No, look straight ahead and listen."

He faced front and gave a small nod.

"I am about to do something, and I think it will cause complete mayhem," I whispered. "If you see the chance, get the guests to run for those woods and hide. Can you do that?"

His jaw grew firm, and he gave another small nod.

"Thank you. Good luck."

My mind raced, guided by a single thought: Now…

I released Jenkins and stepped boldly into the circle.

As I removed the mask that had concealed my identity, cries of alarm erupted from the crowd. I could hear the men racking their firearms, but their threats barely registered.

My attention was solely on Don Diego and the dark entity accompanying him.

Don Diego's arms fell to his sides, and for a fleeting moment, surprise washed over his face, swiftly followed by a flicker of fear.

Clearly, he hadn't expected this interruption, and especially not from the man who he'd left tied up in his office.

A voice rang out among the men, ordering them to shoot me, but Diego held up a commanding hand, a cruel sneer spreading across his face with a challenging stare directed at me.

He shouted to his men in Spanish, words lost to me in the uproar, but the intent was clear: he intended to deal with a "little mouse" like me.

Remaining rooted in the center of the circle, Don Diego gestured menacingly, and to my surprise, the swirling mist coalesced at his command and launched itself toward me with astonishing speed.

I barely had enough time to muster my psychic defenses, creating a protective barrier around myself before Vexarath struck.

That mist enveloped me instantly. It reeked with a sickly smell, like death itself. I could feel it shiver with anticipation, as tendrils reached out like fingers to ensnare me, pulling me into its cold, awful embrace.

I felt my strength and energy being siphoned away, as if it were being drained from the very core of my soul. I heard whispers slithering through his mind, sowing doubt and amplifying my own fears.

You will lose everyone you love…

A wave of dread washed over me. In that disorienting moment, I was sure I didn't have a chance against such a formidable adversary.

Vexarath was no ordinary creature; he was some kind of demonic parasite. His very existence hinged on the host that was Don Diego, needing the energy of sacrificed victims to survive. It thrived on the despair and fear it incited in humans, twisting them into unwilling participants for its dark feast.

I forced myself to suppress the paralyzing grip of doubt, battling against the consuming emotions of failure and hopelessness that threatened to swallow me whole.

I closed my eyes, imagining a barrier of pure, incandescent light enveloping my body like a protective cocoon. A radiant shield to repel the suffocating shadows that surrounded me, stifling my spirit.

I felt Vexarath, still tethered to Don Diego, writhe with discomfort. Summoning every ounce of strength within me, I pushed back against its influence, solidifying my determination against the encroaching darkness. I concentrated, focusing on nothing but the light, the luminous essence that had the power to drive back the malevolent force.

With each breath, I imagined that light expanding outward, asserting my will against the energy swirling around me. Slowly, it relented, receding back toward my adversary. The ominous cloud shifted and coiled before surging back toward Don Diego, whose expression shifted into one of incredulity.

Good.

My actions had sown seeds of doubt in Diego's mind, a flicker of uncertainty that might just give me the advantage I desperately needed.

Suddenly, a searing flash of white light erupted a hundred feet away, instantly scorching the edges of my vision. The blinding glare was immediately followed by a thunderous explosion that rippled through the air like a physical force, sending dirt and grass into the air.

The cacophony ignited a chorus of terrified screams from the hostages. Diego's men instinctively jerked their heads toward the chaos, their grip on the situation loosening as their focus fractured.

I recognized the signature of the blast immediately. It was a Noise-Flash Diversionary Device — NFDD in law enforcement jargon — or as most call it, a flash-bang grenade. The question hammered in my mind: had the FBI finally breached the perimeter? Did this sudden upheaval signal a turning point?

Whether it spelled salvation or further chaos remained to be seen.

I didn't have a second to dwell on it. My eyes locked onto Don Diego with icy focus, watching every twitch, every movement. His hand shot out toward the sheath on his vest — and then froze. His gaze dropped sharply. The sheath was empty.

A surge of triumph sparked through me. Shielding my thoughts with everything I had, I reached into my vest and pulled out his ritual blade. The dark metal gleamed dully in the dim light, but even its shimmer couldn't wash away the horrifying visions that flooded my brain — faces twisted in agony, blood pooling in impossible quantities, cries echoing in the darkness.

Yet, when I glanced up, I caught the raw disbelief etched deep in Diego's face, and a grim, feral grin tugged at my lips.

Suddenly, a guttural roar tore from his throat. His eyes blazed with unbearable fury, wild and untamed. With Vexarath's smoky tendrils still coiled around him like a living shadow, he lunged, a tempest of rage hurtling toward me.

My Aikido training snapped to the forefront of my mind like a lifeline. At the very last moment, with a twisting pivot and a sudden, spinning evasive move, I tried to slip free.
But it wasn't quite enough — his reach was longer, his fury stronger. He missed my midsection, but his sprawling arms crashed against my bad right leg with brutal force, sending me staggering off-balance. The world tipped violently as I spun, then I hit the cold ground hard, landing near the vivid green powder that marked the outer circle.

Don Diego was already rising, his gaze moved to the automatic weapon he'd dropped in the center of the circle. With a spring in his step, he darted forward to seize it, eager, desperate.

I still clenched the ritual blade, its edge glinting faintly under the wan light. The haunted faces of the dead — of all the past victims — surged relentlessly across my vision. Time was slipping away; I had to act, and fast, or I was finished.

Diego lunged for the weapon, dropped to one knee, and lifted it, aiming the barrel straight at me.

Circle...

Though the nightmarish vision of blood and death clouded my sight, I was aware of the buzz. Rolling over, heart hammering in my chest, I scraped the shimmering powder away in one swift, desperate motion. Then, with trembling fingers, I lay the cursed ritual knife across it, creating a crucial break in the magical barrier.

The moment the blade severed the boundary, the effect crashed down like a thunderclap.

The vibrant green wall of energy shuddered and shattered, collapsing inward like brittle glass. The mist coiling around Don Diego's head vanished instantly, evaporating in a swirl of forgotten shadows.

It was as if I'd delivered a crushing physical blow — his body sagged suddenly, his raised hands dropping to his sides. Blinking rapidly, confusion clouded his eyes as he seemed to awaken from some terrible trance. The burning fury waned, replaced by a raw, fragile uncertainty.

At that exact moment, there was another flash of dazzling light, followed by an explosion. Another flash-bang and close enough to make my head ache and my ears ring from the sound.

Several canisters followed this, and as they hit the ground, they sent out plumes of smoke, which I guessed were smoke bombs, to confuse and disorient the terrorists.

Pandemonium reigned. Some masked men ran to Don Diego, and other men ran toward the attack. I was not sure if they were aiding their comrades or seeing Don Diego fall had weakened their courage.

I pulled myself to my feet, my leg giving me another twinge of pain, as one of the masked men reached toward me. Positioned perfectly, I drove my elbow into his masked face with all my strength, sending him stumbling backwards.

I glanced back to see five men helping Don Diego to his feet. Suddenly, one of them yanked a gleaming throwing knife from the folds of his vest, the cold steel catching what little light filtered through the smoke.

Danger…

I felt the buzz, and in a desperate instinct, I spun violently to the side, barely clearing the blade as it sliced through the air with a whistling hiss. The rush of wind kissed my cheek.

The knife thundered onward, propelled by lethal precision and raw power. With a sickening thunk, it slammed into the forehead of another masked assailant, burying itself deep. The man crumpled instantly, his body collapsing to the soft ground as if struck by a sledgehammer.

"This way, this way," a voice shouted, and I looked over to see Mr. Jenkins gesturing to the hostages and pointing toward the nearby forest.

The hostages, with no one holding them, broke away into a run in the direction Mr. Jenkins showed, and I joined them. I had to limp, as the pain in my leg was worse now.

I pushed through the retreating crowd, trying to find Jyanette. Just as I got beyond the circle, she collided with me, her eyes wide with urgency.

"Are you hurt?" I asked, concern lacing my voice.

"Run!" was the only answer she managed. She pulled my right arm over her shoulder to take the weight off my leg and together we bolted into the safety of the dark tree line.

All around us was mayhem and confusion; people scattered in every direction as gunfire erupted and more explosions rocked the resort grounds.

Once Jyanette and I found refuge within the cluster of trees, I risked a glance back. Through the swirling smoke, in the center of the illuminated circle, I saw Don Diego. He gripped his rifle, shouting frantic commands to his men to face their attackers, and then he moved toward the hotel.

"What happened?" I gasped, trying to catch my breath.

"I… I'm not sure," Jyanette replied, panting. "It was when… you did whatever you did while lying on the ground."

"I broke the circle using Diego's own knife," I explained.

"Whatever you did, the guy who was holding me just let go and took off," she said, her brow furrowed in confusion.

I nodded, a surge of understanding washing over me. "Breaking the circle must have severed the controlling power of the masks — probably just temporarily, but I'm sure it shocked all his men."

"Huh?" Jyanette stared at me, bewildered.

"Those masks," I clarified, finally catching my breath. "They don't just hide their identities. The magical symbols on them control the wearers, compelling obedience without question."

"No wonder they do whatever he wants."

The weight of the situation settled like a stone in my chest. "I have to go back to the hotel."

"Are you out of your mind?" Jyanette snapped, her eyes wide with disbelief. "You can barely walk. You don't have that mask to hide your face, and their leader wants you dead."

"I hid Isabella under the stairs, in that spot I put you."

The memory of that small, vulnerable girl flashed through my mind, fueling my urgency.

"Len, for God's sake, she's not your responsibility!"

Just then, another flash of light and explosion rocked the open field nearby, sending a shockwave through the trees. We instinctively ducked behind the trunk of a large tree, the light from the blast illuminating our surroundings like daylight for a moment.

"Don Diego needs Isabella to make his escape plan work. He's still a powerful psychic. If he finds her, she'll never know freedom again. He'll hold her captive, abuse her until she's of no more use, and then offer her up as a sacrifice to his demon."

Jyanette's brow furrowed in confusion. "What demon?"

I shook my head, realizing I hadn't fully explained. "Right, sorry. You couldn't see the dark cloud that hovered around Diego, could you?"

"When you two were facing off?" she asked, her voice shaky. "I saw something. It was faint, like a shadow stretching out behind him. He sent it at you, and you pushed it back."

I blinked, taken aback. "You saw it?"

"Well, at first I thought it was just my imagination playing tricks. Was it real?"

"Yes, it's an entity that Don Diego uses — or that's using him." I could still feel the chill of dread that creature created in me down to my bones.

"I sensed it too. There was something undeniably evil in that circle tonight," she said, her voice barely above a whisper.

I pulled her closer, desperate to gather strength from her presence. "Jyanette, I love you, but Don Diego needs a sacrifice. I can't just sit here while he plans his next move. I have to go back, ensure the rest of the hostages can escape, or he'll slaughter them in cold blood."

She clung to me tightly, her body trembling despite the warm night air. "Don't you dare die on me."

"I'll do everything I can to come back to you. You need to head for the chateaus. Stay close to the woods, and keep yourself hidden."

Another explosion echoed in the distance, the shockwave vibrating through the ground beneath us. Holding her close, I tried to convey every ounce of my love through that embrace. "I love you. I've always loved you."

"I know. Me too."

With a heavy heart, I stepped away, stealing one last look back at her. She moved toward the wood line, low and cautious, her silhouette the promise of what I was fighting for.

Limping as quickly as I could, I wove my way through the dense thicket of trees, retracing my steps toward the hotel where the fighting continued. The sound of automatic gunfire that reverberated through the air was growing closer, mingling with the distant boom of explosions.

An object lying in my path caused me to almost lose my footing. I stumbled forward, using the gnarled trunk of a nearby tree to steady myself.

Looking down in the dim light, I discovered with surprise that I had almost stepped on one of the black skull masks. A terrorist appeared to have hastily discarded it. I flipped it over in my hand and noted that the symbols were untouched, unlike the one I had tampered with.

I didn't dare put it on; I knew all too well that wearing such a mask would link me to the bizarre mental network — and yet there might be some way I could use it.

Clutching the mask in one hand, I limped cautiously through the thick underbrush, my senses heightened. Suddenly, a flicker of movement caught my eye. I squinted into the shadows ahead and discerned a silhouette lurking among the trees.

I froze in place. Like me, the other person was attempting to blend seamlessly into the surrounding foliage, mimicking my stillness with an air of wariness.

I slid behind the trunk of a sturdy oak and whispered, "Psst! Who's there?"

"Who are you?" a wary male voice called back, tinged with anxiety.

It was Jenkins.

"Mr. Jenkins!" I said, both astonished and relieved, "You got away! What are you doing here?"

"Going back to my hotel," he replied, breaking from cover and coming to me, his eyes darting nervously. "There are guests still being held in the ballroom. The bad guys started bolting when you were in that circle with their ringleader. How did you stop him?"

"I got lucky," I said. "I'm going back to free the hostages as well."

"Do you have a weapon?" he said,

"No, I'm afraid not," I admitted.

His brow furrowed, confusion mingling with anxiety. "What's with all the explosions? Do you know what's happening?"

"It's the FBI," I explained, keeping my voice low. "I contacted them."

He halted, scrutinizing me. "How did you do that? All the phone lines and cell towers are down!"

"I have my ways," I said vaguely.

We stood together, staring at the hotel. In the distance, I saw masked men scurrying like ants, and the sporadic rattle of gunfire sliced through the air. Yet there was no one who looked like FBI.

"What is the FBI going to do? Storm the building?" he worried.

"My guess is that they're moving in slowly," I replied, determination fueling my words. "But we can't wait for them. We need to get the hostages out of there, now."

"Is that safe? The FBI are firing mortars at us!" he said.

"They're not mortars," I countered. "Those are flash-bang grenades — designed to disorient rather than harm. They're loud and blinding, but mostly harmless. But, Don Diego is furious and ready to execute everyone in the ballroom. You should stay here."

"Like hell I shall," Mr. Jenkins growled, his resolve hardening. "My staff are in there!"

Another explosion rippled through the air, illuminating the scene with a violent flash on the opposite side of the hotel. The sound of renewed gunfire followed.

Move, now...

The buzz flashed through my mind, propelling me forward.

"C'mon!" I shouted, and together we dashed toward the main building, as best as I could, limping the entire way.

Our timing seemed to be right, as no one stopped us or attempted to shoot us. Don Diego had concentrated his forces at the hotel's front, engaging the FBI and leaving us a window of opportunity.

We finally reached the outer wall of the hotel and came to a halt, panting heavily. I rubbed my right leg, wincing as another acute pain shot through me.

"Are you injured?" Mr. Jenkins' voice cut through the chaos, his face etched with genuine concern. His eyes scanned mine, searching for any sign of blood or weakness.

Clenching my jaw against the dull, nagging ache that throbbed beneath the surface, I said, "I'll be fine." I pointed toward the far end of the corridor. "That door leads into the ballroom. If we can pry it open and get the people out—"

"—Without getting shot," he finished dryly. The weight of the situation settled heavily between us.

We pressed close to the wall, shadows cloaking our movements as we edged forward. The glass door loomed ahead, a fragile barrier between hope and danger. I extended my senses, pushing past pain and fear, reaching out to the terrified souls trapped inside. Their fear was palpable — thick and radiating — like a beacon calling out in the dark.

"What do we do now?" Jenkins' voice dropped to a hush, a whisper meant to match the gravity of our situation.

I glanced down at the mask I held loosely in my hand and, for a moment, a wave of dread washed over me. Why had I even brought this cursed thing? I was afraid of its overwhelming connection to the others' minds.

Then, an idea sparked — dangerous, but maybe my only shot. I realized I didn't have to let the mask control me. What if, instead, I could channel its power—and use it to manipulate the terrorists themselves?

"I have a plan," I said, my voice steady despite the turmoil boiling inside. Without waiting for Jenkins, I veered away from the ballroom door and skirted the hotel's side heading toward the front.

"What are you doing?" Jenkins hissed. "The ballroom is the other way."

Unfazed, I pushed open the unlocked door of the gift shop, stepping inside, into the storage area. Jenkins followed, eyes darting nervously among the shelves. I hurried across the room and collapsed into the nearest chair, the skull mask resting in my lap.

"Why are we here?" Jenkins demanded, his frustration threading through his voice. "We need to get the hostages free."

I met his gaze evenly. "I'm going to make the guards leave the ballroom."

He threw me a skeptical look. "What, you're planning to bribe them with snow globes and keychains?"

A sudden, bitter laugh burst from me, surprising Jenkins and even myself. "No," I managed between breaths, regaining control. "But wait outside the ballroom. I'll come get you soon — once the way's clear."

Though confused, Jenkins nodded and slipped quietly outside and back into the shadows, melting into the night air.

I turned my focus back to the mask, gazing into its empty eye sockets. Wearing it affected my mind and anyone's who wore it. But Don Diego gave his orders without donning a mask. That was the key.

Symbolic glyphs forced submission if you wore the mask. To send orders, I had to stay outside of it. But Don Diego's power had limits. He could send commands to his men wearing the masks but could never truly read what came back. It was a dance of mental energy.

I flipped the skull mask over in my hand, envisioning it as a radio — just waiting for the right frequency. If I could just tune in and take control, I might turn the tide.

Lowering my defenses, I pushed past my fear and pain. This was my chance, for Don Diego was far too busy dealing with the FBI to take the time to search for me with his mind.

I reached out mentally, feeling the chaotic swirl of minds bound by the same psychic web. In the distance, gunfire echoed faintly — explosions shattered the night air — but what rose above it all were the orders flooding into my psyche like a raging storm:

Keep them back…

Shoot, shoot…

Focusing my mind, I fortified my resolve, connecting with the other minds entangled in this mental web. My thoughts rang out with urgency, seeking to galvanize them into action.

Everyone, leave what you're doing and move to the front of the building. Defend the hotel…

My command blazed in my mind, a clarion call slicing through the mental fog. Suddenly, it felt as though an immense, unyielding eye had fixed its gaze upon me. The collective attention of a dozen controlled souls converging, waiting for my direction.

All of you — go! Everyone — now…

Though my mental commands surged with an authority, I could sense a stubborn resistance pushing back. Don Diego's presence lingered, a relentless wind attempting to drown out my voice with counter-orders.

Our previous mental battles had sharpened my awareness —
now I understood his invasive grasp. But I was firm. Drawing
deep on my willpower, I shoved him aside, seizing the strength to
ensure my commands would prevail.

I opened my eyes and stood, only to fall back into the chair as
my right leg gave way.

"Great," I muttered and lifted my head to rest my eyes on the
corner of the room where the crutch leaned against the wall. I
pushed myself to my feet, keeping my weight off my right leg,
and limped over to grab it. I tucked it under my arm. It helped.

Crutch in one hand, skull mask in the other, I made my way
to the door of the gift shop. I cracked the door just as two masked
men ran by on their way to the front of the building.

It appeared my ruse may have worked.

I carefully slipped outside and using the crutch, made my way
around the building to the ballroom's rear entrance.

A sudden rustle startled me — Mr. Jenkins stepped from a
shadowed alcove, face taut with tension. "What did you do,
Mister Wise?" he demanded quietly.

"Call me Len," I said, steadying my voice. "Why? What
happened?"

"Two men ran out that door," he said, pointing at the glass
ballroom door. "Then they ran around heading toward the front
—"

"I know, I saw them."

"I think they were in such a hurry, they didn't close the door."

Together, we crept to the door and gave it a cautious pull. It swung open easily, revealing the remaining hostages inside. They spun toward us, wide-eyed but holding steady.

I turned to Jenkins. "Barricade the big doors. Grab whatever you can — chairs, tables — anything sturdy. We need to keep those doors shut. Now!"

Jenkins nodded sharply and crossed the room, hauling two hefty chairs and wedging them hard beneath the door handles. The scraping sound cut through the tense silence — a barricade springing to life.

My voice rang loud and clear, carrying the weight of command.

"Listen to me! Do exactly as I say if you want to make it out alive!"

All the men and women looked at me and nodded, a spark of hope flickering in their eyes.

I also felt hope — that we might just have a chance.

14. INVISIBLE ESCAPE

"Quickly!" I shouted. "We have to get you out of here!"

But instead of moving, they merely stared back at me, frozen in disbelief.

Panic surged through me. "Come on!" I pleaded, frustration bubbling up as their hesitance lingered.

Finally, as if someone flipped a switch, everyone rose to their feet. We made our way together toward the glass door at the back of the room.

"Mr. Jenkins," I said. "Lead these people into the woods. Get them away from here. You know the grounds better than anyone."

Jenkins pulled away slightly, his gaze sharpening. "Aren't you coming with us?" he asked, concern flashing in his eyes.

"I've got to help someone," I replied firmly. "I need to get her out of here while we still have a chance. Good luck."

Jenkins nodded gravely and stepped forward to face the crowd.

"Everyone," he commanded, his voice strong and steady. "We're moving out one by one. Stay close to the person in front of you, remain quiet, and stay near the wall. Once we're in the right place, we're going to make a break for the woods, one at a time."

With that, Jenkins led the way outside, and the others followed him, stepping into the open air one after another. A few anxious whispers broke the silence, but I quickly placed a finger to my lips, and they fell silent, fear returning to their eyes.

I pulled a chair over and settled down by the door, taking a moment to relieve the pain in my overused leg. The people were rapidly evacuating, but I knew I couldn't let my guard down just yet.

I needed to assist Isabella and get her out from under the staircase. When the final hostage stepped outside, leaving the outside door ajar, I rose and headed for the front of the room, picking up the discarded mask as I went.

Gritting my teeth, I pulled it over my head and focused my mind to protect it from the onslaught of voices. I felt the odd euphoria, and I could hear Don Diego's orders as he tried to rally his men.

I shoved the chairs aside, stepping into the dimly lit hallway. It was eerily quiet; the silence wrapping around me like a shroud. I peered in both directions, scanning for any signs of movement.

Then, a sudden chill engulfed me, as if the air had thickened. I sensed him. I felt Don Diego's presence, like a blade digging into my mind.

I CAN FEEL YOU...

His voice echoed through my thoughts, and a harrowing pain shot through my head, causing me to stagger against the wall.

Pushing onward, I stumbled down the hall and bolted through the doorway that led to the stairs, tearing the mask from my face as I did. I slammed the door shut behind me and hurled the cursed object to the floor, battling the tumult in my mind.

I had been fortunate when I sent the mental order to the others. The sudden loss of his demon companion disoriented Don Diego.

However, now he was regaining his composure and his impressive psychic powers with alarming speed. He was laser-focused on finding my location.

"Isabella!" I called out into the oppressive shadows that clung to the area under the stairs. "It's Leonard, the man who helped you!"

"Leonard?" came her quivering voice from beneath the staircase. "Can I come out?"

Danger…

I sensed the buzz in my mind, and I could feel it pressing down on me like a heavy blanket.

"No, you need to stay hidden for a little while longer," I replied, my heart pounding in my ears as I ran as fast as I could toward the concrete stairs,"But I need the rifle that's under the—"

Danger…

Just as I reached the stack of chairs, I heard the door behind me explode open. Without thinking, I dove headfirst to the concrete stairs, hitting my right leg painfully as I did, and instinctively curling into a protective position.

A deafening eruption of gunfire rang out, echoing violently within the enclosed space. Bullets whizzed overhead, ricocheting off the metal handrail and embedding themselves into the wall above me, sending dust and fragments of concrete raining down.

I shut my eyes, covered my head, and coughed as dust filled my mouth, forcing me into a fit of choking coughs.

"You thought you could best me?" Don Diego's voice boomed, laced with venom and derision.

I could barely hear him above the ringing in my ears.

I raised my head a few inches, peering through the haze of dust to glimpse him.

He stood in the threshold, a wild look dancing in his eyes, the gun still smoking in his grip.

Without hesitation, he dropped the firearm and drew the black knife from his vest. He'd rescued it from the circle where I'd left it. The knife he'd used to kill so many to offer their lives to empower his demon.

The blade glinted with menace in the dim light.

"My hostages are gone," he spat, voice dripping with fury. "Where is the girl?"

Even in the murky shadows, I could clearly see the grotesque, cloud-like aura swirling around him — the demonic entity had returned to him.

Apparently, he'd reconnected with the creature. Vexarath was a ghastly specter, a parasitic force that fed on bloodlust and had nourished Diego's dark desires, while amplifying his host's psychic prowess to a terrifying level.

"You will tell me where she is," he hissed, stepping closer, the knife in his grip and an eager spark igniting in his eyes. "Or, I will relish pulling your skin away layer by layer."

My breath caught in my throat as a wave of fear washed over me. I didn't know what to do, my leg hurt so much I was sure I couldn't get up.

I had to think fast, to survive the relentless wrath of the man and his monster standing before me.

In that moment of despair, a singular thought pierced through my mind. I had to protect Isabella at all costs, even if it meant confronting the beast with nothing but my willpower as a weapon.

"You're allowing that thing to manipulate you," I said, and grabbed the metal rail attached to the wall to pull myself up into a sitting position. "You're not its master; it pulls your strings like a puppet."

The malevolent smile on his face widened, showing a disturbing pleasure in my words. "And I embrace it," he replied, a sadistic glint in his eyes. "This power he gives allows me to eliminate pests like you."

He stepped closer, the knife in his hand, and my exhaustion and fear prevented me from acting.

Just as he drew nearer to the staircase, the air erupted with deafening explosions. Muzzle flashes illuminated the shadows beneath the stairs, stark against the darkness.

Don Diego stumbled backward, a spray of crimson erupting from his vest as gunfire struck true. He fell to the ground; the knife slipping from his fingers.

I sat up straighter, my heart lifting with hope. In that moment, the stack of chairs I had used to shield Isabella tumbled away, revealing her standing there, fierce and ready, the automatic weapon aimed directly at the fallen man.

"You bastard!" she shouted, her eyes savage, focus fully locked onto Don Diego sprawled on the floor.

But she couldn't see what I could see. The sickly, dark cloud that surrounded Don Diego's head extended ethereal tendrils toward her. It appeared to be probing the very essence that surrounded her, searching for an opening.

"Isabella, no!" I called out, desperation clawing at my throat.

The truth dawned on me with painful clarity: she'd wounded the demon's host, and, sensing the weakness, Vexarath sought a new vessel.

It craved murder, a brutal act that would tether it to its new pawn. If Isabella killed Don Diego in cold blood, the creature would seize that moment to bond with her.

Isabella paused, her gaze flickering up to meet mine, the gun unwavering in her grip. "Do you know what he did to me?!" she screamed, anguish and fury in her voice.

Even as I shouted for her to stop, I saw Don Diego scrambling away, his movements frantic as he tried to reach the automatic weapon he'd left near the door.

Isabella's fury ignited once more, and she unleashed a barrage of bullets into the wooden door above him, sending splinters flying, burying him in a cloud of debris.

With the weapon still trained on him, she advanced. First, she kicked away the knife on the floor, then advanced to kick the gun that Don Diego had dropped, ensuring he couldn't retaliate.

My stomach twisted as the misty tendrils continued their relentless advance, stretching out like fingers of smoke, encircling her, eager to ensnare her spirit.

Don Diego lay there, gasping for breath, his eyes wide with shock and confusion as he struggled to comprehend what had unfolded. It was as if he was trying to understand why his fortunes had changed so quickly.

I used the crutch and stair rail to pull myself to my feet, raising my hands in a pleading gesture. I spoke, my voice steady despite the turmoil. "Isabella, don't kill him. Don't go down to his level."

She glanced at me, the weapon still pointed unwaveringly at Don Diego. "He hit me! He molested me!" Her voice was a tempest of rage, each word laced with the pain of her trauma.

As I stood there, the gnawing dread filling me as more tendrils slithered from Don Diego to Isabella. I realized Vexarath was already sinking his hooks into her. It thrived on suffering, exploiting her pain, humiliation, and degradation, turning her justified anger into a weapon against her by turning her into a killer.

I had to reach her before it was too late. The peril of the situation weighed heavier with each passing moment.

"Isabella," I said urgently, locking eyes with her. "That anger you're feeling, that deep-seated hatred, it's not who you are. It's a force trying to take control, to manipulate you. If you succumb to it, you risk becoming a monster as bad as Don Diego ever was."

Her gaze flickered toward me. The glint in her eyes told me she teetered on the brink, poised to leap into the abyss of madness. I felt an icy shiver run down my spine — if she crossed that line and murdered Don Diego, would I become her next target?

I reached out with my mind, focusing intently on the dark cloud-like entity that loomed nearby, trying to form a protective barrier between it and Isabella.

"Listen to me, Isabella! You must resist the overwhelming urge to kill him. That is precisely what this entity wants!"

A flicker of disbelief crossed her face. "What are you talking about?"

"There's a parasitic creature manipulating Don Diego," I explained, my voice urgent and strained. "Now it wants you."

Before I could say another word, Don Diego surged forward with astonishing speed and strength, leaping toward her like a predator lunging for its prey.

Instinctively, she fired the weapon. The shots rang out with a deafening crack, each bullet hitting Don Diego and sending him crashing backward, slamming against the closed door.

For a moment, he stood there, stunned, before sliding to the floor, leaving a macabre trail of crimson blood on the door in his wake.

Isabella lowered the weapon.

The entity was relentless, undeterred by the stillness of Don Diego's lifeless form. It oozed free like a malignant shadow, twisting and writhing with unnatural grace as it slithered down in sinuous coils. Its tendrils stretched toward Isabella, pulsating with a ravenous hunger that set the very air around her trembling.

"Isabella, fight it!" I shouted, my voice cracking with raw, desperate urgency. "It's trying to possess you — don't let it in!"

Her lips quivered, her voice faltering under a crushing wave of confusion, fear... and something darker, something twisting in the depths of her gaze. "I... I don't understand!" Her words shattered the chaos, brittle as glass meeting stone.

"It can't control you if you resist," I called out holding myself upright on the staircase. "Refuse to give in! If you deny it, it loses its grip — don't let it win!"

She turned to me, her vulnerability flickering like a fragile candle in a storm. The dark mist that had surrounded Don Diego now engulfed her head in a swirl of smoky tendrils, coiling tightly. It seeped through her nostrils first — cold, suffocating. She threw her head back, and the mist poured into every opening: her mouth, her ears, wherever it could find entry. A scream tore from her throat as the mist slid deeper, sinking into flesh and bone, merging with her very soul.

In that instant, I understood why with Don Diego it had danced in sinister partnership — a dark, perverse collaboration. He wanted the gifts Vexarath offered. But with Isabella, the creature needed total dominion. It needed to break her free will, to enslave her mind, to possess her entirely.

Panic exploded through me as I stumbled backward, retreating up the stairs, heart hammering with dread. The dim light caught the shimmer of cold sweat on Isabella's pale skin. I watched in horror as the smoky tendrils vanished into her flesh, unraveling and consuming from within — a tempest tearing her apart beneath the fragile mask she tried in vain to hold.

Her eyes — once warm amber pools of life — flickered with chaos, wild storms raging beneath the surface.

I could almost see the demon's clawed fingers raking through her insides, squeezing tighter, twisting her very reality, peeling away the Isabella I once knew like brittle bark from a dying tree.

The room itself seemed to tremble with her torment. A guttural growl bubbled from deep within her throat — half human, half monstrous, cruel and primal: a sound that clawed at the bones of the air.

Then the tremor vanished as if snuffed out by cruel light.

Her eyes snapped open wide. Black voids, endless and bottomless, flecked with violent sparks of red that flickered like dying embers. Her lips curled back in a jagged, unnatural grin — a smile that twisted pain and malice into one, never quite reaching those abyssal eyes.

"Why shouldn't I have it all?" she hissed, voice a whisper that cut through the air. "After everything… he did to me… it belongs to me now."

She bent and picked up the ritual knife from the floor. The blade shimmered wickedly, catching what little light remained. She slid it into her belt, taking possession of the talisman that had killed so many in sacrifice.

She lifted the rifle, aiming it directly at me, her movements deliberate, as if the demon itself guided her hand.

"And you, you want to take it all away," she hissed, each word dripping with venom. "Away from me!"

My heart slammed in my chest like a drum. Behind the darkness, I hoped — somewhere beneath that possessed shell,

Isabella's soul screamed to be free. But the crushing weight of the demon's presence pressed down, suffocating the flicker of light.

I sprinted clumsily up the last few steps, adrenaline propelling me forward as I sought refuge. The ominous bark of the automatic weapon echoed behind me, the force of the shots reverberating through the confines of the stairwell. I hurled myself through the door at the top, the weight of fear heavy in my chest.

I scrambled into the nearby hotel room I had used before. With a frantic motion, I slammed the door shut and engaged the security lock. It felt like a feeble barrier against the storm I sensed outside, but it was all I had.

I fell into a chair, my leg giving way beneath me, trembling from the exertion.

In the chilling silence that followed, I knew acutely that if she followed, the lock was hardly an obstacle for someone so possessed.

I felt tired, my senses dull, the stinging remnants of gunfire ringing in my ears, drowning out any sounds from the corridor.

What could I do now? More crucially, if Isabella was under the influence of the ethereal creature that had given power to Don Diego, what unimaginable depths could she plunge into?

I shuddered at the thought that with the mystical masks donned by Don Diego's followers, she could easily seize control over them as well. They were mere puppets in her quest for vengeance, and I feared what that would mean for me.

Vexarath lurking inside her was a malevolent force. It would undoubtedly recognize me as its only significant threat; I was the one person able to see its true nature.

I had done good things this night. I'd survived, saved my wife, and helped others get through the night alive.

Even so, I now felt that everything had spiraled out of control; what had begun as a confrontation had escalated into something far more dangerous than I expected.

15. RETREATING ODDS

At least the hostages had escaped, which brought me a flicker of hope. I hoped they had removed Jyanette from immediate danger. Don Diego's death was morbidly comforting; his reign of terror was over, and that was one less threat to worry about.

Yet, lurking in the shadows was Isabella, who now bore the burden of demonic possession. I'd encountered possessed people before and had some experience exorcising them — binding the entity and reciting an ancient incantation that still echoed in my memory.

Thankfully, the spell was simple, connected to an age-old practice. But with the heiress caught in the throes of darkness, the solution seemed paradoxically cruel. I needed to bind her and subject her to the ritual that would free her.

Which led to the question: What would I do if she didn't want to be free?

All demonic possessions require an invitation, an acceptance of the evil. Only then could the creature bind and take over. If I could exorcise Vexarath, would she let him go?

My eyes wandered into the nearby bedroom, catching sight of the sturdy wooden cane I had purchased in Las Vegas. An odd sense of relief washed over me at the sight of it. I pushed myself off the chair with the crutch, my legs still shaky, and made my way across the room.

Clumsily, I reached for the cane, feeling its familiar weight as I leaned on it for support. The sensation of the polished wood steadied my nerves, grounding me amidst the pandemonium.

I opened the closet door and peered inside to find my clothes where I had stashed them waiting for me. I realized my disguise had outlived its usefulness and I could finally shed the facade.

It was imperative that I didn't look like the terrorists when the FBI arrived. I took off the tactical vest and the fatigues and changed back into my own familiar attire.

As I dressed hurriedly in the dim light, a sudden spark of inspiration ignited within me. Fumbling through the clutter of my wallet, my fingers brushed against the small, crumpled piece of parchment I kept in it.

I pulled it free, revealing the intricate emblem of the ancient Seal of Solomon imprinted upon the delicate animal skin. The symbol glowed faintly in my mind's eye, its interlocking design—circles, stars, and Hebrew inscriptions—radiating an aura of commanding authority to bind supernatural forces.

I felt a little hope. Unprepared for fighting a supernatural being throughout this entire ordeal, I was now equipped with a weapon. The realization that I had this parchment hidden in my clothes the entire time was both exhilarating and frustrating. I could have used it against Don Diego in that circle.

But I didn't know what I was fighting then.

It took me a while to finish dressing, as my body was tired and bruised. I had pushed myself so hard, and the adrenaline that kept me going was wearing off. I had kept pushing myself out of fear and anxiety. Sitting on the bed, I had an overwhelming desire to lie down and catch some sleep.

Dressed in my own clothes, I returned to the door to peer through the peephole. The hallway lay devoid of any immediate threats. To all appearances, Isabella had not chosen to pursue me. However, there could be other dangers waiting for me.

I pressed my hand against the door, half-expecting to sense a buzz of warning. But I received no precognition.

I unlocked the door and stepped out into the dimly lit hallway, and made my way cautiously down the corridor in the opposite direction from the stairway I'd ascended.

I found what appeared to be the primary staircase, as it was polished stone and gracefully twisted down into the lobby.

I peered down into the dark lobby. The once vibrant area now presented a somber tableau, bearing the unmistakable scars of a recent violent conflict.

Lit only by the dim flicker of emergency lighting that struggled to cast away the looming shadows, I carefully descended the stairs. I saw the shattered remnants of one of the antler chandeliers scattered across the marble floor, reduced to a heap of broken pieces. Overhead, bullets had chipped and scarred the wooden beams. The walls bore holes and chunks missing as well.

At the forefront of the disarray was the concierge desk, now marred with scuff marks and disheveled papers, each crumpled sheet telling a story of the destruction.

FBI agents clad in tactical gear strode in with a grim determination, their expressions focused and serious as they executed their operations. The crackling sounds of walkie-talkies were the only thing piercing through the suffocating silence.

Amidst the mess, I spotted one of the captured terrorists — kneeling, hands cuffed behind his back, and his head bent low. The black skull mask he had been wearing lay discarded on the floor in front of him, an eerie token. Two FBI agents watched him vigilantly, as he stared at the mask, seemingly in a trance.

Outside, through the tall glass doors, I saw several armor-plated four-by-four vehicles standing ready, each equipped with aggressive searchlights. One vehicle illuminated the interior of the hotel, its beams piercing the darkness, while others swept towards the grounds, casting eerie silhouettes across the landscape.

I came down the staircase with my hands raised, doing my best to appear non-threatening in this tense environment. I assumed the FBI had executed their raid on the building, regaining control.

One man guarding the subdued terrorist advanced toward me, weapon raised and eyes narrowed. "You! Who are you?" he demanded, the authority in his voice palpable.

"I'm Doctor Leonard Wise," I replied. "I'm the one who sent the message to the FBI."

With a slight lowering of his weapon, he acknowledged me with a nod before turning away to relay my name over his walkie-talkie, repeating it several times as he requested information from his team commander.

Once the conversation concluded, he leaned toward me, gently but firmly taking hold of my arm. "This way, sir."

"Excuse me," I interjected cautiously, "can you tell me what time it is?"

"Oh-forty-five, sir," he replied.

12:45 AM.

To me, it felt like five in the morning.

I trailed behind the agent as he led me deeper into the lobby, eventually arriving at a window overlooking the hotel pool and the lake beyond. What was once a picturesque view had transformed into a murky canvas of shadows, punctuated by the intermittent beams of flashlights and searchlights as the FBI continued their operation.

In front of the window stood Captain Lauwers in his uniform, next to another man. The stranger had a thatch of thick, dark hair peppered with silver at the temples and cut short, which gave him a distinguished appearance. He wore tactical gear with "FBI" across the front and back in reflective lettering.

Lauwers face opened in a smile, then he glanced at how I leaned on my cane. "Doctor Wise! Are you all right?"

"Just some trouble with my leg," I said.

He took my hand in a warm grip as the stranger looked on, dismissing my escort with a mere nod.

"This is Commander Lou Gurelle," Lauwers explained. "He's with FBI Counter-Terrorism Unit, Los Angeles."

"That's quite a distance to cover," I remarked, surprised at the extent of their response. "How on earth did you get here so fast?"

"I'll tell you, you're the luckiest son-of-a-bitch on the planet, Doctor," he said, taking my hand and giving it a shake. "My team was on training maneuvers in the Eldorado National Forest, about an hour from here. In the middle of the freakin' night, I get a call from Bill McGee, telling me about this resort getting attacked, and asking me what my twenty was."

I nodded. Asking someone their "twenty" was police shorthand for code 10-20, which is a request for location.

"He asked if I had any heavy equipment, and I told him we were training with our new armored vehicles. He told me to get here as fast as I could and to keep an eye out for Doctor Leonard Wise," he chuckled. "Apologies for our delay; on the way, we navigated through a few bureaucratic loopholes before shooting our way in."

"I guess you had a hard time getting into the place," I said.

"Damn straight," Gurelle chuckled. "They blocked the only road in with two vans. We had to smash through them to get in, and they had people with automatic weapons firing at us."

"Those flash-bangs you fired distracted them," I said.

"Yeah, we had a good stock of them, smoke grenades and the launchers," Gurelle explained.

I nodded. "It probably saved our lives."

"What was going on, here?" Lauwers asked, concern written on his face.

I sighed. "A drug delivery, hostages, and human sacrifice."

Both men just stared at me.

"My deputies were running around the entire county," Lauwers said. "The power outage kept us busy. We wouldn't have even come here, except we heard the explosions."

"Doc, do you have any idea who these guys are?" Gurelle asked, "or why they wear those strange masks?"

In as concise a manner as possible, I shared the details regarding Don Diego and his cult of followers, opting to keep the more fantastical elements — namely the power of the magical masks — to myself. Lauwers interjected his opinion as well and between us, we brought Gurelle up to speed on the case from the beginning.

I also told them about the helicopter and the delivery of the cache of drugs.

"We haven't located their leader yet," Gurelle admitted, an expression of frustration creasing his brow. "Oddly enough, they were ferocious in their resistance until about twenty minutes ago. Then they just threw down their weapons and surrendered."

"I saw their leader gunned down. I can take you to him," I offered, eager to be of help.

Gurelle's interest piqued. "Show me."

With my cane supporting my leg, I led him through the dimly lit hallways of the hotel, until we reached the doorway that led to the staircase. I pulled it open, revealing Don Diego sprawled on the floor, precisely as I'd seen him when Isabella had finished him.

Gurelle immediately touched his walkie-talkie, reporting the location and issuing swift commands to his team.

"Did you shoot him?" Lauwers asked as Gurelle wrapped up his conversation on the radio.

"Not me," I replied, glancing down at the lifeless figure sprawled on the ground. "But I would have, given the chance. Isabella Fontaine gunned him down."

"Fontaine?" Lauwers repeated. "Agent Roberts told me she was in San Francisco."

"He was wrong," I said simply.

Gurelle heard what we said, the wheels in his mind turning. "I saw an FBI notice about her. You say she was here, in this hotel?"

"The information about her being in San Francisco was fake, done to get the FBI team to leave," I said.

Limousine…

I felt the buzz in the back of my mind, took a deep breath and concentrated on Gurelle and Lauwers. "The terrorists loaded the shipment of drugs into a stretch limousine with diplomatic plates. Have you located it?"

Gurelle and Lauwers exchanged a glance, then Gurelle met my eyes. "A limousine with diplomatic plates? No. All we found were a pair of vans blocking the road, with the armed men firing at us."

Lauwers shrugged. "It has to be here. The main road is the only way in and out of the resort. There's one other road, but it only leads to the golf course, and that doesn't get you to the highway."

My mind raced through the layout of the resort. There were no hills or major impediments on the manicured lawns. "They could have gone overland."

Gurelle looked to Lauwers, and the captain shook his head. "I suppose they could drive right over the lawns. Why would anyone do that?"

I couldn't tell them I had seen Isabella become possessed by the demon that used Don Diego, and could now lead any remnants of Diego's team. I had to give them a plausible explanation for her to be in the limousine, if we were to recover it and her.

I cleared my throat. "Their leader is dead. Their entire operation stopped. It would make sense to make a run for it with the drugs. They would have to take Isabella with them. Don Diego was going to bring her in case anyone questioned the diplomatic status of the vehicle."

My mind conjured images of the massive quantities of drugs I'd seen crammed into that limo. That kind of stash would be enough to fund anyone's plans. If Isabella had indeed commandeered the limo, Vexarath now possessed her, and would have the knowledge necessary to complete the deal, picking up where Don Diego left off.

Both Gurelle and Lauwers used their radios. Gurelle was ordering an immediate search for a stretch limousine on the premises. I could only hear one side of his conversation, but his team was busy detaining cultists and helping guests navigate their way back to the safety of the hotel.

Lauwers was on the radio with his deputies, asking them if they'd seen a limousine.

Time was of the essence. If Isabella had indeed escaped, every second lost could mean the difference between catching her and watching her slip away into the night with a treasure trove of drugs — an opportunity to rebuild the empire that had just crumbled.

But I had more important things to do.

"Commander Gurelle, Captain Lauwers," I said as they finished their conversations on their radio, "My wife is hiding in the woods. I need to make sure she's all right."

"We're bringing the guests back to the hotel," Lauwers said. "My men will keep an eye out for her."

"We've secured the building and captured the terrorists," Gurelle said. "We have eleven, either dead or secured."

"There were fifteen men besides Don Diego," I said.

"How do you know that?" Lauwers asked.

"The number fifteen was his fixation," I said. "You captured or killed eleven, and I saw Don Diego kill two of them—"

"So you think two got away with the limousine?" Gurelle said.

I was sure of it. "Sounds possible."

"Great!" Lauwers grumbled. "Two heavily armed men on the run in a freakin' limo."

"Is there a map of this place?"

"In the lobby," Lauwers said. "Follow me."

We walked into the damaged lobby, and on the wall was a large map displaying the entire resort. I ran my finger along it.

"If they drove this way, following the stream, they'll end up right at the parkway," I explained.

"They'd have to go through a fence that way," Gurelle said.

"In a limo?" Lauwers pointed out. "They'd go right over it." He pointed at the map. "If you're right, they could access Route 50, whether they're headed into California or Nevada."

Gurelle shook his head, his expression grim. "We're currently engaged in clean-up operations here. I can't send out a team to chase them."

"Well, we could involve both the Nevada and California Highway Patrol," Lauwers insisted, his tone laced with urgency. "But with the cell phone towers down and the lines to the hotel severed, communication is a nightmare." He sighed in frustration, running a hand through his hair. "I think if I head to my office, I can make a call from a landline. Maybe once we're closer to Minden and headquarters, we'll have an active cell tower."

Go along…

The buzz flashed in my head, a sensation urging me to speak out before I could second-guess myself. "Can I come with you?" I blurted.

Gurelle cast a piercing glare at me. "I thought you wanted to find your wife."

"I do," I replied, my conviction wavering as I struggled to process the impulse that had driven me. "But I also need to get in touch with Bill McGee and let him know that I'm okay."

Lauwers exchanged a glance with Gurelle, who shrugged in resignation. "It's going to take us hours to sort everything out here," he conceded.

"The Nevada Energy crew is working to restore power," Lauwers added, worry etched on his face. "A major transformer malfunctioned. They suspect sabotage."

"No doubt," I said.

"Alright, Doc," Lauwers said. "You can ride with me. Maybe you can offer some insights on where this limo might be heading."

Gurelle raised an eyebrow, skepticism clear on his face. "How could he possibly know that?"

Lauwers smiled. "He has his ways. Come on."

I trailed behind Lauwers as we made our way to his car, casting one last lingering gaze at the shadowy outline of the resort, lit by the sweeping searchlights of the FBI vehicles.

A bitter pang of longing went through me as I wished fervently for just a glimpse of Jyanette before we left.

16. DISAPPEARING PURSUIT

We got on the road, shrouded in an enveloping darkness that felt almost tangible. The only illumination in this vast, shadowy expanse was the silver glow of the full moon and the piercing beams of our vehicle's headlights cutting through the night like a blade.

We reached the imposing front gates of the resort, framed by four weather-worn stone pillars. Each pillar supported a set of ornate iron gates.

I instantly noticed a pair of dilapidated vans riddled with bullet holes. They had deliberately placed the vans to create a barricade and block the roadway. Now they wore huge dents where the FBI vehicles had pushed them out of the way. Several bodies lay nearby, men in their black tactical gear, and still wearing the skull masks.

I understood at that moment that Don Diego had never intended for the sleek limousine to pass through those gates. His entire strategy had hinged on a carefully planned alternate route, one that none of us expected. I also understood that Isabella had gained an insight to this hidden path, thanks to the dark force that now controlled her.

Lauwers made a right on the main road and headed east, passing a dark casino and several housing developments that were dark as well, although one or two were lit up by generators as we passed.

Then on the road ahead, the streetlights were on. The return of these lights shocked me; I had grown so used to the darkness that it felt like a revelation.

"Where is your office?" I asked.

"In Minden, about twenty minutes from here," he said, watching the road. "So you were right the whole time."

"How do you mean?"

"Those guys with the masks — damn creepy. But when you did your reading thing, you said they didn't have faces. I guess those masks could count for that."

I nodded, impressed that Lauwers was so thoughtful. I didn't mention the symbols and the incantations that made them work.

There was a beep, and Lauwers pulled his cell phone. "Hey, look at that. I'm getting a signal and a message." He glanced at the screen. "My deputies say that Nevada Energy will have power restored soon."

"That's good news."

I pulled my smart phone and saw that I was now getting two bars. Even though it was the middle of the night, I immediately called Bill McGee, who picked up on the first ring.

"Len, is that you?" Bill said, so loudly I had to pull the phone away from my ear.

"Yeah, Bill. Jyanette and I are fine. I'm with the local police right now."

"Thank God. Laura and I have been worried sick. Did you meet up with Gurelle? He's an old friend of mine."

"Yes, he and the FBI cavalry stormed in to rescue us. They peppered the place with flash-bangs, which scared the bad guys at just the right moment."

"That's what I advised them to do. When are you guys getting home so I can keep an eye on you?"

"Soon, I promise. I've had enough of the desert life."

"Okay. And call Anna. She made quite the persuasive argument. Not that I had to be convinced. She was in tears when I last spoke to her."

"I will. Thanks, Bill."

"Can you try to finish your honeymoon without getting into any more trouble?"

"Working on it."

I ended the call and immediately hit the number for Anna Sokolov.

She also answered on the first ring. "Len, please tell me you're alright."

I could tell from her voice she'd been crying.

"I'm okay, so is Jyanette."

She let out a small sob, then caught herself, cleared her throat and said, "That's good."

"You did great Anna," I said, telling her the truth, but also wanting to encourage her. "You convinced Bill, and he set an armed task force to rescue us."

"I was so worried…"

"You probably saved our lives."

"I-I did?" she said.

"I know you'll be perfect for the Teaching Assistant job. If you can handle this, you can handle anything. Now get some rest."

"I couldn't sleep. Thanks for letting me know," she said.

"Thanks for getting the word out," I said and ended the call, leaning back, feeling a little lighter.

I'd dedicated a lot of time trying to lift Anna's spirits, but now I felt it was more than just altruism. This convinced me I had made the right choice in selecting her to be my ally. A teaching assistant who could communicate without words, who received my thoughts with her uncanny psychic ability, was a rare gift.

That's when it occurred to me. I also possessed a unique psychic gift. I could use it to find which direction Isabella had gone. Closing my eyes, I focused inward, honing my awareness towards the vehicle.

In that instant, I sensed Isabella. It was an odd sensation, like a mental tether. I could also sense that entwined with her was the pulse of something dark and serpentine, a malevolent force thrumming with chaotic energy.

Vexarath.

She sat in the back of the car, boxes all around her. Two men wearing masks were in the front, one at the wheel. The demon had selected these two, as he could still manipulate them using their masks. When Don Diego died, Vexarath cut his losses, and ran away with his new host and two men he could control.

No wonder the remaining terrorists threw down their weapons and surrendered.

I looked out the window and I seemed to recognize the terrain and the buildings we were passing, as well as the empty spaces of the road. This was odd, as I had been asleep in the car when Jyanette drove us to the resort. Then I understood it wasn't my memory I was seeing. It was Isabella's.

Then, in a shocking exchange, I felt Vexarath reach back. His malignant energy lashed against my consciousness like a tempest. I gasped, jolting in my seat as whispers of pain and malevolence scraped at the edges of my psyche. Waves of nausea rolled over me, but I fought back, steeling my mind and pushing against its grip with everything I had, desperately reestablishing my mental shields.

"What just happened?" Lauwers asked, glancing over at me, his voice tinged with alarm as I opened my eyes.

"The limousine came this way," I said, fighting to recover from the psychic onslaught.

"What?" Lauwers said. "What are you talking about?"

"The limousine used this route."

"How could you know that?"

"Let's say the limo came this way," I suggested. "What routes are nearby to get somewhere important, like LA or San Francisco?"

Lauwers frowned. "If it came out here? I thought we decided it was headed straight for the California border."

"Humor me. Are there any advantages to a route out here?"

Lauwers reflected on this for a moment. "If they went out to Route 395, that's a long stretch cutting through Nevada's eastern edge, but it's a straight shot to Los Angeles."

"How long would it take to get there?" I pressed.

"Seven hours to LA, but only 20 minutes to the California border," Lauwers shrugged, eyes narrowing as he adjusted his grip on the steering wheel.

I reached out again, carefully, and I was sure I sensed them on the road ahead.

"I think that's what they're doing. Can you speed up? I think we could catch them."

"Will you recognize it if you see it?" Lauwers asked.

I stared at him in disbelief. "How many stretch limos do you see out here?"

"With the resorts and casinos nearby, it might surprise you," he said, expertly maneuvering the vehicle and speeding up.

"Let's say I'm right. Is there any way we could stop them while they're still in Nevada?"

Lauwers grabbed his phone, his voice urgent as he kept his focus on the road ahead. "If you're right, and that's a big if, I could call and set up a roadblock."

I watched him through the corner of my eye as he dialed. I felt we were getting closer... closer...

Yet I also sensed an impending threat.

Lauwers spoke on the phone, and his voice rose, frustration coloring his words as he argued with someone at the Nevada Highway Patrol.

"I don't have a deputy to spare!" he barked, his voice laced with tension. "All the deputies in Douglas County are restoring power or — no, I'm serious — arresting terrorists! That's right, terrorists!"

He told them of the men armed with semi-automatic weapons and that he was trying to stop a limousine full of drugs.

Finally, he convinced them to send units. "Come from the east on 208 to come in and set up the roadblock at Topaz Lake, it's pretty isolated there this time of night," he instructed, glancing over at me. "I'll switch to your frequency and communicate by radio," he added before hanging up.

I spoke up. "You didn't mention the limo has diplomatic plates."

"Didn't I?" Lauwers replied with a small smirk. "Guess I overlooked that. I sure hope you're right, because if they set up that roadblock and no limousine shows up, it will not go well for me."

"Have faith, Captain," I said.

We fell into silence again, my thoughts racing as I concentrated on the limousine, my eyes searching the road ahead.

I saw the taillights just as the large vehicle turned the corner.

"There!" I said, pointing at the limousine as it headed down the road.

"Damn," Lauwers muttered, and followed the larger vehicle still far ahead of us.

The limo seemed to be aware of us, as it sped up and increased the distance, the pair of red taillights getting further and further away.

"We're compromised," I said. "They know we're here."

"Great! Just freakin' great!" Lauwers cursed, his foot smashing down harder on the accelerator. "How did they know?"

I remained silent, the truth obvious to me. As easily as I reached out to sense Isabella, Vexarath reached back to locate me.

Without waiting for a response, he flipped a switch, unleashing the flashing lights atop the vehicle. Then his siren erupted in a deafening wail, piercing the stillness of the desert night like a banshee's scream as we surged forward into the empty stretch of road.

There was no traffic, no other vehicles to worry about, just us barreling ahead in a desperate chase.

Grabbing the microphone, Lauwers shouted into it with urgency, "Highway Patrol, we are in active pursuit of a stretch limousine on Route 395, currently passing Double Spring. I request a roadblock. Get it in place, now!"

I clutched the edge of my seat, the seatbelt tight around my frame. His driving was much faster than I would have preferred.

The speedometer climbed past eighty miles per hour. It impressed me that the vehicle ahead of us carrying so much weight and length could move with such agility.

The radio sputtered, then crackled to life, a male voice cutting through the frantic energy. "Highway Patrol. Give us five minutes."

"Dammit, we might not have five minutes!" Lauwers shot back, frustration seeping into his voice as he slammed the microphone back into place.

He locked his eyes on the road ahead, fingers gripping the steering wheel so tightly that the veins in his hands stood out like strings. The distance closed between us and the limousine.

Around us was a vast and mostly empty desert landscape. Occasional ranches flitted by, and we zipped past a small casino, its bright lights a stark contrast against the surrounding darkness.

"When we catch up to that limo, I'll need you to handcuff Ms. Fontaine," I said.

"What?" Lauwers blinked, still devoting his full attention to the road. "I thought she was a victim in this situation."

"I know she seems like one, but trust me, there's something I need to do, for her own good," I replied, grasping for an explanation that would suffice. "Do you have a flashlight I could use?"

"There's a penlight in the glove box," he said.

As I opened the panel and reached in, I could see the distant flashing lights of police cars off on the horizon, a sign of our impending reinforcement.

"There's our roadblock," Lauwers announced, a grin creeping onto his face as he pointed toward the approaching scene.

I found the penlight and slipped it into my pocket.

As we drew closer, the roadblock materialized — a formidable line of police vehicles and barricades, firmly set across the highway, looming like a fortress in the vast emptiness of the desert.

Lauwers seized the microphone again, barking commands over the noise of our siren and roaring engine, his tone betraying no hint of doubt. "Prepare to box it in!"

The limousine began to slow down, the driver likely realizing that their escape was nearly at an end.

I held my breath as Lauwers eased off the accelerator. His intense gaze focused on the vehicle in front of us.

Finally, several hundred yards from the blockade, the limousine slammed on its brakes, its driver yanking the wheel sharply, swinging it sideways across the roadway, effectively blocking the road.

Lauwers reacted almost instinctively, pulling over, our tires skidding against the dirt on the side of the road. The squad car jerking to a hard stop about a hundred yards from the limousine. Dust billowed up in the moonlight, curling in the headlights before drifting into the dark.

"Ms. Fontaine is in the back," I said, my voice tight. "The terrorists are in the front."

Lauwers gave a curt nod, already reaching for his radio. He relayed the information to highway patrol, I squinted through the darkness, scanning the distant police barricade. Though too far to make out details, I couldn't see any officers standing — likely they'd already taken cover behind their vehicles, weapons trained on the limo.

"Get out and get behind the car," Lauwers ordered, his tone leaving no room for argument.

I didn't hesitate. The door groaned as I shoved it open and slid out, gasping in pain as my right knee hit the asphalt. I crawled to the back of the vehicle, each step more agony to my overused right leg. Within seconds, I was on the far side of the squad car, and I used my cane to push myself up to peer over the trunk.

Lauwers stepped out next, gripping the microphone. The instant his voice erupted through the patrol car's public address system, the night itself grew tense. "You there in the limousine! Come out with your hands up!"

For a moment, silence. A heavy, suffocating stillness.

Then the front doors of the limousine burst open.

Two figures spilled out, clad in their fatigues and tactical vests. The polished surface of their black masks caught the flashes of red and blue from the police cars, distorting their faces into eerie, shifting patterns of light. Each gripped a semi-automatic rifle with confidence.

Their movements were fluid, practiced — they were professionals.

The moonlight cast their shadows long against the pavement as they lifted their weapons.

Lauwers reacted first, ducking down an instant before the night exploded with gunfire.

A storm of bullets tore through the air, ricocheting off metal, punching through glass. Sparks leapt from the squad car as rounds struck the frame. The deafening cracks of rifle fire mingled with the frantic shouts of officers beyond the barricade.

I dropped, pressing against the car, my pulse hammering.

The assailants advanced, their footfalls barely audible beneath the commotion. They proceeded in a practiced formation, covering each other, the choreography of men who had done this before. The staccato bursts of gunfire sent plumes of dust into the air where bullets struck the pavement.

Then — an answering volley.

The police returned fire in a concentrated barrage. One gunman jerked back as a bullet struck him, his body twisting before he crumpled to the ground.

His partner didn't hesitate, emptying the rest of his magazine in Lauwers' direction before reaching to reload.

Lauwers took the opening. He rose from cover, his aim steady, his expression unreadable, his handgun in a two-handed grip.

One sharp crack — a single, precise shot.

The second man staggered. His weapon tumbled from his hands before he collapsed onto the pavement near his fallen comrade.

Stillness returned as the reverberations of this last shot echoed off the distant mountains.

Lauwers exhaled sharply. The highway patrol was already moving in from the barricade, weapons trained on the motionless gunmen. Their boots pounded against the asphalt as they secured the scene.

Lauwers and I reached the limousine first. His boot struck the rifle of the nearest man, kicking it out of reach of the terrorist's unmoving hand.

I barely noticed. My focus had shifted, my hand already hovering near the back door.

Then—

Danger…

The buzz flared sharply in my mind, like the crackle of a live wire.

I froze.

The last time I had seen Isabella Fontaine, she'd been holding a gun. If she saw me now, with that thing inside her, twisting her thoughts—

She wouldn't hesitate.

She would pull the trigger.

And this time, she wouldn't miss.

17. WITHDRAWN ASSAULT

I took a step back and glanced at Lauwers. He was crouched over the fallen man, his movements efficient. His fingers gripped the edge of the skull mask, peeling it away to reveal a pale, lifeless face beneath. He pressed two fingers against the man's neck, searching for a pulse.

A beat passed. Then another.

Lauwers exhaled sharply and shook his head. "Nothing," he murmured.

The man was dead.

"Be careful opening the back door," I warned, keeping my voice low, "Ms. Fontaine has a weapon."

Lauwers gave a small nod. He approached the vehicle, knocked twice on the tinted glass. "Ms. Fontaine? I'm Captain Lauwers. I'm with the police."

There was a brief silence.

Then, her voice — shaky but urgent. "Yes, please."

Lauwers glanced at me. I gave a slight nod, but my body remained tense.

The door swung open.

Isabella Fontaine practically tumbled out, throwing herself into Lauwers' arms. She clung to him, her body trembling, her sobs raw and unfiltered. "Thank God," she gasped, her voice breaking. "They were going to kill me. They were going to kill me."

She repeated it, over and over, the words tumbling from her in a panicked loop. Tears streaked her face, her breath coming in ragged gasps. Her entire frame shook, her grip on Lauwers desperate, as if she were afraid that letting go would send her tumbling back into the nightmare she had just escaped.

The other officers reached us — one checking the second fallen man, the other peering into the limousine. I took a step closer and glanced inside.

An automatic weapon lay discarded on the floor, its metallic sheen catching the dim glow of distant headlights. I was sure if I had opened the door, she would have used it.

But that wasn't all.

Stacked neatly beside it, nestled among boxes labeled Assorted Snacks, was the real cargo. Drugs. Packaged, and ready for transport.

I took a step closer to Isabella. She still clung to Lauwers, her back to me, her body wracked with sobs, but I didn't pay attention to that.

I focused on what was inside her, thick and dark, like an inky cloud that pulsed and shifted. I sensed that her pleading and tears were all for show, and the entity within was calculating its next move.

I caught Lauwers' eye and, keeping my movements subtle, rubbed my wrists — miming the gesture for handcuffs.

He blinked, eyes narrowing in suspicion. "Why handcuffs?" he demanded. "That's… extreme."

I didn't waver. "Because it's the only way she can truly be free," I said quietly, tension tightening my throat.

Lauwers shook his head, stepping back. "I don't care. You can't just treat her like a prisoner."

My fingers brushed against the worn parchment in my pocket, feeling the faint pulse of the Seal of Solomon. The talisman's warmth was a stark reminder of the battle ahead — an unseen war escalating inside Isabella's fragile body. The demon's grip was tightening, twisting her heart and mind.

"She's not herself," I insisted. "If you want to save her, you're going to have to trust me."

Lauwers paused, eyes flicking to Isabella, who was shivering in his arms, tears glistening on her cheeks.

Isabella's eyes locked onto Lauwers, and she saw the decision flashed hard and cold in his gaze.

Without warning, she whirled around, raising her hands in a blur. In her grip gleamed the black ritual knife, its sharp edge catching the dim light. I realized with a shock — I had completely forgotten she'd slipped it into her belt the moment she killed Diego, hidden beneath her clothes as if it were a second skin.

A scream tore from her throat, wild like a banshee's wail. "He's one of them! He wanted me captured!"

I stumbled backwards, heart hammering, as she lunged forward, swinging the blade in a deadly arc aimed right at me, slicing through the air.

Lauwers froze, shock spreading across his face for an instant, but then he moved like lightning — grabbing her wrists, yanking them up over her head. But Isabella was a wild tempest; she drove an elbow hard into his chest, knocking the air out of him as he stumbled backwards. Her strength was terrifying, fueled by the dark, furious energy of the demon inside her.

Desperation surged through me like ice. I shifted my weight, grasped my cane, and swung it like a bat — the full force landed with a sickening crack against her hands. The knife clattered to the ground, sliding across the roadway.

Her scream was raw pain and rage, "You broke my fingers!" Her voice was almost inhuman, a grotesque howl. But before she could strike again, Lauwers recovered, moving fast. His hands found her arms, prying her away, as he spun her and pulled out his cuffs.

"What are you doing?" Isabella's voice cracked, trembling, a halting mixture of fear and disbelief. The madness in her eyes flickered with something fragile beneath. "You don't understand what's happening!"

"We're not safe," I said, swallowing the lump in my throat. "None of us are — unless you're restrained."

Lauwers tightened his jaw, the weight of the moment pressing down hard on him — torn between protecting her and trusting my warning. "Ms. Fontaine, I'm sorry," he said, his voice cold as steel as he clicked the handcuffs around her wrists.

"No! No cuffs!" she shrieked, thrashing wildly against the unyielding steel. "You don't get it! It was them! Those men — they kidnapped me! And he helped them —" Her voice broke, before locking her gaze on me with blazing, furious clarity. "Are you seriously listening to him?"

Lauwers's face darkened, jaw clenched like iron. His grip tightened on her arm as he said, voice low and edged with hard skepticism, "We stopped them from dragging you across state lines because of Doctor Wise. You'll calm down once this is over."

His voice was steady, professional, but when his gaze flicked up to meet mine, it was hard.

"I told you so," was all I could manage.

"Yeah," Lauwers replied grimly, a shadow of resigned acceptance in his voice. Then his eyes flicked down, and I glanced down to see blood on my shirt. "Are you okay? You're bleeding."

I looked down and found the fabric torn, soaked with a dark red stain. My fingers trembled as I peeled open the shirt to reveal a shallow cut on my skin. "It's nothing," I muttered, though the ache beneath whispered otherwise.

"There's a medical kit under the passenger seat of my car," Lauwers said. "Why don't you take Ms. Fontaine to the car and get it?"

I nodded silently, eyes never leaving Isabella's haunted, restless form. "Ms. Fontaine," I said softly. "I can help you."

Isabella bared her teeth, suddenly lunging forward despite the cuffs locking tight. "You're wrong! He's one of them!" Her voice cracked, raw with terror and betrayal. "If you trust him, you're as much a part of this as those men!"

Lauwers looked between Isabella and me, doubt flickering in his eyes. His free hand hovered near his weapon, as if unsure whether this was a rescue or an arrest.

"Stop it!" I barked, taking her arm. Sweat dotted my forehead as I felt the demon reaching out, trying to influence Lauwers. "I'm the only thing standing between you and losing yourself."

She shook her head, tears streaming down her pale cheeks, voice barely a whisper now. "I don't know what's real anymore… but I know you're lying."

Lauwers visibly flinched, and I was afraid Vexarath was affecting him, influencing him, but he spoke up. "I don't think Doctor Wise was part of kidnapping you," he muttered, the conflict raging in his expression as he released her to me. "But whatever this is, I want this over — fast."

I tightened my grip on Isabella's arm, nodding toward the car. "Fine. Just let me be alone with her in your car. Her in the back me in the front."

Lauwers hesitated, then gave a stiff nod. "I'll give you the time you need. But as soon as we've examined the car, I want to release her."

Her body slammed against me one last time, a primal scream tearing from her throat. "You're making a mistake!" she warned. "If you don't stop now, there won't be anything left of me — or you."

I kept moving, pulling her along, brought her to the car, and pulled open the rear door.

Isabella yanked her arm from my grip and took a step back. "I am not going in there," she said, her voice teetering on the edge of control.

"You are going in there," I said, my voice low, unyielding. "Or I'm picking you up and putting you in there."

For a moment, I thought she might run. Her breath came fast, her body taut like a coiled spring. Then something changed.

Her face — those delicate features — contorted in a heartbeat. Her eyes darkened, her skin rippling like liquid shadow. A grotesque transformation overtook her: her jaw stretched unnaturally, her mouth curling back to reveal jagged teeth. Sharp, ridged horns pushed through the dark waves of her hair, twisting upward like gnarled roots.

Her voice, no longer her own, rumbled from deep within. "Release me." The words were guttural, an ancient rasp, vibrating with something other than her voice.

Then — just as suddenly — it was gone. The horns, the jagged teeth, the monstrous visage all melted away, leaving only Isabella standing there. A beautiful woman. A hostage.

If I hadn't seen it with my own eyes, I might have thought I imagined it.

The sudden shift still dazed her; her breath was uneven. Taking advantage of the moment, I shoved her inside the car, forcing her legs in and slamming the door before she could resist.

The real battle was only just beginning.

I threw a quick glance toward Lauwers and the other officers. They were still busy with the limousine, securing the scene, their focus locked on the two dead men and the stockpile of drugs hidden within. None of them had noticed.

Good.

I slid into the passenger seat, yanking the door shut behind me. It wasn't much privacy, but it would have to do. I reached under the seat, found the medical kit, and quickly put salve and a bandage on my wound. I had been lucky, it had just grazed me. If I hadn't moved back when I did, I would have needed an ambulance.

As I finished and put the kit away, a low, gravelly voice hissed from the back seat of the police cruiser, thick with a malevolence that crawled under my skin like icy fingers. "I'll kill you."

"I'm sure you'll try," I said, my tone flat, detached. From beneath my coat, I pulled a fragile parchment, its edges worn; in the other hand, a borrowed penlight.

I flicked the tiny beam across the ancient paper, and the intricate Seal of Solomon blossomed into view — the ornate design inked in symbols older than memory.

A rancid hiss slithered through the cramped space, the stench of sulfur overwhelming the stale scent of the car's vinyl seats.

Isabella — or rather, the malevolent force imprisoned within her — recoiled violently, as if struck by invisible blows.

"No — stop! It burns!" Her voice cracked menacingly, torn between the brittle whisper of Isabella and the monstrous growl lurking beneath.

"You are bound," I intoned, voice steady, fingers gripping the parchment as I prepared to reclaim her soul. "Release Isabella."

The creature snarled, the voice twisting deeper, darker. "She belongs to me now. Forever."

I swallowed the panic I felt, inhaled slow and even. The ancient ritual was the only light against this darkness.

"I conjure thee, O Creature of the Flame and Shadow," I intoned, the words heavy with power and pain, words I'd uttered before — words that banished horrors even worse than this.

Suddenly, a violent shudder wracked Isabella's slender frame. Her eyes seized wide, irises devoured by endless blackness as if the abyss itself gazed back. She thrashed, wrists cuffed tight, a puppet fighting against invisible strings.

"No!" The entity's roar was a soundless scream, a raw, guttural promise of violence. "I will hunt you down to the very end of existence!"

My voice rose to meet the fury, cutting like a blade through the darkness. "Be ye accursed, damned, and eternally reproved." Every word burned with the fire of ancient wrath.

The car lurched violently, a monstrous force ramming and clawing from within, shaking the cramped metal cage like a beast hell-bent on destruction.

"NO!" The demon's fury crescendoed, raw and panicked.

"By the three principles — Alef, Mem, Shin — I command you, Vexarath, release this vessel and be cast back into the void!"

The air inside the car crackled with unnatural energy. Flashes of shadow and light danced wildly across the cracked windshield, illuminating the interior in grotesque bursts that painted her twisted features with nightmarish clarity.

Isabella's spine arched unnaturally, her mouth parting in a mute scream that stretched the air into something suffocating and monstrous. The silence howled louder than any scream, a dark void that pressed into my soul.

From her open mouth issued a vile, inky black smoke like a living shadow unleashed from the depths of hell itself. The air even where I sat grew heavy and acrid, choking the breath from my lungs as that demonic essence clawed its way back to its true, terrifying form.

It slithered and roiled, a writhing mass of darkness pressing against the cold plexiglass partition that separated us from the cramped confines of the police car's backseat.

The smoke thickened rapidly, an unnatural fog crawling like a sinister plague through the confined space behind the barrier. It pulsated with malevolent life, tangible and suffocating, swallowing all light and hope.

My heart hammered as I stared, straining to see — anything recognizable — but Isabella was gone, vanished behind that black fog.

Only the oppressive blackness remained, alive and waiting, as if the demon had never inhabited a human shell but was now reclaiming the nightmare it was meant to be.

The vehicle jolted again, harder — metal groaning in protest — as if some titanic, unseen force fought to shred existence itself just to hold on.

"I cast you, Vexarath, into the deepest Abyss, beyond time, beyond mercy!"

With one final, bone-rattling shudder, the nightmare broke.

Silence fell like a heavy shroud.

The thick, choking darkness that had swallowed the back of the car thinned, retreating as if some unseen force was violently dragging it out from the very air itself.

Slowly, the shadows peeled away like night dissolving in the dawn, revealing Isabella slumped against the worn seat. Her body was unnaturally still, collapsed and twisted as if drained of every ounce of strength.

She trembled violently, every shiver wracking her fragile frame like a leaf caught in a storm. Cold sweat clung to her skin, slick and clammy, pooling at the hollow of her neck and soaking through her clothes. Her breath came in short, ragged gasps, desperate and broken, like a drowning woman hauled up from the depths, choking on air that refused to fill her lungs.

The silence in the car pressed in around us, thick and suffocating, broken only by the wet, rasping noise of her struggling breath — the sound of a nightmare refusing to release its grasp.

Her head lifted slowly, and the darkness that had enveloped Isabella's eyes was now gone, leaving behind the fragile glow of human light, dull and flickering but unmistakably hers.

Tears carved silent trails down pale cheeks. "I… I couldn't get free," she whispered, voice shattered and raw, a haunted prayer swallowed by the dark. "I couldn't get free," she repeated, a broken mantra that echoed in the shadows of the night.

My passenger door flew open.

Lauwers stood there, breathing hard, his face tight with confusion and frustration. "What the hell is going on?"

I needed to catch my breath. "Had some trouble with the penlight," I said, slipping the parchment back into my pocket.

Lauwers shot me a look. "Are you kidding? It looked like you were setting off fireworks inside my car!" He put his attention on Isabella, concern tightening his expression. "Are you alright, Ms. Fontaine?"

Isabella swallowed hard and sat up straighter. "Y-yes," she said, her voice shaky but regaining strength. "I think so."

I met Lauwers' eyes. "You can take the cuffs off now, Captain."

He hesitated, his gaze shifting between me and Isabella, but after a moment, he pulled the keys from his belt and opened the back door. He reached for Isabella's wrists, unlocking the restraints.

She was unsteady as she stepped out onto the pavement, rubbing her wrists where the metal had bitten into her skin.

"Will you be okay here with Doctor Wise?" Lauwers asked, still observing her and casting a nasty look at me.

She nodded. "Yes. Thank you."

She eased herself back onto the seat, with her feet planted on the pavement, shoulders slumped, staring up at me with the back door open.

I looked at her — really looked at her. Any trace of the polished, elegant woman I had first seen in my vision was gone. Her face was bare, vulnerable. She looked so young.

And completely human.

The air around us felt different now — lighter, cleaner. An oppressive weight that had hung over Isabella like a shroud had lifted.

She rubbed her arms, as if trying to shake off a lingering chill. Then, after a long, shuddering breath, she looked up at me.

"I wasn't me," she said, a tone of awe in her voice. "I had all these plans rush through my mind. Get to LA, make a sale, get back to my compound, create more followers." She met my eyes. "But none of that was me. It was like I'd become him, become the man I killed. How is that possible?"

"A force possessed him, worked with him, a parasite," I explained. "When you killed him, it took you."

She frowned. "You could see it, couldn't you?"

I nodded.

"How did you…" she started, then hesitated. "I mean… how did you do what you just did?"

Her voice was raw, edged with something fragile, filled with fear.

I met her gaze, steady and unflinching. "I've dealt with possessed people before," I said simply.

Her expression flickered, like she was trying to make sense of something impossible. "Possessed," she repeated, rolling the word over as if testing its weight. Then she nodded, a slow, hesitant movement. "That's what it was."

She pressed a trembling hand to her temple. "I felt… powerful. Invincible. But … it wasn't really me." Her voice dropped to a whisper. "I can't even explain it. It was like I was watching from somewhere far away, like my body wasn't mine anymore."

"It was the entity," I said finally. "The same one that gave Don Diego his power."

A shadow passed over her face. "You told me not to agree. Not to let it in." She closed her eyes, shaking her head as the memory surfaced. "But I wanted to kill him so badly... I wanted it more than anything. And then, suddenly, it was inside me."

Regret bled through her voice, laced with exhaustion and something deeper — shame.

"How do you feel now?" I asked gently.

She swallowed hard. For a moment, she didn't answer. Then her shoulders slumped, and the tears came, silent at first, trailing down her face. She wiped at them hastily, as if embarrassed, but they wouldn't stop.

"I feel like..." Her voice caught. "I feel like I want to see my father."

We were there for hours. The coroner and the forensic team took forever to arrive. While the Medical Examiner methodically documented the scene, while the Crime Scene Investigators snapped endless photographs, measuring distances, marking bullet casings, and murmuring among themselves in hushed, procedural tones.

Then came the wait for the tow truck. I never understood why they couldn't just drive the damn limousine away. The engine still worked, didn't it?

But protocol was protocol. After gathering the evidence, the Highway Patrol officers rolled the vehicle out of the middle of the road, pushing it to the side like an oversized carcass.

Isabella climbed fully into the patrol car, curled up on the back seat, and shut the door. She didn't say a word — just lay down, her head resting against the hard vinyl, and within minutes, she was asleep.

I fought my exhaustion for a while, leaning my head back, watching the occasional flicker of headlights sweep across the night. But eventually, sleep pulled me under, dragging me into restless dreams laced with shadows and echoes of the voice that had come from Isabella's throat.

I only stirred when the car rocked slightly. Lauwers had gotten in, the rustling of his jacket and the creak of the seat signaling our departure. As the patrol car rumbled down the road, I let myself drift in and out of consciousness, my mind balancing on the thin line between awareness and sleep.

When the car finally came to a stop, Lauwers shook me gently.

I blinked, groggy, and lifted my head. A sliver of pale light broke through the Eastern sky, stretching thin against the horizon: the first whisper of dawn.

Glancing out the window, I recognized the building immediately. The townhouse. The same one Isabella had been staying in before the men with masks abducted her.

I got out, relying on my cane to get me on my feet and keep me there. The night's events had caught up with me — my body ached, my mind felt sluggish, and my knee throbbed. But I forced myself to focus.

Several unmarked vans lined the street in front of the townhouse. Armed men in full tactical gear stood at attention, their weapons at the ready, their eyes scanning the area. My pulse jumped slightly — until I noticed the illuminated FBI lettering emblazoned across their vests.

Lauwers and I flanked Isabella as we approached the front door. She walked stiffly, as if moving required every ounce of strength she had left. Upon entering we encountered silence; only the low hum of conversation from the next room reached us.

Then, as we entered the main area, a dozen sets of eyes focused on us.

A tall man in his fifties with dark hair and a mustache pushed past the agents, and went to Isabella with words of *"Mi ángel. Mi pequeño."*

My angel. My little one.

"P-Papa," Isabella moaned, and flung herself into his arms, a fresh burst of tears in her eyes. And her father held her, weeping as well.

Agent Roberts stood with Commander Gurelle, along with two of his agents, their expressions unreadable. But my gaze locked onto the couch — where two people sat side by side.

Agent Marcus Calvin sat next to my wife. She looked worn and scared, and I was actually glad that Marcus was there to help her. My jealousy had been stupid, and if he helped her get through any of this night, I was grateful to him.

Jyanette saw me and shot to her feet. And then she was in my arms.

She collided with me so hard I nearly stumbled, her arms winding around me like she never wanted to let go. I felt the dampness of her tears soaking into my shirt, her breath hitching against my shoulder.

I felt tears in my own eyes as I held her just as tightly, letting my forehead rest against hers.

"I was afraid I was going to lose you," I whispered.

"Not a chance," she whispered back.

"I have some questions…" Agent Roberts started, stepping toward us, his eyes unreadable.

Lauwers cut him off with a shake of his head. "Later for that. You can question them tomorrow. Right now, I'm taking them back to the main hotel."

Roberts looked like he wanted to argue. His jaw tightened, his shoulders squared — but then he met Lauwers' gaze. Whatever he saw there was enough to make him rethink his approach. He exhaled through his nose, muttering something under his breath, but ultimately, he gave a small nod and backed off.

Lauwers wasted no time. Without another word, he ushered us toward the car.

The ride back to the main building was quiet. The weight of the night sat heavy on all of us. Outside the car windows, the first hints of morning light stretched across the sky, a cold, pale blue creeping in at the edges of the darkness.

By the time we pulled up to the main building, the resort had come back to life — at least in small ways. They had restored the power and light spilled from the windows, casting long golden streaks across the pavement. Shadows of movement flickered inside — staff members trying to restore some semblance of normalcy after everything that had happened.

Jyanette and I held onto each other as we made our way through the lobby. The place remained in shambles — with overturned furniture, broken glass, and signs of a struggle still uncleared. But none of that mattered. Right now, the only thing keeping us upright was each other.

Only one elevator was operational. An armed FBI agent stood inside, his expression unreadable, his posture rigid. He didn't speak as we stepped in, just pressed the button for our floor at our request and stood silently as we ascended.

We stumbled into our room, the weight of exhaustion pressing down on us like an avalanche. The door clicked shut behind us, locking out the rest of the world.

Jyanette turned the shower on, and steam quickly curled into the air, thick and warm.

Throwing off our clothes, we stepped in, allowing the water to rush over us, washing away the dirt, the sweat, the lingering stench of fear.

For a long moment, we simply stood there, the heat soaking into our bruised bodies, easing the tension from our muscles. I ran my hands over her skin, tracing the injured or bruised places, reminding myself that she was here. Alive!

Safe.

She did the same for me, fingers moving gently over my bruises, over the scars both fresh and old.

I dried her and she dried me, our motions slow and tender, as if we were afraid we might break each other.

And then we fell into bed.

Jyanette curled against me, her breath warm against my skin. Her fingers slid over my chest, tracing soft, barely there patterns.

"Love me, Len," she whispered, her voice fragile and raw, carrying the weight of everything we had endured.

"My leg," I said, and she looked at how bruised and swollen it was.

"Then you just lie there," she said.

I cupped her face, pressing her lips to mine — soft at first, then deeper, more urgent.

She lay atop me and bodies became one slowly, carefully, as if rediscovering each other after a long separation. There was no rush, no desperation — only a deep, aching need for connection. For reassurance.

The night had left us battered and bruised, but in each other's arms, we found solace.

There were sighs, moans, and even tears — grief and relief tangled together in a wordless confession of love and survival.

When it was over, with our bodies spent and the exhaustion finally taking hold, we lay wrapped together, our breathing slow and steady, our hearts beating in sync.

Sleep pulled us under.

And for the first time in what felt like forever, I didn't dream of darkness.

18. EBBING ANSWERS

An insistent knocking jolted Jyanette and me awake. A quick glance at the clock told me it was just past one in the afternoon. Considering we'd only crawled into bed at dawn, neither of us had gotten nearly enough sleep.

Groggy and disoriented, I pushed myself up, wincing as my stiff muscles protested the movement. My knee was twice the size it should have been, and only my cane kept me upright.

I grabbed one of the hotel robes and stumbled toward the door.

The brightness of the hallway was blinding as I squinted at the two figures standing before me — Marcus and Roberts.

"Hey, Len, sorry for disturbing you," Marcus said with a sheepish expression, his tone apologetic.

"What's up?" I muttered, shielding my eyes from the light and barely stifling a yawn.

"We need to get you and Jyanette on record about yesterday," Marcus explained. "May we come in?"

I groaned, stepping aside to let them enter. Roberts scanned the room like a man hunting for incriminating evidence. It was a habit of his, one that made my skin crawl.

"Give me a few minutes to get dressed," I said, heading back to the bedroom.

Jyanette was already up, pulling on a pair of jeans and a fitted sweater. Her hair was a tousled mess, and she still looked half-asleep as she peered at me. "Let me guess — Marcus and Agent Roberts?"

"Who else would bother us?" I replied.

She groaned. "God, I was hoping we'd at least get to sleep in."

It took me a few minutes to get ready, and by the time I emerged, Jyanette had set up the hotel coffeemaker, brewing two cups of much-needed caffeine.

I decided our uninvited guests could fend for themselves.

Sitting side by side on the sofa, steaming mugs in hand, we faced the two agents. Marcus seemed a little uneasy. Roberts sat on the edge of his chair like a coiled spring.

"So, what do you want to know?" I asked, taking a slow sip of my coffee.

Marcus barely had time to open his mouth before Roberts cut in. "How did you know we were going on a wild goose chase when we left?"

I arched an eyebrow. "The spirits whispered it in my ear."

"Don't get cute with me, Wise," Roberts snapped, his voice rising. "You're involved in all of this, and I don't know how yet."

Jyanette's voice was sharp as a blade. "Len saved lives. If it weren't for him, a lot of the guests of this resort would be dead right now."

Marcus cleared his throat. "We've spoken to guests and the hotel manager. They confirmed you got them out of the ballroom and to safety."

"Yeah," Roberts sneered, "and they also mentioned you were wearing one of those masks — like the terrorists."

I met his gaze without flinching. "I used it as a disguise so I could move about freely."

Roberts pushed to his feet, pacing like a restless predator. "Really? Then explain why Captain Lauwers said you insisted on going with him and that you did something to Ms. Fontaine in a police car."

"She was in the back seat and I was in the front," I said. "All I did was calm her down."

Roberts glared at us, anger in his eyes. "I want a full report on every action you've taken since we left."

I let out a short, humorless laugh. "No."

His jaw tightened. "What?"

"I'm a private citizen. I don't work for you, and I don't work for the Bureau," I said, my voice edged with steel. "I did what I could to help, and you ignored my advice at every turn. Go file your own damn report, Agent Roberts, and leave me out of it."

Roberts jabbed a finger in my face. "You're involved, Wise."

"Yes, and I almost got killed," I said evenly.

Marcus glanced between us, then sighed. "I think we should leave, sir."

"That's the first good suggestion I've heard," Jyanette said.

Roberts still had more to say. "Wise, I'm going to look into you so hard you'll think you're getting an exam from a proctologist."

I shook my head. "Makes sense, since you're an asshole."

Fuming, Roberts spun on his heel and stormed toward the door. Marcus hesitated for a beat, shooting me and Jyanette a look of pity before following him out. The door slammed shut behind them, and the room fell into silence.

Jyanette shook her head. "You do have a way with people…"

"So do you," I said, still fuming. "I was tired of that jackass pushing us around."

Jyanette, lounging on the sofa with her arms crossed, watched me with a knowing look. "I agree. But, Roberts made bad choices, and now he's scrambling for someone to blame."

I scoffed. "Sorry, I'm out of patience with him."

She broke into a mischievous smile. "Well, you getting all masculine and protective? That turns me on."

I looked at her, surprised. "Really?"

She stood, offering her hand to help me get up. "Let me show you," she murmured, leading me toward the bedroom. "Honeymoon, remember?"

Hours later, after making love and sinking into a deep, dreamless sleep, we woke to the soft glow of the setting sun creeping through the hotel curtains. We took our time getting dressed, the weight of the past day still clinging to us like an unseen shadow.

By the time we made our way down to the lobby, it was night and the hotel had undergone a remarkable transformation.

Workers scrubbed away the destruction from the attack — at least on the surface. The floors gleamed, the shattered glass was gone, and the faint traces of industrial cleaner had replaced the lingering scent of smoke.

But the walls and ceiling still bore scars — bullet holes pockmarked the plaster, and a few splintered columns stood as silent witnesses to the night's violence.

Behind the front desk was Mr. Jenkins, looking better than the last time I saw him — upright, composed, and far removed from the man who had faced down Don Diego with quiet defiance. As soon as he spotted us, his expression brightened.

"Dr. and Mrs. Wise," he said warmly, coming around the desk to shake my hand with both of his. "I can't tell you how grateful I am for what you did. If it hadn't been for you—"

I smiled. "I should thank you, Mr. Jenkins. You have more courage than almost anyone I've ever met. You stood up to Don Diego, and you took charge of the hostages escaping—"

He flushed red, embarrassed by my compliment.

"Was anyone seriously hurt?" I asked, needing to know.

His smile faded slightly. "Thankfully, none of the guests. But a few of us — including me — had a trip to the hospital."

"Are you all right?" Jyanette asked.

"Fit as a fiddle," he said and indicated the gauze bandage on his head. "My head required several stitches, but I got a chance to sleep,"

"What about Ken Hastings and his wife? Do you know if they're alright?"

"They're both fine," Jenkins assured me. "He also went to the hospital, no internal organ injured from that blow to his stomach. He's back at the hotel now."

Jyanette's stomach growled softly. "What's the food situation?"

Jenkins smiled. "We've set up a buffet in the ballroom. With all the police and emergency personnel it seemed the best thing to do until we get everything back to normal. But it should do the trick. Please, go in and help yourselves."

Hand in hand, Jyanette and I stepped inside. What happened next caught me completely off guard.

The moment we entered the ballroom, conversations stilled, and heads rotated in our direction. The silence made both of us stop walking.

At first, there was a smattering of applause — one or two people rising to their feet, clapping hesitantly.

But then, like a ripple spreading across a still pond, more and more guests stood, their applause swelling into a wave of gratitude that filled the vast room.

Jyanette and I stood frozen, caught in the unexpected moment. The sound of clapping grew louder, echoing off the walls, until it became an overwhelming roar. Faces — some familiar, some strangers — faced us with gratitude, admiration, even awe.

I wasn't sure what to do. Should I nod? Bow? Say something? Instead, I just stood there, stunned, my fingers tightening around Jyanette's as I felt the weight of what we had done settle over me in a way it hadn't before.

We had saved these people.

Not because we had to. Not because we were heroes. But because, in that moment of crisis, it had been the right thing to do.

A warm squeeze on my hand brought me back. Jyanette, ever composed, leaned in slightly. "Just smile and wave," she whispered, her eyes shimmering with unshed emotion.

So, I did.

As we made our way toward the buffet, people stepped forward to shake our hands, to offer their thanks. Some clasped my shoulder, others embraced Jyanette, murmuring words of gratitude, their voices thick with emotion.

"You saved my wife — thank you."

"I don't know what would've happened if you weren't there."

"God bless you both."

It was humbling. Overwhelming.

I met every gaze, accepted every handshake, returned every tight, grateful smile.

And for the first time since that long, harrowing night... I felt that maybe we had done something that truly mattered.

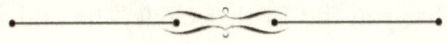

I wanted to head home the next day, eager to put the nightmare behind us and return to some semblance of normalcy. But my new wife had other plans.

"With all the attention focused here," Jyanette reasoned, "this is probably the safest place to be in the entire country right now. Besides, you need time to recover. And," she added with a grin, "we never got our spa day."

I could argue about many things, but not with her logic. Or her stubborn streak.

By the second day, the resort had returned to life. Guests trickled back to the pool and the beach, laughter and clinking glasses filling the air once more. Restaurants reopened, the scent of grilled seafood and tropical cocktails mingling with the breeze.

Work crews arrived early each morning, setting up scaffolding, patching bullet holes, and repairing shattered glass. It was strange how quickly the world went on, how efficiently people swept away the scars of violence to return to comfort.

By the third day, things were mostly back to normal — though guests still approached us, some with gratitude, some with curiosity. I was especially relieved to see Ken Hastings and his wife again, both in fair shape, though Ken still sported a spectacular black eye.

We had dinner together that evening, and Ken — never one to leave a mystery alone — leaned in, lowering his voice conspiratorially.

"Tell me what you did in that circle," he said, eyes gleaming with intrigue. "What made what's-his-name lose his damn mind like that?"

I took a sip of my drink, keeping my expression neutral. "It was the FBI," I said. "The flash-bangs, the smoke. I just got lucky with the timing."

Ken chuckled, shaking his head. "I don't know, Len. You got awful lucky that night."

And he wasn't wrong. I had gotten lucky. In more ways than one.

News crews swarmed the resort, reporters setting up cameras and staking out every angle of the attack. They phoned our room relentlessly, and when we ignored those calls, leaving the phone off the hook, they found our cell phone numbers.

The reporters went digging into my background, some even unearthing details of my cases in New Jersey.

They wanted an interview, a statement — anything.

My answer was always the same: "No comment."

Jyanette and I finally got our spa day, and as I lay face-down on the massage table, the masseuse took one look at me and let out a low whistle.

"Damn," she muttered. "You got beat up real bad. Is there anywhere I can work that won't hurt?"

Surprisingly, the massage helped, kneading away the stiffness and the tension in my body. By the next day, I felt a little more like myself again and could walk without the cane if I wanted.

Jyanette was right. Staying had been the better choice.

Finally, the day came for us to return to New Jersey. As we made our way to the front desk to settle the bill, the staff bustled about, back to their usual routine. Mr. Jenkins stepped out to greet us, a warm smile on his face.

"Someone has taken care of your bill," he said, sliding the paperwork away. "Even your spa day. We won't charge either of your parents. Someone has paid for your entire stay."

"Who did that?" I asked.

"Ambassador Fontaine."

Jyanette and I exchanged a look of surprise.

"Isabella's father?" I said.

"Yes," Mr. Jenkins said. "However, let me tell you, if he hadn't done it, I would've paid for your stay out of my own pocket."

I hesitated, then reached out to shake his hand. "Thank you," I said, meaning it more than I could express.

"Come back anytime," he said. "You will always be welcome here."

With that, we headed for the airport, returned the rental car, and boarded our flight home.

Back to New Jersey. Back to reality.

There would be no masked gunmen or hostage crises, but I knew better than to think life would be quiet for long.

Something would happen. It always did.

Trouble had a way of finding me, whether I wanted it to or not.

EPILOGUE

T he car service pulled up to the familiar stone house in Mountainview, the tires crunching on the gravel circular driveway.

It had been over three weeks since we'd last set foot here, and it felt like an eternity.

The house stood just as we had left it — solid, warm, welcoming — its hand-cut stonework and dark-beige siding bathed in the golden light of late afternoon. The large windows gleamed, reflecting the rustling trees that framed our home.

Hand in hand, Jyanette and I made our way in our private entrance, taking in the comforting scent of pine and earth. As soon as we stepped inside, a knock echoed through the foyer.

Before I could take a single step toward the door, it swung open, and Mrs. Higgins burst in, her face a mix of relief and overwhelming emotion.

"I haven't seen ye since the wedding," she exclaimed, her voice thick. "And I heard about what happened on the news." Without warning, she pulled me into a hug, her grip far stronger than her compact frame suggested.

"Oh," I gasped, wincing as she squeezed my bruised ribs. "We're fine, Mrs. Higgins, but — maybe go easy?"

She released me immediately, her eyes wide with remorse. "Oh, I'm so sorry, Doctor. I'm just glad ye made it through in one piece."

She went to Jyanette, who welcomed her embrace with a laugh. Mrs. Higgins stepped back and held her at arm's length, giving her a once-over as if to reassure herself that she was truly unharmed.

"Look at ye both," she said, shaking her head with an affectionate smile. "A proper married couple ye are now."

I grinned, wrapping an arm around Jyanette's waist. But as Mrs. Higgins studied us, her smile faltered slightly, replaced by something more pensive, something unreadable.

"What is it?" Jyanette asked, chuckling.

"No, not at all," Mrs. Higgins replied, but her expression remained serious. "Ye two get settled first, and then, dear, would ye come see me in the kitchen?"

"Um — sure, Margery."

With a last nod, Mrs. Higgins disappeared down the hall, leaving us in silence.

Jyanette raised an eyebrow. "Okay... is it just me, or was Margery acting a little weird?"

"Hard to say," I admitted. "But you know, Mrs. Higgins is probably a better psychic than I am, so I'd take her seriously."

"I always take that woman seriously, Len."

We spent the next half hour unpacking, hanging clothes in the closet and tossing others into the hamper. The sheer amount of laundry we'd accumulated over the past weeks made me groan.

"I swear, if I see another hotel laundry bag, I'm going to lose it," I muttered.

Jyanette laughed, kissing my cheek before heading toward the door. "I'd better go see what Margery wants before she comes back to drag me there herself."

I busied myself checking my phone and setting up my laptop, just as there was a sound at the house's front door.

I made my way down the long, polished hallway that connected our private wing to the heart of the house. The soft hum of voices and the faint clatter of footsteps grew louder as I approached the front door, where Jyanette and Mrs. Higgins stood side by side, warmly welcoming guests inside.

Just then, Bill McGee and his wife Laura crossed the threshold, their faces bright. Close behind them was Anna Sokolov, her presence adding a youthful touch to the gathering.

I caught Jyanette's eye and felt a jolt of curiosity. Her expression was unusual—something flickered in her gaze, a strange mix of anticipation and tension I couldn't quite place. What secret had Margery whispered to her that left her like that?

Before I could dwell on it further, Bill spotted me and closed the distance in an instant. With a booming laugh, he swept me into a bear hug, his hand thudding heavily against my back.

All three carried vibrant, colorful gift bags that seemed to burst with promise, their smiles wide and infectious — a perfect prelude to the excitement filling the room.

"Surprise!" Bill exclaimed, stepping back with an enthusiastic grin. He was my height and broad shouldered, a contrast to Laurie who was a tall, thin brunette. "We couldn't let you two start your married life without a proper celebration!"

"Ooh, let me open some champagne," Mrs. Higgins said, running off to the kitchen.

Jyanette smiled. "This is such a lovely surprise!"

Laura looked us over, her eyes sparkling with excitement. "You don't seem to be too badly wounded for once."

"For once," Jyanette agreed. "Though we have a few bumps and bruises."

Anna stood slightly behind them, her expression a mix of joy and shyness. Her blond hair was in a pageboy cut, and she wore a simple dress. "I hope it's okay that I came too."

"I thought you wouldn't mind," Bill said. "So we gave her a ride."

"Of course, Anna," I said, looking at the bag she carried. "But you didn't have to buy us anything."

"I got my first paycheck as your new Teaching Assistant," she announced, which drew cheers from everyone. "And I finally figured out the computer this week."

"I knew you could do it," I said, my voice filled with pride.

Mrs. Higgins came out with a tray with six glasses on it. Four had a lighter colored amber liquid and two held a darker color bubbly drink.

"Champagne, and sparkling apple juice," Mrs. Higgins announced.

We all went into the living room and sat.

Anna looked at the tray as she sat in one recliner. "I guess one sparkling apple juice is for me,"

"You're not driving," Bill said. "And I won't report you."

Anna glanced at me. "Is it all right?"

"Please," I said, and we each took a glass. I took the apple juice and, to my surprise, Jyanette took the other. There was a toast, and we all took a sip.

Bill and Laura exchanged knowing glances before Bill spoke again. "We wanted to give you something personal, something that reflects your journey together." He reached into one of the gift bags and pulled out a photo in a silver frame. "I had your brother send me the photo from the wedding, and we had it framed."

"We haven't even seen them yet," Jyanette said, excited.

It was a great shot of Jyanette in her wedding dress and me in my tux. Both of us looked thrilled.

Laura chimed in, "And we also brought something for your future adventures." She handed Jyanette a beautifully crafted leather journal. "It's for you to document your experiences together — all the ups and downs, the joys and challenges."

Jyanette's eyes lit up as she accepted the journal. "I love it! I can't wait to fill it."

Finally, Anna stepped forward, holding out a small box wrapped in simple brown paper. "I wanted to give you something special," she said, her cheeks slightly flushed. When Jyanette opened it, she found a delicate silver bracelet adorned with charms representing love and friendship.

"It's lovely, Anna! Thank you so much!" Jyanette said and rose to pull Anna into a warm embrace.

As we settled in the living room, laughter and conversation flowed easily among us. I told them what had happened at the hotel, and how we had narrowly avoided a disaster.

As I recounted our adventure, Mrs. Higgins whispered in Jyanette's ear and the two of them left the room.

As I was finishing up, Mrs. Higgins brought in Jyanette, and for a moment, I felt alarmed. Jyanette's face was pale, her eyes wet, her expression unreadable.

"Everything all right?" I asked, as all of us turned to face them.

"Um… y-yes, I guess," Jyanette stammered, but there was something in her voice that said otherwise.

Bill rose. "Is anything wrong?"

Mrs. Higgins reached out, placing a reassuring hand over Jyanette's. "Tell them, dear."

"Tell us what?" I said.

"Well, it's nothing bad, y'see," Mrs. Higgins said and shook her head. "It's just… I had a feelin'. So before you got home, I made a wee purchase."

Jyanette hesitated before reaching into her pocket and holding out a small plastic stick.

I took it, puzzled. It was a simple flat white plastic rod with two very clear pink lines at one end.

I stood, feeling as if I were floating, my mind trying to understand what I was seeing. "Is that… what I think it is?"

Jyanette's face glowed with delight. "Yes. It's a pregnancy test. And it's positive."

I stared at it, then back at her. "But the doctors said you couldn't—"

"It appears they were wrong, Mr. Wise," she whispered, a single tear slipping down her cheek.

The room exploded with cries of "Congratulations!" and excited screams from both Laura and Anna, who ran to Jyanette and hugged her.

Bill grabbed my shoulders and said with his big booming voice, "Len, you're going to be a father!"

I was speechless, my throat tight with something I had never felt before — something bigger than joy, bigger than shock. It was awe.

The women released Jyanette, and she folded into my arms, and we held each other, our tears mixing as Mrs. Higgins giggled beside us, Anna clapped her hands, and Laura was crying as well.

This was a miracle. A life we had never expected, never dared to hope for.

Yet a chill hummed beneath the surface, a sinister whisper crawling at the back of my mind. Something broken lurking within this miracle. Something I could not yet see.

Imperfect...

FREE PREVIEW

IMPERFECT IN THE MIND

DOCTOR WISE BOOK 14

ARJAY LEWIS

MIND
BENDER
PRESS

PREVIEW

T he room was sealed tight — no sound could penetrate, no light could seep in. Frank opened his eyes once more to the oppressive void of utter darkness. But even this crushing blackness was his only refuge, the thin veil between him and the constant torment he endured all day, every day.

How long had his captor held him here? Time had lost all meaning; it stretched and frayed into an endless nightmare.

It felt like an eternity, but something deep inside whispered it couldn't be more than a week… no, maybe just a few days.

He pulled the threadbare blanket tighter around his thin frame. He'd lost so much weight, even though they fed him regularly — meals as hollow as his will to live.

It was the machines. Those infernal devices, siphoning away his very soul, grinding him down piece by piece until only emptiness remained.

A sudden click echoed through the stillness — he gasped as a switch flipped outside his enclosure. A harsh, electric flash illuminated the chamber as the machines roared to life.

Overhead, the fluorescent lights flickered on, casting sickly shadows that danced across the walls. The shrill hum of the radionic devices filled the air, a sinister symphony of twisted science and dark obsession.

He could see now, his eyes slowly adjusting to the dim light. The walls, cold and lined with polished black wood panels, seemed to absorb every stray bit of light, focusing all attention on the labyrinthine machinery. The air reeked of ozone and something ancient— like the scent of burnt parchment mixed with a sharp tang of metal. A blend of occult mystery and ruthless technology.

Dominating one side of the room behind a thick plexiglass panel scarred with arcane scratches, stood a massive workbench, cluttered with an array of radionic systems. Antiquated, gleaming brass boxes with faded analog dials and sliding plates were among them. Other devices were sleek and modern, boasting digital readouts that flickered like ghostly eyes.

The Scientist had entwined each machine with bundles of cables in twisted, chaotic arrays, connecting oscillators, amplifiers, and smooth input slates — etched with strange symbols that seemed to writhe under the pale light. Photographs, strands of hair, powdered minerals — each placed carefully as if sacrificed to unseen gods.

Neon indicator lights blinked rhythmically, pulsing in time with the relentless frequencies surging through metal veins.

Nearby, a collection of Hieronymus machines stood like silent sentinels of forbidden knowledge. Brass triangles spun slowly, discs whirred, and calibrated needles trembled on glass faces covered in a labyrinth of etched glyphs: arcane runes, planetary symbols, cryptic scripts designed to focus energy beyond mortal reckoning.

These machines were a grotesque marriage of art and science, the twisted legacy of the maddened genius Tom T. Hieronymus, who had sought to transcend reality itself. The strange hum burned through Frank's brain, threatening to drive him mad.

Frank gazed through the transparent partition. The inscriptions shimmered faintly, as if alive under the electric hum — a language meant to pierce the veil between this world and something far darker.

He knew every device. He had to. Once he had been a college professor — a man of reason and knowledge — before the divorce shattered his life, before the unbearable loss of his little girl twisted everything into ash.

After that, the drugs, the despair, the slow but crushing descent into oblivion. He'd lost everything—home, family, self—until all that remained was the raw, raw pain and this hellish chamber.

He longed to escape with every shattered fiber in his being. Even the nightmares of the streets with their dangers and filth, seemed preferable to this mechanical tomb.

The door slid open behind the glass partition, cutting through the silence. The Scientist entered.

Tall, gaunt, and impossibly pale, his posture radiated a strange energy — one that reeked of madness and cold calculation. His skin stretched taut over angular cheekbones, giving him a visage as skeletal as death itself. His wild mane of coarse gray hair stood defiantly in every direction, pulled back carelessly into a chaotic ponytail, as if betraying the fractured disorder of his mind.

He approached the machines, and his eyes — an unnatural, fierce green — seemed to glow with fanatic fervor.

With a deliberate motion, he flipped a switch, and a small box mounted on the wall crackled to life.

"Good morning, Professor Thompson," he intoned, voice cold as ice. "I trust you slept well."

Frank pushed himself up on the narrow cot, clutching the thin blanket like a lifeline. His voice was a croak. "Let me out of here, you son of a bitch."

The Scientist regarded him with a detached amusement. "And what good would that serve, after all we've accomplished? I'm sorry, Frank — but you're looking ill."

"It's the goddamn voices," Frank rasped. "Those damned machines screaming in my head. Turn them off. Let me rest. Just for a few days."

The Scientist smiled — a cruel, bone-chilling smile — his teeth resembling the jagged edge of a skull grin. "We're so close," he whispered. "After today, you will no longer be my prisoner. Either we achieve our goal... or descend into madness."

Summoning every ounce of fading strength, Frank lunged at the plexiglass, pounding his fists against it with a desperate fury that echoed through the chamber. The sudden onslaught made the Scientist recoil, surprise flickering across his cold features.

"What is it you want?!" Frank screamed, voice raw with pain and rage.

The Scientist's grin deepened, spreading like a malevolent shadow. His voice was a low hiss, venomous and resolute.

"Perfection."

TO BE CONTINUED IN

IMPERFECT IN THE MIND

DOCTOR WISE BOOK 14

AUTHOR'S NOTE

Good to see you, follower of the odd.

What I wanted with *Vanished In the Mind* was a big event, and I hope you feel I pulled it off: bad guys, high stakes, a lot of danger. I loved that the villain was a dark mirror version of Len himself.

My inability to visit Lake Tahoe forced me to research the area and its resorts online. Most of them are on the California side of the lake, but I wanted to keep my focus on Nevada.

The concept of the magical skull masks came to me early, and I loved the idea so much, I used AI to generate the image that we used on the front cover.

I also have to confess that I planned out from the beginning of the series the news at the end of this book. I will not reveal what the surprise ending is here, in case you (like me) are one of those people who read the notes in the back of the book before reading the book itself.

As always, I owe much to my wife, novelist Debra Snow, who puts up with me, and my editor Libby Broadbent, who also has to put with me, but not as much as my wife. Libby always finds the core problems with my books and makes wonderful suggestions on how to fix them.

The next book, *Imperfect In The Mind*, will bring Len back to Mountainview and home, and return him to the group of supporting characters you all know, as well as a couple of surprise guests!

I hope you'll join me then!

—Arjay Lewis

ABOUT THE AUTHOR

Known as the "Wizard Of Odd", Arjay Lewis is an actor, magician, and multi-award-winning author.

I write tales of the strange and the horrifying.

I have spent my life as an entertainer, amusing people as a street-performer in the 1970s; a Broadway and casino artist in the 1980s; a party performer in the 1990s and 2000s; a cruise ship performer in the 2010s.

Stories have always been in my mind, and I have been writing since the 1990s. My reason to write is simple: to entertain. I write the type of books that I like to read: murder mysteries, strange tales of unnatural gifts, odd happenings and horror.

Please visit my web site and sign up for my mailing list to be "in the know" for upcoming books. Visit me on Facebook, Twitter, or my Amazon Author page.

And thank you for reading. You are the reason I write.

www.arjaylewis.com
www.facebook.com/arjaylewis
www.twitter.com/arjaylewiswrite
www.amazon.com/Arjay-Lewis

ALSO BY ARJAY LEWIS

Doctor Wise Series
Fire In The Mind
Seduction In The Mind
Reunion In The Mind
Haunted In The Mind
Devotion In The Mind
Asylum In The Mind
Specter In The Mind
Vengeance In The Mind
Echoes In The Mind
Infection In The Mind
Justice In The Mind
Ritual In The Mind
Vanished In The Mind

Horror
The Muse
Kept In The Dark
The Vanishing
Digger

Romantic Suspense
(with Debra Snow)
A Study In Murder

NYPD Wizard Detective
The Wizards Of Central Park West
The Vampires Of Greenwich Village
The Werewolves Of Washington Square